Praise for

"With an interesting location, compelling characters, and lots of Christmastime charm, Liz Johnson has created a story that will sweep you right into the holiday spirit."

Melody Carlson, recipient of a *Romantic Times* Career Achievement Award; author of *A Royal Christmas*, *Second Time Around*, and *The Happy Camper*

"*Meddling with Mistletoe* is the perfect book to get you in the holiday spirit. Fans of Denise Hunter and Karen Kingsbury will be delighted with this Christmas romance that's akin to a Hallmark movie in book form."

Sarah Monzon, author of *All's Fair in Love and Christmas*

Praise for *Beyond the Tides*

"An emotional and witty story, featuring flawed characters who must learn to reconcile their own shortcomings, *Beyond the Tides* is highly recommended."

Midwest Book Review

"Johnson kicks off her Prince Edward Island Shores series with this heartwarming romance. . . . Johnson's fans will eagerly anticipate the next installment of this promising series."

Publishers Weekly

Praise for *The Last Way Home*

"Johnson's sweet, small-town romance filled with strong emotion continues her Prince Edward Island Shores series."

Booklist

"This testament to the power of family and God's forgiveness will have readers eager to see what Johnson does next."

Publishers Weekly

Praise for *Summer in the Spotlight*

"Johnson sets out a tender, slow-burning romance woven through with an earnest message about overcoming one's past and the restorative power of second chances. Series fans will savor this feel-good finale."

Publishers Weekly

Sometimes you Stay

Books by Liz Johnson

PRINCE EDWARD ISLAND DREAMS

The Red Door Inn
Where Two Hearts Meet
On Love's Gentle Shore

GEORGIA COAST ROMANCE

A Sparkle of Silver
A Glitter of Gold
A Dazzle of Diamonds

PRINCE EDWARD ISLAND SHORES

Beyond the Tides
The Last Way Home
Summer in the Spotlight

Meddling with Mistletoe
Sometimes You Stay

Sometimes you Stay

A Red Door Inn Romance

Liz Johnson

Revell

a division of Baker Publishing Group
Grand Rapids, Michigan

© 2025 by Elizabeth Johnson

Published by Revell
a division of Baker Publishing Group
Grand Rapids, Michigan
RevellBooks.com

Printed in the United States of America

Library of Congress Cataloging-in-Publication Data
Names: Johnson, Liz, 1981– author.
Title: Sometimes you stay : a Red Door Inn romance / Liz Johnson.
Description: Grand Rapids, Michigan : Revell, a division of Baker Publishing Group, 2025.
Identifiers: LCCN 2024047878 | ISBN 9780800744892 (paperback) | ISBN 9780800747121 (casebound) | ISBN 9781493450633 (ebook)
Subjects: LCGFT: Christian fiction. | Romance fiction. | Novels.
Classification: LCC PS3610.O3633 S66 2025 | DDC 813/.6—dc23/eng/20241029
LC record available at https://lccn.loc.gov/2024047878

Most Scripture quotations, whether quoted or paraphrased by the characters, are from the Holy Bible, New International Version®, NIV®. Copyright © 1973, 1978, 1984, 2011 by Biblica, Inc.® Used by permission of Zondervan. All rights reserved worldwide. www.zondervan.com. The "NIV" and "New International Version" are trademarks registered in the United States Patent and Trademark Office by Biblica, Inc.®

Some Scripture quotations, whether quoted or paraphrased by the characters, are from the King James Version of the Bible.

Cover illustration: Nate Eidenberger
Cover design: Laura Klynstra

Published in association with Books & Such Literary Management, BooksAndSuch.com.

Baker Publishing Group publications use paper produced from sustainable forestry practices and postconsumer waste whenever possible.

25 26 27 28 29 30 31   7 6 5 4 3 2 1

For Shannon, Sarah, Kathy, Judy, Maeleah, Toby, Melissa, Ray, Kimberly, Tami, Kim (and Rick). And Julia and Troy too!

You know who you are and how special you made my first shared tour of the island.

Thank you for your encouragement.
Thank you for your warmth.
Thank you for your friendship.
I will never forget our PEI memories.

This is how we know what love is: Jesus Christ laid down his life for us. And we ought to lay down our lives for our brothers and sisters.

1 John 3:16

One

Lucretia Martin wasn't willing to call a single corner of the world home. At least not for more than a few days. And she would know. She'd seen nearly every tourist trap and secret alley of every city worth visiting. She'd eaten croissants at the coziest Paris café and sipped tea from vendors in a bustling Turkish bazaar. She'd seen the Colosseum lit up at night and Machu Picchu on an unusually sunny day.

She'd seen the most amazing things the world had to offer, and none of them had tempted her to stay put.

But the view of North Rustico Harbour on her phone's screen as she panned across the landscape was almost enough to change her mind.

Almost, but only that.

She had to admit the quaint and colorful buildings on the far side of the bay held a certain appeal, beautiful and soothing. The rich green pine trees overlooking the water surrounded her with their spicy scent as the whisper of the waves lulled her into a sense of calm. Maybe it was a false feeling of peace, but she leaned into it anyway.

She had no problem understanding how someone might decide to settle here. For a time.

Cretia inhaled from deep in her chest, dragging in the salt-tinged air as the sun caressed her face. The late spring breeze off the harbor cut through her sweater and whipped her hair in front of her eyes, far too much for a good selfie. But the weather was perfect for capturing the swaying branches of the trees that lined the sun-bleached boardwalk, which wrapped around the rolling blue water.

Her phone on a stabilizing arm, she panned across the weather-beaten businesses. Bright yellow and blue paint chipped off the wooden walls, evident even at this distance. Turning slowly, she caught the row of houses beyond the bluff across from where she stood. With a quick spin, she captured the embankment dotted with pink and purple wildflowers. They bobbed and danced and stretched toward the water.

Feeling that same tug, Cretia hopped off the gray boards onto a short dirt path. It couldn't even be ten feet long and ended at a cement bench. When she peered over the edge, she paused. She'd never seen purple water. Perfect emerald green? Stunning blue? Yes. She'd seen the shorelines that made the postcards on almost every continent.

But purple?

She checked her screen to make sure it captured the way the blue water mixed with the red earth beneath it.

Suddenly the wind gave her a shove, and she nearly took a step forward to catch her balance. A step that would have taken her right over the edge and five feet down into the water.

Scrambling back, she chided herself. "Careful there, Cretia."

She didn't have time to waste cleaning up after a spill like that. She knew from experience that a clothed dip in the ocean would take up far too much of her limited time on Prince Edward Island. She needed to spend her days exploring and recording the island's beauty, not searching out a laundromat and waiting for her clothes to be cleaned.

After her first accidental dive into the French Riviera, she'd decided to let her clothes just dry and then packed them with the rest of her clean clothes before moving on. Big mistake. Everything in her suitcase had taken on a decidedly fishy smell.

After that fiasco, she'd discovered the joys of hotels that offered laundry service. But her trip to PEI was short enough that she hadn't bothered to book a hotel with that particular amenity.

Better to stay on dry land.

Stepping back from the edge, she lowered her phone and spent a moment just enjoying the breeze on her face. Temps back in Arizona would be pushing a hundred already, but the late April weather on PEI was barely warm, still a hint in the wind of the cold the island had survived that winter.

She had some good footage of the area now. When she returned to her hotel room in Charlottetown that night, she'd put it together with a voice-over. Not that she'd think too much about that yet.

She tended to do better without a script anyway, describing the way this place made her feel, explaining how the woman in the seat next to her on the flight into Charlottetown had been from North Rustico. Ginger had gone on and on about how lovely the area was. Though it hadn't been on her original itinerary, Cretia quickly added this section of the north shore—part of an island that a lot of people thought was merely fictional.

She couldn't have been the only child who'd thought Anne's world of Prince Edward Island was too idyllic to be real. And with a little searching, she might just find out she'd been right. No place could be that perfect.

She wasn't looking for the island's seedy underbelly or anything. Her followers weren't interested in dark and depressing. They wanted a real-life look at places they hadn't heard of or considered visiting. They wanted unexpected experiences and gorgeous views.

And so far, PEI was shaping up to offer a lot of gorgeous views.

It all seemed . . . well, like when she'd read Anne's story as a child and dreamed that she'd be sent to live with Marilla and Matthew. It was just that. A dream. Too good to be true.

She would only be on the island for two days, so she'd have to get moving if she was going to find the unexpected. Opening her carry-on, she tucked her stabilizing arm into it beside her tripod and other equipment. While she'd parked about half a mile away, she'd wanted to have easy access to her gear. Toting her lightweight rolling bag made that easy.

After shoving her phone into her backpack and slinging it over one shoulder, she grabbed her bag's extended handle and strode toward the boardwalk. It was only a few feet of dirt between the bench and the even gray planks, but the toe of her shoe managed to catch a tree root, and she hissed as her ankle twisted.

She tried to put some weight on her foot, but fire shot up her leg, and she jerked her knee up. Taking a few deep breaths, she rubbed at the bare skin between her slip-on sneaker and the cropped hem of her jeans.

It didn't seem swollen, but even a little pressure felt like a hammer to her ankle.

With a sigh, she sank to the edge of the boardwalk. She needed a minute or two. Gently she rotated her foot.

Or three.

She'd seen a few people out walking their dogs earlier, but it was an early morning—well before the start of the tourist season—and there wasn't a soul in sight from her angle.

Parking down by the dock had seemed like a smart idea that morning. There had been plenty of spaces, and she never complained about an opportunity to stretch her legs. Not when so many of her days were spent in airplane seats.

Heaving a big sigh, she closed her eyes and gave her ankle another twirl.

Maybe a little better. Not perfect but better. She could get to her car and then find somewhere to get ice and elevate it for a while.

But first she had to get to her car.

She squinted at the four wheels on her carry-on. She'd tried leaning on the handle once in Florence, and the whole thing had flown out from under her. Utter betrayal. Total embarrassment.

Ironic because she had accepted it from a sponsor and endorsed it in part because of the way it rolled so smoothly.

She wasn't about to replay that scene on a different continent. So she sat there until a lobster boat chugged into the harbor. Then another.

With each growling engine, she tested her range of motion. Some improvement.

She'd take it.

Pushing herself up on her good leg, Cretia squared her

shoulders. Then she took a tentative step on the tips of her toes.

A groan tried to escape, but she swallowed it down. Clearly nothing was broken. She was just going to be a little bit sore. It wouldn't be the first time.

Grabbing the handle of her unhelpful bag, she hobbled toward the dock, pausing every few steps to catch her breath and let the pain ease.

Halfway to the dock, her face was damp with sweat despite the cool air, and she was fairly certain her cheeks had turned a not-so-pretty shade of red. Dabbing at her forehead with the sleeve of her sweater, she nodded as a jogger rounded the bend in front of her.

The woman in bright pink leggings slowed, then pulled out one of her earbuds. "Everything okay?"

Confirmation of those not-so-pretty cheeks.

Cretia forced a smile. "Thank you. I'm fine."

With a second concerned glance, the woman gave a quick nod, tucked her earbud back into place, and picked up her speed.

This day was turning out to be less productive than she'd planned. But at least she had a few shots of the harbor and the boardwalk. And after a decent night's sleep, her ankle would be good as new. Or at least good enough.

She just had to get to her car.

Hobbling on, she let out a sigh of relief as she rounded a bend to see the bustling dock ahead. Almost there.

Fishermen crawled off their boats, unloading equipment and oversized coolers. They hefted awkward wooden traps with ease, hollering to each other from boat to boat. It was a choreographed dance.

One she should be recording.

She grabbed her phone from her backpack and didn't bother to zip it all the way up as she hurried toward the dock. Ignoring the sting in her ankle, she slipped into the action, hunting for the best angle. She passed a man at least a foot taller than her, his brown overalls covered in wet patches. But he gave her a broad smile beneath his bushy beard. The other men were almost as big, grizzled but somehow kind. One gave her a wink as she zoomed in on him.

"Hey there, sweetheart," he called.

Cretia laughed and waved at him before spinning to watch a boy probably still in high school toss a round mesh trap of some sort to a man on a boat. The man was an older version of the boy, his lips whistling a cheerful tune. He caught the trap by curling his fingertips into the twine, then tossed it into the stern like he'd done it a million times.

When she swung back to the boy to record his second throw, she turned right into a solid wall. It grunted but had no give, and her ankle screamed as she stumbled backward. Twisting hard to take any weight off her right foot, she turned toward the harbor.

Suddenly the ground disappeared, and she clawed for purchase on anything, only managing to wrap her arm around the handle of her suitcase with those stupid wheels that rolled along far too agreeably.

She didn't so much hear a splash as feel it, her chest breaking the surface of the water with a clap. And then everything was silent. Except the rushing of her blood through her veins and the bubbles from the scream that insisted on ripping from her throat.

The water swallowed her, pressing in from every angle, squeezing her lungs, and dragging her down.

She opened her mouth to scream again, but the water rushed in. It was salty and heinous, and she couldn't spit it out without inviting more in. When she blinked, she saw nothing but black. And then her eyes were on fire. Her throat gagging. Her lungs crying for air.

Her soaked jeans and sweater dragged her farther below the surface.

She clawed at the water, arms flailing to find anything she could pull herself up on.

Only then did she realize she was still holding her phone. And the open backpack on her shoulders—which contained every bit of electronic equipment she owned—was going to drown her.

Not today.

Scissors-kicking as hard as her denim-clad legs would allow, she fought for the surface, fought for even a single breath of air.

Come on. Come on. She could make it. She had to. The water couldn't be that deep. She couldn't have sunk too far.

Ditch the backpack.

Not going to happen. Not now. Not after everything she'd done to get to this point.

Just when her lungs were ready to implode, her head broke the surface and she snatched a breath. She also caught a glance of something huge and furry lunging off the cement dock right at her.

Bear.

Bear!

It was all she could think as a splash echoed through the water.

Perfect. If the water didn't get her, a bear attack definitely would.

She could see the Instagram headlines already. POPULAR TRAVEL INFLUENCER MAULED ON GENTLE ISLAND.

Oh, the irony.

Muscles trembling, she kicked toward the dock, praying one of those friendly fishermen would help her before her limbs gave out or the bear did any real damage. The rolling waves had carried her only a few yards from the cement wall, but from where she struggled just to keep her head above water, it seemed an impossible distance.

Suddenly an enormous hairy head slid under her arm. Pushing against its snout, she fought for freedom. If she lost a finger or even a whole hand to its razor-sharp teeth, so be it. At least she'd be alive.

She tried to kick and scream, but the water prevented both, her legs useless, moving in slow motion. Sinking, she held her breath.

Every moment, she expected the pain of the animal's bite. Maybe it had already come, but the freezing water kept her fully in shock.

Her head broke the surface again, and she gasped a deep breath, filling her aching lungs until they remembered their job. With no more strength to fight, she let the animal at her side propel her.

A hand came out of nowhere, snatched her under the other arm, and pulled her up and over the edge of the dock like each of her limbs didn't weigh a million pounds. She was pretty sure they did at this point.

Then someone was ripping off her backpack, and she fought their hands.

"Calm down. It's okay. I'm not stealing your bag."

She'd heard that from a pickpocket in Europe too. But before she could turn far enough to get a grip on her backpack, an enormous hand thwapped her between her shoulder blades. Then again. Harbor water and bile burst out of her, and she folded over, leaning on a trembling arm at her side.

"Would someone help Joe Jr. out of the water?"

The words reached her as though she was still underwater. They weren't for her. She was pretty sure. But she didn't know where or who they came from.

Another coughing fit tore from her throat, and she squeezed her stinging eyes shut. When she could finally breathe normally again, she risked a squint into the sun.

And into the face of a man she hadn't seen on the dock before.

He squatted a few feet in front of her, his forearms resting on bent knees. The wrinkle between his eyebrows didn't detract from the smooth ridge of his nose. And she imagined that without the tight line of his mouth, he might have a nice smile.

"You all right there? That was a nasty fall."

As soon as she shook her head, she realized she couldn't stop. Her whole body began to tremble, her teeth chattering.

"You must be freezing." In a second, he pulled off his yellow flannel overshirt and wrapped it around her shoulders, pulling the neck closed beneath her chin.

It didn't help much. The wind still cut through her, and she couldn't stop twitching.

"Anyone know her?" he asked over her head, and a low

mumble of uncertainty came from the fishermen who had surely witnessed the whole scene.

His gaze came back to meet hers. "Where are you staying?"

"Char-Char-Char—"

"Charlottetown?"

She nodded.

"Tourist?"

She managed another jerk of her chin, but the rest of her body had gone nearly numb.

"Well, you won't make it back to—"

Suddenly the giant black body that had leapt at her—and saved her—bounded to their side. His whole body shook, water flying off every piece of fur and coating them both.

The man waved off the beast with a laugh. "Joe. Come on now. Can't you see the lady's been through enough?" Then his tone softened as he reached forward and scratched the big head behind its ears. "Good job, boy."

Finally she turned toward the animal and managed to get a clear look. It wasn't a bear but nearly as big. And twice as furry, his black hair shaggier than the sheepdogs she'd seen in Scotland. Big black eyes stared back at her above a dark snout. A wad of drool on his jowls joined the water dripping to the ground below.

She would have recoiled if she'd had an ounce of adrenaline left. Instead, her arm decided to give out on her, and she slumped toward the ground. Before her head could connect with the gravel, the man grabbed her shoulder and scooped her to his chest.

"Whoa there." He stood up slowly. "Let's get you somewhere warm and dry."

Two

Finn Chaffey was not in the habit of carrying women—especially ones he hadn't officially met. One of the many clueless Newfoundland dogs on his farm that didn't want to go back to where they were supposed to be? That was a regular occurrence. Pretty tourists soaked in harbor water? Not once.

But the moment he had helped her stand, he knew she wasn't going to make it far. Certainly not the twenty-minute walk to his place on the far side of the three-way intersection, across from the dairy farm. With each hobbling step, she cringed, her shoulders hunching beneath his shirt.

She'd probably twisted her ankle when she fell into the water. After bumping into him.

He'd been too busy reining in Joe Jr.—who was far too excited about their daily walk—to notice her until it was too late. Until she'd bounced off him and gone airborne.

Her predicament wasn't entirely his responsibility. Just mostly.

Not that he'd have left her to fend for herself even if he

hadn't been at fault. He liked to think he'd have gone in after her if Joe hadn't been there. The dog couldn't learn to find a piece of Limburger cheese in an open barn. But underwater rescue was in his blood.

He reached out to give his buddy another head rub, and Joe Jr. was right there, still a little damp despite his energetic shimmy.

The swimmer hadn't been able to shake off the water as easily, and her whole body continued to shiver.

One steadying hand on her elbow, Finn quickly scanned the scene. Mike and Bobby had returned to their boats, finishing the day's work. Most of the others were headed in that direction. His truck was at home, and if the girl had a car nearby, her key fob probably wasn't going to work after that dunking.

He knew one family on Harbourview Drive that wouldn't balk at him showing up with a half-drowned stranger.

"Think you can make it about ten minutes down the boardwalk?"

She nodded, then stumbled on her next step, grabbing at his arm.

Yeah. This wasn't going to work.

"Do you mind?" He wasn't quite sure what he was asking, and the raise of her eyebrows said she didn't know either.

But there wasn't a smooth way to put it into words. At least not into words he knew. So he leaned down to hook his arm behind her knees, but she hobbled back, stuffing her fist to her mouth to muffle a low groan.

"I'm all right. I can make it." The pinched lines around her lips contradicted her words.

Putting his hands on his hips and staring her down like

he would an ornery goat, he said, "At the rate you're going, it'll be a lot longer than ten minutes."

Her shoulders twitched, and she crossed her arms, hunching in on herself.

"You're cold and wet. Let me get you somewhere warm, and then we'll figure this out."

She opened her lips, and he was sure she was going to make another argument. Nobody had time for that. Instead of waiting for her, he scooped an arm around her back and the other under her knees, lifting her against his chest.

She let out a soft "eep" and pushed against his shoulders. His grip slipped, and he nearly dropped her. With a cry, she slung her arms around his neck. Whole body trembling, she leaned into him.

"You're warm." She sighed and pressed her face into his neck.

Not for long. He could feel the icicles forming where the wind met the damp tracks she left around the collar of his white T-shirt.

"Let's get somewhere we can both be." He started toward the boardwalk, careful not to jostle her. This wasn't exactly the walk he'd planned, though he took this path through the dock and around the harbor most days.

Before he got more than a few steps, she croaked, "My backpack."

He paused to make sure Joe Jr. was pulling his weight, and the dog indeed had her bright orange bag between his teeth. The top flap hung open, and water still dripped a trail as Joe trotted along. Everything inside had clearly been doused in salt water, and anything electronic was probably ruined. So he said only, "Got it."

She sagged against him, letting out a loud sigh.

Two minutes of silence shouldn't have been awkward, but it was. He'd never been this close to a stranger. Was rarely this close to personal friends. The last girl he'd held against his chest had been Jessie Sloan—aged fifteen months. And that was only to make sure she didn't run off while her mom rounded up the others from Sunday school.

Clearing his throat, he said, "I'm Finn, by the way. Finn Chaffey."

She nodded into his neck. "Cretia Martin." She emphasized the last syllable with a long *e*, the mumbled name almost sounding Spanish.

Good. Introductions out of the way.

"Thanks," she said. The single word was more breath than sound, and he almost missed it.

"You're welcome."

"I thought your dog was a bear."

"A lot of people do." He chuckled. "Guess he just has one of those faces."

She giggled too, the sound low and throaty. Maybe her laugh always sounded like that. Or maybe it was a by-product of swallowing half the harbor. He had a sudden desire to know for sure. But that would have to wait.

"Almost there." He jogged up the steps from the boardwalk to the road above, holding her a little tighter to keep her from bouncing too much. Joe Jr. had no such concerns, bounding up the steps and racing across the road, not even bothering to look both ways. He leapt into the front yard of the two-story blue house with the white porch and bright door.

"Joe Jr." Jack, Marie and Seth Sloan's eldest, raced down

the steps from Rose's Red Door Inn and dove into the dog's side. Joe happily dropped the load he'd been carrying, letting his tongue hang halfway to the ground as he slobbered all over the boy. Jack had to be seven or eight, but the dog was at least twice his size. And a total sucker for a good ear scratch. Jack had his number, and Joe wiggled and writhed in the grass as he basked in the attention.

The front door opened, and Marie poked her head out. "Jack, what are you—" Her eyes swung from her son, and her eyebrows shot beneath her dark curls. "Finn? What happened? Who's—"

"This is Cretia. We had a little accident in the harbor." He offered a helpless shrug.

"Come in. Come in." She waved them into the Victorian-staged foyer and past the round wooden entry table with a perfectly fanned spread of travel magazines, not even a word about the sporadic drips in their wake that marred her perfect floor.

Ignoring him, Marie put a hand on Cretia's shoulder. "Are you hurt?"

"R-r-rice."

"You're hungry? I can make you something warm to eat."

Cretia shook her head, more water falling onto his arm from her long black ponytail. "My bag. My electronics." Her teeth resumed chattering as soon as she stopped speaking.

Marie's forehead wrinkled as Finn turned back toward the yard, where Cretia's backpack had landed with an audible squish when Joe Jr. let it go in favor of little-boy hugs and belly rubs. Whatever was in that bag probably wasn't going to make it. But he wasn't going to be the one to tell her.

Thank God for Marie Sloan, who had never met a situation she couldn't take charge of. "We'll take care of that after we make sure you're all right. Come into the kitchen." Marie wasn't even a step in that direction when she angled her head and called down the hallway, "Julia Mae, will you bring me some big towels? Now." She paused and gave them both a quick once-over. "Lots of them!"

They took a quick path across the dining room, weaving between a few of the mismatched four-top tables. They weren't set with tablecloths or place mats at the moment, but the rich white wainscoting and deep blue paint on the walls reminded him how stunning the room could be dressed up in its Sunday best. As they flew through the swinging door that led to the kitchen, the little jingle bell above the door rang its greeting.

"Let's sit you down here," Marie said, pulling out a wooden stool from along the middle island and leaning in close to Cretia's face when he set her there. "Where does it hurt?"

Cretia wrapped her arms around her middle and curled in on herself, shooting an uncertain glance in his direction. Could she feel his absence too? It was an unusual tingle deep in his chest, not strong, just . . . present. A noticeable change. Cold where they had managed to keep each other tolerably warm together.

Only it was cozy in the house. Maybe the real chill came from being apart. He crossed his arms in a losing attempt to ward off the strange feeling.

"Julia, where are you?" Marie called.

"Coming!" The voice of the little girl was muffled behind

a stack of neatly folded beach towels taller than her head. But she moved quickly, nearly running into the corner of the island counter.

Putting a hand on her dark curls, Finn stopped her before she could do any real damage and grabbed two of the towels off her stack. "Thanks, squirt."

He whipped one to full size and threw it around Cretia's shoulders, then rubbed up and down her arms from shoulders to elbows and back. She still twitched and quivered, but maybe not so much from the cold as the adrenaline that had likely coursed through her. And the rush of it leaving her body.

He didn't stop, though. A bit of contact might be comforting.

To her or himself, he didn't know.

Either way.

Marie spread another white towel over Cretia's lap and then threw one at him. Finn raised an eyebrow, but Marie only gave him a roll of her eyes. He swung it around his neck and patted at a few wet spots on his shirt before turning back to Cretia.

Slowly the tension in her shoulders began to ease, and the clacking of her teeth slowed. After a few more minutes, she took a shaky breath.

"I'm sorry to be such a bother." She inhaled again, raising her shoulders and posture. "I'll— Let me clean up your floor."

Marie bent slightly at the waist until her face was directly even with Cretia's line of sight. "I'll handle that later. First, are you all right?"

Cretia tried to pull the towels off and move to stand, but

Finn put a heavy hand on her shoulder. "She must have hurt her leg when she fell in. She couldn't walk on it."

Cretia shot him a hard look, which softened as soon as she turned back to Marie. "I twisted my ankle. Before. On the boardwalk. I was a little off-balance and ran into a column or something when I was getting some footage on the dock." She waved the phone still in her hand. There was no way it had survived the ordeal, but she didn't look ready to let it go, her fingers holding it like a vise.

Finn chewed on his lip and dragged a hand through his hair. She hadn't exactly run into a column. "Um, actually . . ."

"Finnegan Chaffey." Marie's voice turned all things mom. "Tell me you didn't push this poor thing into the harbor."

"Of course not! I was just trying to wrangle Joe Jr., and she bumped into me." He shot Cretia what he hoped was an apologetic grimace. "I'm sorry. I didn't mean to send you over the edge." Literally.

Her dark eyebrows pulled together. "I ran into you?"

He offered a one-shoulder shrug, the best he could do at the moment.

"But I didn't even . . . You weren't . . . I didn't see you there."

"I didn't see you either. Until it was too late." He tried for a smile. "Maybe we're even?"

Marie harrumphed. "Not likely, mister."

Yeah. He knew she was right. "What can I do?"

"First things first." Marie ran a towel over Cretia's dripping hair. "A shower and some dry clothes."

Cretia's eyes flashed wide and fearful. "My carry-on. Did you see it?"

Finn cringed. "It's in the harbor. Somewhere. But if it had any sort of buoyancy, the waves could have carried it halfway to Newfoundland by now." Maybe not quite that far, but their only real hope of recovery was if a lobster boat crew mistook it for a buoy. Not real likely. Though she did not need to hear that at the moment.

"That's . . . that's everything . . ." Cretia struggled to find her words and her breath, which came out in quick pants. Her wide eyes turned even more wild. Her smeared eye makeup had been funny at first, but combined with the unhinged look in her eyes, she was more than a little bit terrifying.

Marie shot him a look that seemed to ask just who he'd brought into her home, and he could only shrug. He had no idea.

"Do you have another suitcase?" Finn leaned in, offering a reasonable solution. Surely, she had some other clothes somewhere. "Did you leave it at your hotel in Charlottetown? I can help you get that back."

Little lines appeared between her gently arched eyebrows as she began to shake her head. "No. That's— Everything I own is in my carry-on and backpack."

Marie sucked in a quick breath, and Finn backed up so fast that he bumped into the white-tiled counter that ran the length of the wall.

"Everything?" he asked slowly. He had to have misunderstood. No one carried *all* of their earthly belongings in two bags. Next to large bodies of water.

Cretia merely dipped her chin, her gaze dropping to her folded hands in her lap.

"I'm sure we can find you something to wear while we

wash your clothes," Marie said. With a hand under Cretia's elbow, she guided her toward the back stairwell.

"Please. Can you rice my electronics?" Cretia thrust her phone at him.

Finn accepted the metallic blue device and glanced toward the front yard where Joe Jr. had dropped her bag, but it didn't help to make sense of her words. "Rice?"

"Put them in uncooked rice. Cover them all the way. It might pull the water out."

"Sure. Yeah. I can do that." He nodded toward Marie. "You go clean up, and I'll . . . rice your electronics."

Cretia's features pinched tight for a moment, but finally she allowed herself to be ushered away, limping with each step.

Finn flipped the phone over in his hand a few times. It looked fairly new, one of those ones with a fancy camera and a huge screen. Then again, he didn't have much to compare it to. He still used a flip phone that required old-school texting techniques. Not that he texted much. Or did anything but take business calls and reach out to his parents every now and then.

He was certainly no expert, but one of the guys in town had dropped his fancy phone in the harbor once. Brandon had complained for weeks that the so-called water-resistant feature was a scam because his phone never did turn on again. The screen on Cretia's was mostly black, save for three small patches that flickered neon colors and two horizontal cracks that it had probably sustained either going into or out of the water. He had a feeling that elaborate features wouldn't save this phone from the trash bin. Rice or not.

Still, he set the phone down and jogged toward the front yard to find Jack and Joe Jr. playing a game of tackle tag, Joe's happy barks mixing with Jack's squeals of laughter.

"Jack, can I leave Joe with you for a minute? I'll be right back."

Jack looked up as Joe Jr. pushed him to the ground. "Sure, Mr. Finn!" he said from somewhere beneath the furry beast, who looked up with a dumb grin.

"Be good, Joe."

The dog answered by letting loose a big dribble of slobber.

Finn could only laugh as he picked up the squishy backpack and set it on the porch before jogging down the road toward the town grocery. He made the trip past the harbor in half the time it had taken with Cretia in his arms and crossed the street at the three-way stop. In the store he picked up six bags of white rice.

Jasmin Brandy, who had been in the same grade as him, raised her eyebrows when he plopped the bags down at the checkout. "The church having a potluck I didn't get invited to?"

"No. I have to *rice* some electronics."

"Rice? Is that a verb?"

"Apparently so. You think this is enough?"

Jasmin chuckled. "I don't even know what that is."

At least he wasn't the only one out of the technology loop. But her response didn't answer his question. "Hang on. I'm going to get some more." He ran back to the shelf and grabbed the last three bags. Just in case.

"You going to need a sack for these?"

He looked at the twenty pounds of rice and frowned. "Yeah."

Jasmin rang up a green reusable grocery bag—just like the five he had at home—and filled it.

Swinging the bag over his shoulder, he waved and headed back to the inn. On the front porch, he picked up Cretia's backpack and headed for the mudroom, where he quickly found a plastic bucket. After filling it halfway with the long-grain white rice, he shoved her phone in until it was covered. Then he opened her backpack.

Digging through a stranger's personal effects felt like an invasion of privacy, so he peeked inside first.

Each of the three sections in the main pocket were carefully organized. The sleek silver laptop in the middle sloshed when he pulled it free, and he grimaced. He didn't see how rice could combat that, but he shoved it into the bucket anyway. Then came a tablet about three times the size of her phone.

Next was a stick with a claw on one end and an elbow of some sort in the middle. It didn't look like any piece of electronics he'd ever seen. But better not to risk it. He shoved that into the rice too. And every charging cord he could find in the main and smaller front pockets.

When he reached into the front pocket, his fingers brushed something that wasn't electronic and that felt a whole lot like soggy bread.

Jerking his hand away, he peered in. Water-logged white paper outlined the shape of a dark blue passport. With precision pinching to avoid the paper, he pulled the passport free.

He had no business opening it, but he did anyway.

Lucretia Sonora Martin. Hometown: San Luis, Arizona, USA.

Every wrinkled blue page was covered in colorful stamps.

At least, they had probably once been identifiable as stamps. Now they were smeared, ink running and blending together into a messy watercolor.

Thankfully the passport was made of better stock than the mushy printer paper he'd come in contact with. Carefully smoothing the pages, he hung it over the edge of the bucket, praying it would dry enough that it wouldn't need to be replaced.

He didn't even know the closest place she could apply for a new one. Certainly not on the island. Maybe Halifax. But that was a full-day trip.

To make sure he got all the electronic equipment out of her bag, he turned it upside down and dumped out everything else, which clattered to the mudroom floor.

The fob for her rental car—thankfully the kind that had a physical key snapped inside so she'd be able to drive it back to the airport in Charlottetown. A stainless-steel water bottle, which clanged and bounced and then rolled away. A soggy pair of rolled socks and a wad of fabric that looked suspiciously like underclothes.

Not that he was in the habit of looking at women's unmentionables.

With a nudge of his boot, he pushed them all into one pile, including a wet clump of paper. It looked like the island map given out at the airport rental car counter.

He gave the bag another shake, but nothing else broke free, so he poked his head inside one more time. There had to be more in there. A purse of some sort? Keys to her home? Lip gloss? A snack, maybe?

The only thing inside was a single photograph—an old-school Polaroid. The woman in the picture looked like an older version of Cretia, but the setting didn't make sense. She appeared to be sitting on a recliner, a giant cat curled up in her lap. But something was piled up on her right. And her left. And behind her.

The more he stared at it, the less the photo made sense.

Suddenly the Polaroid was snatched from his fingers.

"Who said you could look through my things?"

Three

Cretia slapped the old picture to her leg, away from Finn's prying gaze. Though his eyes looked more remorseful than curious at the moment.

"I'm sorry. I was just . . ." He waved a hand toward her wilted backpack and a small pile of her things. Including a once-fresh pair of underwear.

Her cheeks flamed, and she scooped up the mess from the floor, hugging them against the sweatshirt Marie had loaned her.

"I didn't want to miss any electronics." With the toe of his brown boot, he pushed a red plastic bucket across the floor. It was half-filled with white rice. Just as she'd asked.

Through gritted teeth, she managed, "Thank you."

"I'm not sure it's going to help, though." He frowned at the bucket, and she hated that he was probably right.

A lot of experts no longer recommended rice for rescuing waterlogged electronics. But it was the only thing she'd been able to think of after her own dunking. Her laptop was almost certainly a lost cause. And even if her phone lived up to its water-resilient promises, she'd seen the cracked screen.

She'd tried to get it to turn on as Finn carried her to the inn, but there had been nothing but a few limp flickers.

Everything that her warm shower and fresh—albeit snug—clothes had done to restore her humanity disappeared. The sure knowledge that she had lost everything replaced whatever hope she'd managed to drum up beneath that fabulous rain showerhead.

A jagged sigh fought its way out, and she opened one eye to stare at both her rescuer and the bearer of bitter news.

Finn was larger than she'd realized. Though she shouldn't have been surprised. He'd picked her up like she was nothing—like he hadn't even noticed the roundness of her hips and thighs that online trolls loved to comment on. His shoulders stretched his white T-shirt as he shoved his hands into the back pockets of his jeans. Behind his light brown beard, he probably had a baby face, and she had no guess at his age. The only thing she was certain of was the compassion in his brilliant blue eyes.

"I really am sorry about all of this." His voice rumbled, and she hugged her scant belongings even tighter.

She didn't know how to respond, so she looked right into his face and gave him only the tiniest nod.

"I'm warming up some chicken noodle soup," Marie called from the kitchen. "You'll stay, Finn."

He didn't look away but responded to Marie as though she'd asked a question. She hadn't. "Thank you. But I can't stay long. Joe Jr. will be hungry soon, and I need to check on the kids."

Cretia blinked, and it was enough to jerk herself out of the trance of Finn's gaze. His left hand was still hidden in his back pocket, and she tried to remember if he'd been wearing a ring. He could still be married even if he didn't have one.

Not that it mattered. She would be on the island for just one more day. And then she'd never see Finn Chaffey again. Just like every other man she'd crossed paths with over the last four years, except for the occasional meetups with other digital content creators.

"I guess he's earned a treat today. He did save Cretia, after all." Marie's voice carried a hint of a chuckle.

Behind his bushy beard, the corners of Finn's mouth ticked up. "Silly dog," he said just for the two of them in the mudroom. "He was bound to do something right eventually."

Cretia sucked in a quick breath, something deep in her stomach tugging her toward Finn. She took an inadvertent step on her sore foot and stumbled toward him.

Catching her elbow to keep her upright, he nodded toward the kitchen. "Let's get you some ice for your ankle."

She nodded and led the way, refusing to let him see her wince with each step. When she was all settled at the island counter, her foot resting on another stool and a pack of frozen peas cradling her ankle, Marie set a beautiful bowl in front of her, the pottery painted in a swirling glaze to match the island's signature reds and greens.

"The inn isn't open yet for the season, so the food options are limited to what I can get my kiddos to eat. And what I can cook." Marie smiled at Finn as she set a bowl down in front of him too. "Do either of you want a grilled cheese?"

Cretia shook her head, but Finn perked up. "Got cheese from Mama Cheese Sandwich's shop?"

The spoon almost to her mouth, Cretia burst out with a laugh, nearly spraying chicken noodle soup across the white-tiled countertop and beyond. She covered her mouth before making a mess of the otherwise spotless kitchen.

"Caden wouldn't let me bring any other cheese into this house." Marie winked at Finn. "Coming right up."

Even if it hadn't been part of her job to find the hidden treasures and quirky bits of the places she visited, she would have asked about that name. "I'm sorry . . . Mama Cheese Sandwich?"

With one eyebrow raised, Finn looked up from slurping a spoonful of his own soup. "Yeah. Mama Cheese Sandwich."

"Is that . . . a thing? I mean, like, a store or a place or a . . . person?"

Marie chuckled as she set to work buttering two thick slices of bread. "Yes, Mama Cheese Sandwich is a person. Her son Justin owns Kane Dairy."

That did not answer all of her questions, but as Finn dove into his soup, Cretia took a careful sip of hers. Warmth spread down her throat and through her chest. When it reached her stomach, she suddenly realized just how empty she'd been. She'd meant to stop for something after the boardwalk, and that had been hours ago. Now she couldn't seem to scoop up the savory chicken and broth fast enough.

"You sure you don't want a sandwich?" Marie asked with a sharp look at her almost empty bowl.

"Um . . ."

"Yes. She wants a sandwich," Finn said, his gaze pointed. "That's the only right answer to a question like that."

"Oh, really?"

He shoved his giant spoon into his mouth. "Trust me on this."

Trust him? She barely knew his name. And that he had kids. And that he had a dog the size of a boat.

And eyes that could put her in a trance.

All of those things did not add up to trust.

But her stomach did not need any such assurance. It growled loudly, and she chuckled. "That does sound good, actually."

"One more grilled cheese coming up." At the stove, Marie flipped Finn's sandwich before buttering two more pieces of bread.

"And the cheese is from someone whose son owns a dairy?" Cretia ventured again.

Still at the stove, Marie had her back turned to them, her shoulders bouncing in time with her chuckle. "Kathleen Kane—Mama Kane to most of the folks in the area. Her husband owned the dairy, and she made the best cheese sandwiches. Gave them out to kids playing with her son or anyone who was hungry, really. About thirty years ago, a little girl named Natalie accidentally called her Mama Cheese Sandwich. I guess it stuck."

That made sense. Kind of. Cretia had seen plenty of wild usernames on social media, but this was different. She had a sudden urge to meet the woman who let everyone call her by such an unusual name. If only she had time.

"And you grew up here? With Justin and Natalie?" Cretia asked.

"Oh, no." Marie shook her head as she delivered Finn's sandwich. He had half of it in his mouth before she could continue. "I moved here about twelve years ago and helped get this inn started. What about you? What brings you to the island, Cretia? Are you traveling alone?"

She should have anticipated the question but still nearly choked on her response. "I'm a digital content creator."

Finn peered at her over the last bite of his sandwich, his eyebrows pinched together. "A what?"

Cretia shrugged like she'd just said she was a nurse or teacher or had any other regular job. "I travel around the world and create video content about the interesting places I go. I recommend some lesser-known destinations and tips for making the most of vacations and how to travel on a budget. I'm a travel vlogger."

"And people . . . pay you to do that?" Finn asked.

"Um . . . sort of." She took a deep breath through her nose to keep herself in check.

"Sort of? How do you sort of get paid?"

Her cheek twitched as she tried to keep her tone even and pleasant. "I have sponsors and followers and subscribers."

"But what are they paying for?"

Marie swept toward them, a second plated sandwich in hand. "Leave her be, Finn. Just because you don't understand what she does doesn't make it less valid."

Finn scowled—at least Cretia thought that's what was happening behind his whiskers. "I just don't understand. How do you make a living doing nothing?"

Her blood went from a simmer to a boil in an instant, heating her skin from head to toe. "Nothing? You think I do nothing?"

"No, I didn't mean—" Finn stumbled over the bite in his mouth, crunching on the bread.

Marie thumped him on the shoulder. "Put a sock in it, Finn. You've already got your foot halfway down your throat. You barely have room for your sandwich."

He grimaced. "Sorry. I just . . ." Confusion still covered his face as Marie gave him another sisterly smack.

Explaining how someone could make a living by posting videos online was never easy, especially to the technologically averse or the ones who questioned everything. And Finn struck her as both.

She wasn't uber wealthy or anything, but she had a healthy nest egg. And everything else went toward new adventures and more content. She had no other bills, no other responsibilities.

Besides, her finances weren't any of his business. She wasn't asking him—or anyone else—for help.

Except for when she'd taken a swim in the harbor that morning. But he'd already admitted that fiasco was more than a little bit his own fault.

She didn't need his charity. Or Marie Sloan's, for that matter.

"Thank you very much for lunch. How much do I owe you?" Cretia reached for her phone but found her pocket empty. "I can . . . I'll send you some money as soon as I'm back online."

"Don't be silly." Marie's words sounded like a song, the notes sweet and airy. "You don't owe me anything. It was just lunch."

She'd heard that a few times from pub owners in Ireland. And once from a man in Oregon who thought a free meal had earned him some other favors. He'd gotten himself a knee to his sensitive bits for that.

After so many years alone on the road, Cretia had learned how to read people. Fast. Marie posed no threat. And Finn wasn't dangerous, just a little clueless. And apparently rude. Though she couldn't forget his earlier compassion.

But that didn't mean she needed to stick around.

Pressing her lips into a thin line, she lowered her foot to the ground. Her stool scraped as she pushed back, her ankle only giving a little twinge to remind her of the mishap. "I think I better go. But thank you again. I'll send you some money for lunch as soon as I can."

Marie shot a glance at Finn before rushing around the island. "You're in no shape to go anywhere. And your things. You don't have—"

"I'll figure it out." She took a step toward the mudroom to retrieve the extent of her belongings. Diminished though they were.

"Your shoes are soaking wet, and your clothes are still in the washing machine."

"I . . . um . . ." Cretia glanced down and plucked at the sweatshirt covering her. She couldn't very well walk out of the inn in another woman's clothes. Especially when she would probably never be back. "I'll mail these to you?"

Marie's eyes filled with worry, and she glanced at Finn, signaling him with a nod.

He jumped to his feet so quickly that he sent his own stool clattering to the ground as he finished the last slurp of his soup. Holding up one hand, he scooped up his overturned seat, then slid in front of her. "Please, wait. I'm sorry. I swear that my mom taught me some manners. I spend all day with dogs and other animals, and I sometimes forget."

"Dogs?"

As if on cue, the dog barked from the yard, and Finn smiled. "Joe Jr. and a bunch more."

She'd heard Finn call the dog that after he rescued her. And the name plucked at an old memory she couldn't quite put her finger on. Maybe the dog's dad had been named Joe, and his name was as simple as that. Still, she couldn't help but ask for clarification. "Joe *Jr.*?"

Finn nodded slowly. "He's . . . Have you ever seen *While You Were Sleeping?*"

That was where she knew the name from. It had been one of her mom's favorite movies, and they'd watched it over and over when she was a kid.

"Like the character in the movie, my dog is just a little bit of a doofus. My mom decided it fit."

Cretia's concern must have shown on her face because Finn immediately waved his hands and tried to clarify his words. "He's well-intentioned. Very sweet. But just a little bit . . . off."

She didn't know what that meant exactly—or if she should be offended that Finn had sent his not-quite-all-there dog to rescue her. "Compared to what?"

"To the other Newfoundlands I breed."

"All right . . ." She wasn't sure what she was supposed to do with that information. Knowing there were more bears around town wasn't exactly adding to North Rustico's appeal. Especially if they had their breeder's temperament.

Cretia shook her head to clear it, then glanced around Finn at the bucket in the mudroom. Even her passport looked like it could use a rest. Her laptop and tablet had probably succumbed to the same fate as her phone—damaged beyond repair. All of them would have to be replaced.

Thank goodness her content automatically saved to the cloud, and she had videos scheduled every day for a couple weeks.

Squaring her shoulders, she managed a loose smile for Finn. "I appreciate your apology, but I just need to get to an Apple store. And then I have a ticket to Iceland."

Finn's eyebrows bunched together. "The only apple store on the island is connected to an orchard."

"Excuse me?"

Marie slid into her peripheral vision and pressed a warm hand to her shoulder. "It sells apples grown on trees—not electronics."

"You're telling me there's nowhere on the island I can replace my things?"

Marie shook her head slowly. "You might be able to get something at a box store, but they don't carry large supplies. Usually they have to order what you want. Especially if it's a high-end item."

Cretia swallowed hard against a suddenly dry mouth. All of her information was accessible—so long as she had some sort of device. Without one, she had no record of her plane tickets. No reservation number at her hotel, whose name she couldn't even remember. And no way to navigate the island, let alone get off of it.

A rope around her lungs pulled tight, and she gasped for breath.

She'd been in some sticky situations, even had her backpack and the laptop within it stolen once. But she'd never felt quite so helpless before. She'd always had something— usually her phone. Her most important tool. Her lifeline.

Without it, she was stranded. In a foreign country.

When she'd been robbed before, she'd gone to the US embassy. They'd managed to get her a new passport. Yes, there had been enough bureaucratic red tape to cover a house. But at the end of the day, she'd had her passport shortly after the local police were able to retrieve her electronics.

She'd never been more thankful for the Find My Device feature.

This time, she knew where her things were.

On a mudroom floor.

In a bucket.

Covered in rice.

And highly unlikely to ever function again.

Cretia cleared her throat. "Do you know where the local US embassy is?"

Finn and Marie made eye contact, a knowing look passing between them.

"The embassy?" Marie said after a long silence. "It's probably in Ottawa."

Cretia let out a heavy breath. She hadn't gotten an A+ in geography, but she knew Ottawa wasn't on PEI—and Canada was huge. She wasn't bebopping across Europe right now.

"But there's a US consulate in Halifax." Marie's words rose in tone and hope. "That's where I went to begin my paperwork when I decided to stay on the island."

"Halifax?"

"Nova Scotia," Finn supplied with a small shrug.

"How far away is it?"

"About a four-hour drive." Marie frowned. "Each way."

And in a completely different province. Cretia hadn't rented her car to leave PEI. She'd barely rented it for another day.

She was completely on her own.

Stranded.

Suddenly she felt like she might be sick, her stomach twisting painfully on the once delicious grilled cheese. Her hands began to shake, and the throbbing in her ankle found its way to her temples, each beat of her heart pounding another nail into her skull.

When she swayed, a large hand—a familiar one—cupped her elbow, and Finn slipped to her side. "Hey, it's gonna be all right. We'll figure it out."

Easy for you to say.

Maybe her facial features betrayed the direction of her thoughts because Marie swooped in with her own promise. "So, here's the thing. I owe Finn here a favor for letting my toddler terrorize his animals."

"That's an exaggeration," he said with barely a glance up. "I wouldn't let anyone—even Jessie—*terrorize* those animals."

Marie raised her eyebrows in a knowing motion that all mothers seem to have mastered.

Finn ducked his chin and mumbled, "She might have pulled on a few tails and chased a couple puppies. But they were bigger than her. I'm certain they were not traumatized."

With a quick roll of her eyes, Marie turned back to her. "Regardless of the emotional trauma inflicted, I owe Finn a favor. And it would seem Finn owes you much more than that."

No one even raised an eyebrow.

"So, how about you stay in one of my guest rooms until we can get this all sorted out?"

"I couldn't—" Cretia began, but Marie interrupted her with a tone that brooked no argument.

"You're in no shape to drive to Charlottetown today—or to make decisions about tomorrow. Once your clothes are clean and you've had a good night of sleep, it'll all be manageable."

Surprisingly, Cretia had a feeling Marie might be right.

Four

Finn trudged into his kitchen, tearing open the top envelope he'd grabbed from the mailbox at the end of his lane. He didn't really need to open it to know what it said. But maybe he was a glutton for punishment. Approvals didn't come in envelopes. Rejections did.

That didn't stop hope from rising in his chest as he flipped open the single sheet.

> *Dear Mr. Chaffey,*
> *We regret to inform you*

That was all he needed to read, all he needed to know.

It shouldn't have been a surprise—although the first three banks had at least bothered to call him to reject his loan application. He made a move to crumple the letter but then tossed it on top of the pile of invoices on his desk.

He dropped his chin to his chest to let out a long sigh, then groaned as his nose came in contact with his shirt. Oof.

That was ripe. Which was saying something coming from someone who had spent most of his life in a barn.

But he didn't reek of hay or dirt or hard work. He smelled like the harbor. Like rotten fish and salt and seaweed. It was beyond unpleasant.

Joe Jr. trotted up to him, slurped up a drink of water from the bowl along the wall, and then nipped at the hem of his shirt. A low growl came from deep inside the barrel-chested dog. Apparently, Joe agreed.

Finn gave the dog a good ear scratch with one hand. With the other, he grabbed the back of his shirt and yanked it over his head before chucking it toward the laundry room. "Is that better?"

Joe woofed and slobbered into his hand.

"Good boy," he said, slipping his friend a biscuit from the tin on the counter.

When the crunching quickly ended, Joe looked up with big black eyes, silently begging for more. Crouching down, Finn rubbed his giant head between both hands. Joe's fur was thick and coarse, his ears soft and pliable. "You think you earned a second treat today?"

Joe nearly smiled at the familiar word. He *had* jumped in to rescue Cretia that morning. No hesitation. No stumble. He'd looked better than some of the dogs Finn had trained as rescue swimmers.

Of course, those dogs performed as they'd been taught ninety-nine percent of the time. Joe did as he was told about one percent.

Still, he'd picked today to do as he was asked, so Finn reached for another bone-shaped treat. Without him, Finn would have had to plunge into the harbor to save Cretia.

"Thanks for sparing me a cold swim." And making sure Finn had the strength to carry her to the inn.

Even if she had made his shirt smell like a cesspool.

The memory of her exhausted smile flashed across his mind's eye, pulling at something low in his gut.

Joe crunched his cookie and trotted off to his enormous pillow in the living room as though he was the goodest boy who ever was.

Ridiculous dog.

Shaking off thoughts of his pet and the pretty woman Joe had rescued, Finn grabbed a fresh T-shirt from the basket on top of his dryer. It was a little wrinkled, but there wasn't a body in the barn that would care. He stepped through the back door and strode across the lawn toward the traditional red building and gray-shingled roof visible from a kilometer away. His grandfather had built it nearly half a century before, though it had only recently started housing a cow.

As far back as Finn could remember, the barn had only been for the dogs his family bred and trained. It kept them warm in the winter and cool in the summer and kept them away from any other wildlife.

Until recently.

Not that his bunnies and cow were strictly considered wildlife. But over the last few years, Finn had brought in a few strays.

As he slid the door open and stepped into the dim light, one of those strays greeted him with a low moo.

"Hey, Roberta." Finn strolled across the tidy cement floor and patted the black-and-white former milk cow between the eyes. Or rather, beside her lone eye. The vet had had to remove the other thanks to a nasty infection. A permanent reminder of her previous living conditions. "Got enough to eat there?"

The old girl mooed again, contentedly chewing on her hay. But his question seemed to set off decidedly less satisfied calls from every other corner of the floor. The three goats in the next pen bleated like an entire herd. The dogs barked like they'd been starving for days. Even the rabbits in his homemade hutch chirped especially loud.

The cacophony nearly made him miss the ring of his phone, but the vibration in his back pocket made him jump. He jerked the phone free, flipped it open, and pressed it to his ear. "Hello?"

"Finnegan." The deep voice needed no introduction, but he offered one anyway. "It's your dad."

Finn smiled as he tucked the phone between his ear and his shoulder so he could grab a pallet of hay for the goats. "This is a surprise."

"I thought you might be feeding."

"I am."

His dad offered a throaty chuckle. "Your mother always says I have perfect timing."

Finn offered an obligatory laugh. They both knew his mother said no such thing. Never had. Thomas Chaffey was notoriously late, and only Bea Chaffey's sainthood had kept them married for nearly thirty-five years.

"What's up?" Finn asked as he opened the gate and stepped into the goat enclosure. Jenna immediately ran to him, butting her head against his legs to get at the meal in his hands. Her two kids kept their distance, prancing in the far corner and eyeing him with their strange horizontal pupils.

"Your mother heard there was an accident at the harbor

today. Aretha Franklin just called from the Bahamas. She heard it from Kathleen, who heard it from . . . well, never mind. Are you all right?"

"Yeah. Yeah, I'm fine. A tourist fell in the harbor. And it was kind of my fault."

With the mama goat adequately distracted by fresh hay, he strolled toward the kids, who tried to escape to the small pasture behind their pen. If not for the locked gate, they would have been long gone. Squatting before them, he slowly held out his hand to let them investigate it. Not even a month old, they still wobbled a little on their spindly legs, but they were definitely warming up to him, seeing as he'd been supplementing their feeding with daily bottles of milk.

"Kind of?"

His dad's delayed question made him jump and nearly lose his balance. Swaying to stay upright, he scared off the kids, who staggered toward their mother for their own dinner.

Finn pushed off his knees and stood slowly. "She bumped into me. Actually, she sort of *bounced* off of me."

His dad said nothing, but Finn had no problem picturing his questioning eyebrows.

Finn dumped out the goats' water tub and scrubbed it clean with the brush that hung from a nail on the back wall. "I don't know. I wasn't paying attention. I was just taking Joe Jr. for a walk—"

His dad snorted a laugh. "Enough said."

"He's not that bad, Dad. He's just . . ." Finn chewed on his lip as he searched for the right description for his sidekick. The dog had always been just a little bit off. While the rest of his litter had been easy to train, Joe had been a big goofy pup. And he'd grown into a big goofy dog.

His dad probably knew by now that there weren't exact words for Joe, so he asked only, "Is the girl all right?"

"Uh . . . mostly. Physically. Her stuff is ruined, though. But I set her up at the Red Door. Marie is taking care of her until we can figure it out."

"You're going to help her get her gear sorted?"

"Yeah. I'll check in on her tomorrow. I'll make sure she can get whatever she needs." Assuming those electronics weren't as much as the new tractor he'd been eyeing or the expansion on the barn he'd been dreaming of, he'd be willing to cover the cost of replacements. Not that she was likely to let him. She'd been pretty stuck on paying Marie for a simple lunch. But at least he could offer.

"Good man."

Finn rubbed at his chest, right over the center of the warmth that spread through him. It didn't matter that he was thirty-three. His dad's approval still mattered.

"So, how's the new litter?"

With a chuckle, Finn walked toward the puppies in question. Stretching up on their back legs, they pawed at the fence, barking for dinner, a drink, and affection. "Not so new. They're at least twenty pounds now." Reaching through the chain links, he stroked the soft black fur, fluffy and mostly clean. For now. He'd given them all a bath after a romp in the pasture the night before, but two of them had thoroughly rolled in their hay bedding.

Ringo gnawed on his knuckle, his puppy teeth not quite sharp enough to break skin.

"Already? How are they shaping up? Ready to start training?"

Finn gave the four pups a harder perusal. "Good shape, strong. And good dispositions."

"Good. Good." There was a longing in his voice, and Finn knew that his dad would rather be training this litter than be anywhere else. Except at his wife's side. But after almost a year of tests and more years of painful joints, his dad had been diagnosed with rheumatoid arthritis. He physically couldn't keep up the business, so he'd passed it to Finn more than ten years before.

And his mom had done what she could always do. She'd talked her husband into her heart's desire—a home with a harbor view in Summerside, steps from a coffee shop that was purported to have the island's best oatmeal lemon bar.

"You can come visit anytime, you know," Finn said.

"Same goes to you. Your mother was just saying we haven't seen you in far too long. Busy saving damsels in distress, I suppose."

Finn chuckled. "Cretia isn't what I'd call distressed." She would have marched out of the inn and probably all the way back to Charlottetown on a bum ankle if Marie hadn't stopped her.

"Cretia? Sounds like you're awfully friendly already." There was a note of teasing in his voice, but Finn couldn't defend himself fast enough.

"Well, I couldn't carry someone whose name I didn't know."

He nearly bit off the tip of his tongue. He'd opened a world of questions without thinking about it.

"You carried her to the inn? You should have led with that."

Before Finn could explain that it had all been quite

innocent—and necessary—his father hollered away from the phone. "Bea! Come here! He picked her up and carried her."

"What?" his mother shrieked from somewhere deeper inside the house. "Where? Why? Is he going to see her again? Soon? You know he's in his mid-thirties. We were married at nineteen."

Finn sighed and scrubbed a hand down his face.

That response was exactly why he hadn't started by telling them that he'd held her in his arms. Cretia was a stranger. A strong, smart stranger—with long black eyelashes that shaded dark chocolate eyes. And high cheekbones. And smooth pink lips.

Not that he'd looked that closely. Besides, none of those things changed the fact that she wouldn't be around long enough for him to get to know more than how her soft curves fit into arms.

Which had been nice.

Really nice.

Of course, he hadn't given that more than a passing thought besides how she'd started off so stiff, pushing away from him, nearly fighting him. The fear that had clenched his gut when he'd nearly dropped her. And the moment she'd finally given in, sinking against his chest. Warm where they touched.

This was not a topic of conversation he was eager to have with his dad—and especially not his mom. Individually they'd dropped more than a hint or two that they'd like him to keep the family tree going. Together, they were relentless.

"She couldn't walk. That's all. I was just helping her get to the inn so she could dry off."

"But you're going to see her again?" his mom called from the background.

"Yes," his dad said. "He already told me he's going to help her replace her things. It was his fault she fell in, after all."

His mom cried out, and he could picture her covering her mouth. "Oh, honey. No. Did you push her in?"

"What? Why would I push her in?" Raking his fingers through his hair, he sighed. "It was an accident."

"Joe Jr.," his dad supplied by way of explanation.

"Oh." His mom didn't need more.

"Listen, guys, I've got to finish feeding and spend some time with the pups."

"Okay," his mom called. "But bring her down here when you get a chance. We want to meet her."

Yeah, that wasn't going to happen. But he said only, "We'll see."

"Say hi to the Fab Four for us," his dad said in lieu of a goodbye.

With a quick "I will," Finn flipped his phone closed and shoved it into his pocket.

Squatting down in front of Ringo, who was still pressed against the fence, Finn scratched his ears through the chain link. "You going to set the rhythm for this group?" he asked.

The pup barked a joyful response. More likely he was just hungry, so Finn set about measuring the all-natural kibble into four silver tins. The puppies had only been eating solids for a few weeks, so he added a dash of water over each to keep them soft.

Balancing the puppy-sized bowls, two in his left hand and two in the crook of his left arm, he let himself into the kennel with his other hand. John, Paul, George, and Ringo loped toward him, tangling between his legs. Their little black faces looked up with eager expectation, and their high-pitched yaps filled the barn from floor to wooden roof beams.

"Hey now, everyone calm down."

They did not.

Not that he'd expected them too. And the sound of his voice only seemed to rile them up, making them hop on his feet and wag their long tails.

He'd just begun training them, so he didn't bother giving them a command as he leaned down to put their dishes next to each other. This evening was about socializing them. Playing with them. He'd been gone far longer than he'd planned, and he needed to help them get rid of some of their energy.

Three little rumps lifted right in the air as the heads disappeared into their bowls. John, sporting his green collar, jumped a few times, and Finn gave him one more head scratch before pointing him to the bowl.

He couldn't remember the last time they'd had a litter with so few puppies. For the last few years Maisey had delivered at least seven with each litter. One year she'd had twelve.

Four was an anomaly. Four boys at that.

He'd really had no choice but to name them after the Beatles, his dad's favorite band. Finn still had all their albums on vinyl, and he'd fully planned on naming Joe Sgt. Pepper. Until his mom got the idea in her head that Joe Jr. was the only option. There had been no arguing with her.

But one of these days, Finn was going to have a Sgt. Pepper. Then he wouldn't be the only one in the Lonely Hearts Club.

And maybe his folks would back off a little bit.

And maybe he wouldn't feel quite so alone.

Not that he was by himself. Six adult Newfoundlands barked from the adjoining kennel separated by a solid wood fence, and Finn strolled over to feed them too. They all rushed toward the food, jostling him and each other for position. All except for Bella, who waddled with her very pregnant belly. The vet had said she was carrying eleven, and Finn prayed they all survived.

"Hey, pretty girl." He squatted at her eye level, running a gentle hand from the top of her head to her swollen side. "How you feeling? 'Bout ready to have these kiddos?"

She slobbered all over his shoulder.

He'd take that as a yes.

In a few days he'd set up a whelping bed and move her into the birthing room off the front of the barn. She was probably still a week or so away, but this was only her second litter, and he'd rather be ready just in case he'd misjudged her.

With eleven more pups on the way, he had no business feeling lonely. He had more than enough work to keep any man busy. And more than enough mouths depending on him to feed them.

And his dad depending on him to carry on the Chaffey legacy. Both the family business and the family name.

But managing one didn't leave much time for the other.

Sure, he'd thought about marriage and a family of his own a few times over the years. Not a particular woman—just the concept. And he liked the idea. Coming inside on a cold December day to a warm hug and a soft kiss. Sitting across the table from a kind smile. Sharing the weight of the business and his dad's expectations. Waking up every morning next to the woman he would love for the rest of his life.

All good things.

Except he'd never met anyone he wanted those things with.

Sweet girls. Pretty ladies. Kind women. He'd met every single one in North Rustico, PEI. Before moving to Summerside, his mom had paraded half the female population of the north shore past him.

Not a single one had made his heart hammer against his ribs.

Until he'd picked up Cretia. And set her down. And stopped her from leaving.

Scowling, he tried to force himself to think about anything else. To not see her face every time he blinked.

This was ridiculous. He barely knew her. And what he knew made no sense. How could someone make a living by traveling around the world?

It couldn't be safe. It probably wasn't smart.

And when she gave up on her ludicrous lifestyle, she'd head back to her home. He wasn't an expert at US geography, but he thought Arizona was about as far from the island as you could get and still be in the States.

In the meantime, she'd gallivant around the globe— assuming her passport hadn't been ruined—and probably be even farther away.

But when he'd set her on the floor at the inn, he'd felt her absence deep in his gut. Somewhere not far from his heart. There had been a hollowness, like he was missing something.

How could he miss someone he'd known for exactly fifteen minutes? Besides, they'd barely said two words to each other. And, of course, the minute he had spoken, he'd shoved his foot in his mouth.

He'd never felt this way before, and he didn't quite know

what to do. Except ignore the feeling. That was probably his best option. But he had to help her replace her electronics. He could disregard whatever his gut said for as long as it took to get Cretia back on the road. Then it would just be him and the Fab Four again. And a few dozen other animals.

He'd probably barely see her anyway. He had work to do.

"Come on, boys." He held the gate open, and the puppies tromped onto the open barn floor. "Let's go outside and play."

Five

After a night in the coziest bed she'd ever slept in, Cretia woke to find her clothes folded in a stack on the desk in her guest room. Marie had asked if she could sneak in that morning and drop them off. She'd also left a fresh towel that smelled of sunshine and wildflowers.

The whole day before had turned into a bit of a blur in her memory. After the excitement of the morning and the following adrenaline crash, she'd napped for most of the afternoon. But she still hadn't woken feeling rested.

Marie had invited her to join the Sloan family for dinner, but Cretia had skipped the meal in favor of inspecting her electronics.

Just as she'd expected. They were hopeless. All of them.

Surrounded by disappointment, she had crawled back into the comfy bed while the sun was still up.

With the warm sunrise, the day felt a little more manageable. Cretia skipped the shower but washed her face with the inn's complimentary cleanser before donning her clothes, savoring the familiar jeans that hugged her waist but left plenty of room for her hips and thighs. Running her fingers through her dark waves, she tried to make sense of her hair but knew it was mostly a lost cause. All of her travel-size hair potions were somewhere in the harbor.

And her electronics might as well be.

She pinched the bridge of her nose as more memories from the day before rushed back to her. Finn and his beast. Losing everything. Her twisted ankle.

She stepped forward gingerly, which elicited a small twinge across the top of her foot. Nothing more.

At least she wasn't seriously injured. And a quick inspection showed barely a bruise and no visible swelling. Nothing to keep her from getting back on the road.

Except her electronics.

Taking a deep breath, she eased open her door and stepped into the hallway. The inn was mostly silent, save for the friendly scratch of a tree branch against the window at the front of the house. Its bright green leaves were a beacon, an invitation to settle beneath its shade.

She didn't have time for that.

Tiptoeing past a row of closed wooden doors on each side of the hall, she remembered that Marie had said the inn had no other guests at the moment. Which explained why she'd had her first uninterrupted night of sleep in years. No slamming hotel doors or the thunder of little feet running up and down the hall. No cars driving along busy streets outside her window.

Surely, being the only guest in the house contributed to her brain shutting off as soon as her head hit the pillow. Well, that and the mattress that welcomed her like a long-lost friend. And the lavender-scented sheets. And the utterly exhausting day.

The old Victorian house felt homier than any other place

she'd stayed in her travels. Or before, for that matter. It was lived in and loved on, child-size jackets hanging from pegs on the mudroom wall above the bucket of rice, nonsensical pictures covering the front of the stainless-steel refrigerator in the kitchen.

The inn was far from empty. It was just . . . peaceful.

Cretia shook her head to clear away her ridiculous thoughts before taking a careful step onto the wooden stairs. The hand-rail held steady as she cautiously made her way toward the foyer and front door, the third-to-last step squeaking under her weight.

"Cretia? You awake?" Marie's voice sounded like it had come from somewhere near the kitchen, so she moved in that direction.

"Yes." When she pushed open the swinging door with the jingle bell, she found two little girls eating breakfast at the island. One was maybe five or six. Cretia had seen her briefly the day before but hadn't realized she was an exact copy and paste of her mom—all inquisitive blue eyes and brown curls. The other was a few years younger. From her high chair, the toddler grinned, unconcerned with the red jam smeared across her cheeks.

"Mama said we had to be quiet because you needed rest after your . . ." The older girl looked at the ceiling for a second before finishing. "Or-ordeal." Her eyes narrowed, and then she nodded firmly. "You look okay to me."

"Julia Mae." Marie sighed as she slipped into the room through a side door. "You can't decide that for someone else. You don't know how she feels."

Julia Mae frowned at her mom but finally nodded a re-luctant agreement.

Marie gave her daughter a soft kiss on top of her curls before turning toward the door with a warm smile. "How are you feeling, Cretia? How's your ankle?"

"Better. Much better. Thanks to your bag of peas."

Marie's smile grew. "I'm glad someone appreciated them. The kids refused to eat them."

"Daddy too," Julia Mae offered.

With a chuckle, Marie conceded. "Yes, Daddy too."

Cretia cracked a smile at the sweet exchange, letting herself wish for just a moment that she had memories like that from her own childhood.

"Did you sleep well?" Marie bent over to wipe the cheeks of her youngest.

"It was lovely. Really. The best I've slept in years."

Marie beamed up at her.

"I'll pay you for the room as soon as I—"

Marie shook her head quickly. "We've covered that. You don't owe us anything. I'm returning a favor to Finn, who definitely owes you."

Cretia opened her mouth, but Julia Mae filled the silence instead. "Mama says we're not supposed to argue with her. She says when she makes a decision we have to go with it. It's for our own good. Even if we don't understand."

Cretia nearly snorted. Of course, Marie had to have had that conversation with her precocious daughter.

But Cretia wasn't part of her family, and she wasn't about to give in. She didn't take charity from anyone. She had more than enough in her bank account to rent a room, so if Marie didn't let her pay for it now, she'd do so later.

"So, do you know what you're going to do today?" Marie asked.

"Um . . ." Cretia bit the corner of her lip and shot a glance at the mudroom, where the bucket of rice and ruined electronics still sat. "I suppose I'll get to work on replacing my things."

Marie frowned, her gaze shifting over her shoulder toward the room off the kitchen. "I want to help, but our computer guy is upgrading our system this week. I only have my phone to make bookings right now."

Cretia waved off her concern. "No worries. I'll figure something—"

"Finn can help you."

Finn, who thought her job was a joke. Finn, who had all but pushed her into the water. Finn, who had dug through what was left of her personal things.

Finn, who had raced to the store to buy a bucket's worth of rice the minute she'd asked.

"He has a . . ." Marie paused. "Well, he can help you order what you need."

Marie's pause made her teeth clench, but Cretia finally nodded. "Yeah, yesterday he said he'd help me figure it out."

"He lives a few minutes out of town. My husband Seth picked up your rental car last night. You're parked right out front, and the keys are next to the rice bucket."

"Thank you. But he didn't have to—"

"Nonsense. I traded him for dish duty. He got the better end of the deal. Trust me."

Cretia didn't know how to respond, which wasn't a problem since Marie kept going.

"Finn lives just down the road. It's about a five-minute drive or a twenty-minute walk—if you're feeling up to it. Do you think you can make it on your own? I have to take the girls to an awards ceremony at Jack's school this morning. But I'm sure Finn can help you figure out your rental car situation too."

A bubble of something like uncertainty rose in her throat at the thought of navigating this town on her own. Of course, she knew it was the size of a postage stamp. And sure, she'd found her way through a hundred international cities. But always she'd had a map as close as the tap of her finger.

This time she was *alone* alone.

Except for the people here who insisted on helping her.

She swallowed at the worry, but it only seemed to grow.

Just fake it until you make it.

That had been her motto when she'd booked her first flight out of Phoenix. And it hadn't changed, whether it was holding her head high and walking with a purpose through an unfamiliar airport or using the two semesters of French she barely remembered in Paris.

Fake it until you make it.

She'd keep moving forward into the unknown until it made sense, until she was confident in the next step. Until then, she'd hold her head high and pretend she knew what she was doing.

Plastering a smile on her face, she forced out a perky, "I'll go see him in a little bit, then."

"Can I get you something to eat? Our kitchen isn't officially open, but you can help yourself, or I can get you . . ."

"Mom's real good at toast."

Marie shushed Julia Mae with a chuckle, but Cretia jumped in before she could continue. "I'm fine."

Marie hoisted her youngest out of the wooden high chair and set her on the floor. "Okay. We'll be back this afternoon. Feel free to come and go as you like through the back door."

Nodding toward a folded yellow flannel sitting on the edge of the counter, she added, "Will you take Finn his shirt while you're over there?"

The shirt he'd literally given Cretia off his back when even her bones had been shivering.

"Sure. But you'll have to point me in the right direction."

"Go through the intersection and past the bakery on your left. You can't miss it. Smells like cinnamon and sugar from heaven. Finn's is the green farmhouse across from the Kane Dairy sign."

Following Marie's directions, Cretia had no problem finding the bakery—and making a mental note to come back to it. Indeed, it did smell like heaven, and her stomach growled as she imagined the treats coming from its ovens.

She'd decided a walk sounded nice after being inside most of the day before, and the flat road didn't bother her ankle much as she ambled past the gray house set up on a little hill. She lifted her nose for another sniff, and the sun's rays made her skin tingle.

As she strolled out of the bakery's reach, her mind wandered to thirty minutes before and the useless pile of rice in the bottom of the bucket. She'd pretty much written off her electronics the night before, but she'd checked for a miracle just in case. Her phone screen had barely flickered when she tried to turn it on. And her laptop hadn't done any better.

Her tablet at least had pretended to turn on, the screen blinking a few times—though mostly green lines. Then it froze. No poking, prodding, or cajoling could bring it back to life.

She'd seriously considered throwing it across the kitchen for the pure satisfaction of watching it explode against a wall. But she wouldn't repay Marie's kindness by risking any damage to her pristine kitchen—every white cabinet spotless and tiled counter wiped clean. Marie had joked about her own cooking skills—or lack thereof—but everything about her kitchen screamed that it was loved and cared for. There were no stacks of dirty dishes in the sink. No slices of moldy bread by the stove. No overflowing trash bags in the corner. This was the kitchen she'd dreamed of as a child. Just like the ones she'd seen on the DIY TV shows.

Instead of throwing her tablet, Cretia had dropped it back in the bucket, gathered up Finn's shirt from the counter, and marched past the wall of shelves across from the coats in the mudroom and out the door.

By the time Cretia cleared the memories from in front of her eyes, there were only pine trees and hayfields in front of her. The two-lane road continued, dipping and twisting, but there was no telling where it led. No sign of the promised dairy farm or Finn's green house.

She'd probably been too lost in her thoughts and taken a wrong turn. Must have.

But when she whipped around, she realized she'd walked right by it all. The big white house next to a Kane Dairy sign that proudly announced "North Rustico's Favorite Cheese" beside a stack of yellow wheels. A red arrow on the grass-green wood pointed toward a small structure added to the end of the white barn. The neon sign in the window read "Open."

Maybe this was the home of Mama Cheese Sandwich— and the cheese that had melted not only in her sandwich but also in her mouth. Cretia could still taste the sharp cheddar and spicy pepper jack combination. She needed to stop by the dairy store too.

Across the street, right where Marie had told her it would be, sat a square two-story farmhouse. The green exterior didn't match the grass or blend in with the tree in the front yard. It wasn't teal like the bowl she'd eaten out of the day before. It was softer than that. Quieter than the island's natural hues. It wasn't harsh or hard on the eyes. The front boasted white trim and sweet shutters. It was . . . serene. She took a deep breath and realized she was smiling. For absolutely no reason. Other than that it was a pretty house.

At least on the outside.

Her gut twisted hard, the muscles in her face falling as she strode down the gravel driveway. She had no business assuming anything about the interior of Finn's home, but her mind still pictured the worst. Always.

Not that she'd seen the inside of any personal homes in a while. Hotels. Inns. B and Bs. Train stations. Airports. Those were the spaces she'd occupied. But homes were . . . different.

Homes were private.

Homes were places where secrets were never thrown away. Her shoulders tensed as memories of her childhood flooded through her.

Finn had said he had kids. Maybe he'd made a home for them that he was proud of. A home where they could invite friends over. A home filled with the scent of lavender pot-pourri or home-cooked meals.

Finn and his . . . wife?

She hadn't bothered to ask the day before. To be fair, she'd been recovering from a dunk in the harbor and had a few other things on her mind. But still. She should have asked. Marie hadn't mentioned a partner that morning—only that Finn would help her.

Maybe he was a single father.

Plenty of single fathers ran around pulling strangers from the water and carrying them like they weighed nothing. With strong arms. And a warm smile that seemed to come from his core. Dripping in seawater, she'd needed that warmth. And he hadn't disappointed.

Yeah, there were lots of single dads like that.

Probably.

Cretia let out a loud sigh, ready to bang her forehead against the dark wood of the front door. She was overthinking this. Per usual.

Finn's life was none of her business. What was on the other side of the door didn't matter either. She needed to get off this island and back to her regularly scheduled life.

It was just a house. A boxy farmhouse.

She didn't have to live there. Whatever it looked like on the inside, it wasn't her problem.

She didn't even have to go inside.

There. Easy enough. She'd just stay on this side of the threshold. She'd hand Finn his shirt through the open door. And then she'd walk away.

A little voice inside her whispered a not-so-gentle reminder that this plan conveniently failed to account for replacing her electronics and calling the rental car company—and the help Finn might offer.

Maybe he had a laptop that he'd bring out to the front stoop so they could enjoy the sunshine.

Sure. That was a totally normal idea. But she wasn't going

to know how this would play out until she talked with him. And that required getting him to the door.

Forcing her hand into a fist, she knocked twice and waited. The house was still. No children's voices, no barked greeting from Joe Jr.

She knocked again, louder and longer this time.

Still nothing. Maybe the kids were at school. Maybe Finn was at the same awards ceremony that Marie had hurried off to.

"Come on, boys! Go get it!" The voice was unmistakably Finn's, though Cretia couldn't figure out exactly where it was coming from. Or who he was talking to. Until a chorus of high-pitched barks followed.

Cretia followed the sound of playing dogs across the yard and toward the big red barn. The sliding door on the front side was closed, so she tiptoed around the end of the building, running a hand along the bright wooden planks, the paint smooth and unmarred by time and sun.

The barks grew louder and more frenzied until Finn broke through them. "Sit." He cleared his throat. "George." He sounded both mildly annoyed and amused, and Cretia hurried toward him, curious if his expression matched his tone.

"Good boy, Ringo." His praise was immediately followed by the telltale sounds of a dog devouring his crunchy treat.

When Cretia finally rounded the corner, the scene before her was not what she'd anticipated. Finn stood in the center of a small fenced-in corral, a fluffy black puppy under one arm and three identical copies around his feet, jumping at his knees. Behind him, a full-sized Newfoundland was rooting for something in his pocket.

"Joe, stop it," Finn said over his shoulder.

She barely recognized Joe Jr., all dry and fluffy, his tongue lolling out of the corner of his mouth. The dog's big nose didn't stop his mission.

"I'm going to put you inside," Finn threatened.

Joe remained undeterred. But suddenly his nose tipped into the air, and he looked around Finn's leg. With a guttural woof, he bounded toward her, nearly tripping over his own feet. He wasn't nearly as scary on land when she didn't think he was about to jump on top of her. But he was still a beast—immense and intimidating.

Except there was something like a goofy grin on his face and maybe a bit of joy in his bark.

He plowed into the chicken-wire fence, shaking his head over the top and sending drool flying toward her. She raised her elbow as a shield just in time for his slobber to coat her arm instead of her face.

"Cretia!" Finn's eyes flew open wide, and he fought his way free of the three puppies trying to trip him. "I'm sorry. Joe isn't used to having— That is, what are you doing here? How's your ankle?"

With one hand she held out his flannel while trying to surreptitiously shake her other arm dry without wiping Joe's slobber on her clean sweater. "It's fine—much better today. Marie asked me to bring this . . . Actually, I wanted to say thank you. To you and Joe." The latter happily accepted her rub of his head. "You didn't have to pull me out of the water or take me to Marie's, and I wasn't very . . . appreciative yesterday."

"More than understandable. That was quite an ordeal. And I was a little bit . . . well . . ."

"Judgmental. I think the word you're looking for is judgmental. And nosy."

A grin broke through his beard, crinkling the corners of his eyes as he finally took his shirt. "Yes. Those things. I'm sorry about that." He adjusted the puppy under his arm with a shrug of his shoulder. "Maybe we can start over?"

"All right." She moved to shake his hand but realized they were both full. "I'm Lucretia—Cretia—Martin." She laid heavily on the last syllable again, emphasizing the long *e*.

His eyebrows rose and his forehead wrinkled. "Mar-teen?"

She nodded firmly. "It's Spanish."

"And I'm Finn Chaffey."

"Finnegan," she clarified.

He frowned. "To my parents and a select few women who enjoy bossing me around."

"So, just Finn?"

The puppy under his arm wiggled, apparently bored with their conversation, so Finn put him down and he joined his identical siblings.

"Marie doesn't have internet at her place right now. But she said maybe I could borrow yours to order some new equipment."

"The rice didn't work?" He didn't sound particularly surprised, but there was a note of sadness in his voice.

"No. They're all shot. My phone won't even pretend to turn on. I think the salt water demolished it. I need to borrow a computer with internet. It won't take me very long."

His gaze darted toward the house. "I'm . . . Can you wait an hour? I just started with the puppies, and I'd like to keep them on schedule." Something like hope flashed in his eyes. "You can join us."

Cretia looked around for evidence of what they'd been

up to but spotted only a few tennis balls scattered across the green grass. "For what exactly?"

"Puppy training." Finn waved at the four pups. "Or, more precisely, puppy socialization. It's good for them to be around other people, to get used to various voices and smells."

"And I'm other people?"

He motioned for her to climb over the fence, which reached to just above her waist. Clearly he thought she was some sort of track and field star. She was the queen of walking tours and the occasional sprint to catch a train. But leaping fences was not on her résumé.

She shook her head firmly as he sized up her proportional height.

"Um . . . do you mind if I . . . again?" He was already leaning down to scoop her up and over, and before she could respond, her feet landed inside the corral.

"Do you do that a lot? Pick people up, I mean. It seems like you've had quite a bit of practice."

He chuckled from somewhere low in his chest, the sound reverberating and making the dogs bark. "Not people so much." He nodded toward Joe Jr. "Not until I met you anyway."

She wasn't sure how she was supposed to take that, but Finn didn't stick around to clarify. Turning toward the puppies, he caught their attention and brought them into a line in the shadow of the barn. Holding out a treat between his fingers, he commanded them to sit, with mixed results. The two in the middle did as they were told. The one on the far left spun in a circle, chasing his tail, while the other caught sight of a dragonfly and leapt after it.

But the minute Finn rewarded the middle two with treats

from his pocket, the other two rushed him for equal treatment. "Uh-uh," he said firmly, holding his open hand toward their noses. After a few more attempts, they finally obeyed and received their biscuits. "Good boys," he cooed, giving them extra ear scratches.

At her side Joe gave a little *ruff*, pressing his damp nose into her hand. Cretia stroked his soft fur from between his eyes to the back of his head, but she couldn't take her gaze off Finn. He moved with a steady assurance that both commanded the dogs' respect and spoke of a deep love for the little guys. Every action practiced yet relaxed, putting them all at ease.

"You want to come play with them?" he asked from his squatted position, pushing the sleeves of his gray Henley up to his elbows.

It took her a moment to realize he was talking to her, but she agreed before she could think about the consequences of getting on the ground with the black furballs in the only clothes she owned.

The pleading faces with big black eyes could not be denied, and she sat down in a particularly soft patch of grass. Joe circled at her side and plopped down along her thigh. Then four little bodies jumped against her, nearly sending her backward. Their warmth and silky coats invited hugs and snuggles.

"Meet John, Paul, George, and Ringo."

"The Beatles?"

Finn shrugged as he stood and strolled toward them. "They're definitely a Fab Four."

Six

Most visitors to the barn looked at twenty-pound dogs and thought they were well on their way to full grown. They forgot that these Newfoundlands were barely puppies, complete with wiggling tails, squirming bodies, and heaps of energy.

Cretia seemed to have no such misconception.

Finn put his hands on his hips as he watched her play with them, her scratches teasing and joyful. There was no surprise and less fear in her expression, her eyes alight with laughter. And the puppies responded in kind, happy yips filling the yard.

"Ow!" she said, pulling back from Paul and giving him a soft glare and a contradictory belly rub.

"Sorry. They're still a little bitey—new teeth and all."

She looked at the side of her hand and laughed. "I noticed. But thanks for the warning." Her smile returned in a flash, her attention back on the dogs. As she flipped her mass of dark waves over her shoulder, his stomach took a similar spin, and he nearly choked on his own tongue. His heart slammed into his ribs. Then again for good measure.

Sweet cinnamon rolls, she was beautiful.

It wasn't just the way the sun made her black hair glow like obsidian or the deep tan of her skin or the pert line of her nose. It was all of those things and the slightly crooked front teeth in her smile. And the light in her eyes. And the dimple in her left cheek. And the joy in her laughter.

No wonder people watched videos of her exploring the world.

She was literally in his backyard, and he couldn't seem to take his eyes off her any more than the puppies could stay away or Joe Jr. could leave her side.

Finn squinted at the older dog, who lay along her leg, his chin resting on her knee and his eyes closed. Joe didn't sit calmly beside anyone for very long. Even Finn. But five minutes in, he hadn't moved a muscle, despite the Fab Four nipping at his ears and tail.

"Are you just going to stare at us, or are you going to join in?"

The tips of his ears burned, and Finn shoved his hands into his pockets as he dropped his gaze to his boots. "Sorry. You're good with them. You have a dog when you were a kid?"

Something like pain flashed across her face, but she schooled it back to neutral so fast that he couldn't fully identify the emotion. "No. We had . . . cats. But I always wanted a puppy. Just a little one."

"Why didn't you get one?"

She shook her head. "No reason, really. My mom just . . . I guess she thought they wouldn't fit into our home." Her tone carried something deeper than the easy dismissal, but her expression confirmed that she didn't want him to push.

"Well, you're welcome to play with these puppies or any of my dogs as long as you're here."

"Thank you." She picked up a tennis ball, rolled it toward her extended feet, and John tumbled after it. "How many dogs do you have?"

"Eleven for now. More on the way."

Her jaw dropped, her mouth hanging open for several long, silent seconds. "More? Why would you want more? How do you even keep up with them?"

Finn chuckled, swiping his hand through his hair. "It's what I do. I breed and train Newfoundlands."

Those telltale lines between her perfectly arched eyebrows appeared. "Why?"

He snorted a laugh as he plopped to the ground, facing her. John tromped over and dropped the ball in his hand, and he rubbed the pup's ears. "Because it's what we've always done. It's what my dad did and his dad."

His explanation didn't make a crack in the confusion written across her face. "But why? I mean, what do you do with them?" Paul with his blue collar jumped into her lap, and she hugged him close as though protecting him from ending up in a cage somewhere.

"Oh, you know. They end up here and there."

"Here and where? In good homes? Like, where they're cared for?"

With a chuckle and a shake of his head, Finn grabbed George under his front legs and stared into his little face. His slightly sour puppy breath easily carried the distance between their noses, and George barked with glee. "You think I'd spend months raising these guys only to send them off to be mistreated?"

The tight line of her lips began to relax, but worry still flickered in her narrowed eyes.

He couldn't remember the last time anyone in North Rustico—let alone on the island—had questioned his care for the dogs. It was his name on the business, his family's reputation on the line. Her doubts stung like a snapped rubber band. Not that he didn't deserve them after he'd questioned the validity of her job the day before.

Forcing a loose grin into place, he said, "Most of them are raised as rescue dogs."

"Like what Joe did for me yesterday." Her voice was small, almost apologetic, and Joe looked up at the sound of his name before resting his head back on her leg and feigning sleep.

"Exactly like that. It's in their blood. They're strong swimmers, fearless in storms. Good trackers."

"And the rest of them? You said *most*."

"A few go to good homes—families who want a new friend. And a few become therapy dogs."

Her nose crinkled, confusion in her eyes.

"They help people with high anxiety, neurodivergence, and PTSD challenges. Because of their size, they can be intimidating, but they have such gentle spirits that they tend to calm down those around them. My dogs have gone to therapy clinics, nonprofit organizations for veterans, and individuals needing some support."

She started to crack a smile. "I've seen plenty of emotional support animals on airplanes, but I can't picture one of your Newfoundlands fitting under the seat in front of me."

Just the idea of Joe Jr. trying to squeeze under a chair made him chuckle. "Yeah, they're more the open spaces kind of therapy. Not exactly portable when they're full grown—unless you have a big truck."

She matched his smile and pointed at the Fab Four. "What about these guys?"

"They're already sold to a couple of rescue teams in Newfoundland and Labrador."

The corners of her mouth dipped. "That sounds like hard work. It's cold up there."

Ruffling Paul's thick coat of black curls, Finn shook his head. "These guys are made for that kind of weather. And when they put on another hundred and thirty pounds, they'll be nearly impervious to the snow."

Her glance shot up from the pup in her arms. "A hundred and thirty?"

With a shrug, he chuckled. "Give or take. Joe Jr. is pushing one sixty, and he was the runt of his litter."

Cretia looked like she'd swallowed her tongue. "*He's* the runt? But he rescued me like I was nothing. And you . . ." Her gaze dipped, shadowed by her full eyelashes.

He remembered. Plunging his arm into the water and pulling her out. He'd had to do it more than once with dogs that refused to leave the harbor during their training. At least she hadn't fought him like they sometimes did. But he said only, "There was a lot of adrenaline in the moment."

"Well, like I said before, thank you."

"I'm happy to help for as long as you're here."

The muscles in her neck contracted around a swallow as Ringo pounced on her leg. "So could I borrow your computer for a few minutes?"

"Marie sent you down here for that?" He couldn't contain a snort at the irony. Marie had to be up to something. Not that Finn wasn't happy to offer his setup and eager to make up for his misstep the day before, but there were a dozen other places Marie could have sent Cretia. Even Brooke in the front office of the church would have been happy to share her sleek new laptop.

"Was she wrong? I can go somewhere else if there's a public library or something. I don't mean to be a bother."

He reached to pat her knee, but Joe Jr.'s head snapped up and a low growl came from somewhere deep in his body. It wasn't threatening, just a caution. Slowly pulling his hand back, Finn tilted his head at the dog. Joe had clearly decided that Cretia was his person—his to protect, his to save.

Only Finn didn't know who or what she needed to be protected from.

He shook off the questions rolling through his mind and caught her gaze. "You're not a bother. It's just that . . . Never mind. I'm happy to help."

Her mouth pinched slightly, lines appearing around it. "Do you have time now?"

With a glance toward the barn, he said, "I just need to feed the kids really fast. It'll only take a few minutes."

Her face twisted in confusion, her lips pursing to the side as the wrinkles between her eyebrows returned. "Aren't they at school?"

"School?"

"Yeah. Marie went to an awards ceremony or something for Jack today. Do they go to the same school?"

"Do they go to the same school?" He tried to stop himself from repeating her words. He just couldn't figure out another way to make sense of what she said.

Cretia nodded slowly. "Yes. The same school. Or are

they older?" She shook her head. "No, you're younger than Marie, aren't you? I mean, you look younger. Not that she looks old. It's the beard. Your beard is throwing me off. But maybe you had kids really young." She sucked in a sharp breath and blinked twice. Slowly. Decisively. "I'm sorry," she whispered. "That should have been inside processing."

"Inside processing?" Again with the parroting. He could bite his tongue off.

The prettiest shade of pink bloomed in her cheeks, and he couldn't look away, even as George gnawed on his wrist.

"I . . ." She looked toward the hayfield on the other side of the corral fence and tucked her dark hair behind her ear. "I spend a lot of time alone, but I do better when I can verbally process things. It's no big deal when I'm on my own. A little more awkward when it spills out in front of other people—or worse, the person I'm talking about."

A chuckle bubbled deep in his chest. He tried and failed to cover it with his hand.

The color in her cheeks deepened, stretching toward her neck, and she pressed her fingers to her throat. "I swear, I'm better in front of the camera."

"I don't think it's possible you could be more charming."

Her eyes flew to meet his, her gaze tangible. The skin on his arms tingled under the weight. It wasn't like the touch of the sun on a cool day. It was like a welcome fire, rushing through him. Unlike anything he'd ever experienced before.

His own neck began to burn, and he swallowed hard against the lump there. "You're right, processing that inside would have been less awkward." Tacking on a grin, he added, "But no less true."

"Okay." Her nostrils flared and her lips twitched. "So you need to feed your kids? And then you can help me?"

"Indeed. Maybe you want to help *me*?"

She gulped audibly. "You want me to meet your kids?"

Pushing himself off the ground—to the clear dismay of George, whose green collar jangled as he wiggled and jumped, begging for more attention—Finn winked at her. "I think you'll like them. They're pretty friendly."

Cretia shifted to her knees, and Joe let out a long yawn while stretching his body to find a new comfortable spot. "I used to be a nanny, but it's been a long time since I was around little kids. I don't know if I'll be much help."

He managed to smother his chuckle this time as he imagined her reaction to the kids waiting for their lunch. She was in for a surprise. "Sure you will. It's not hard." Reaching out his hand, he nodded to indicate she should take it.

She reached for him as though moving through water, slow, thoughtful.

But there was nothing gradual about the rush of lightning that zipped up his arm when her fingers touched his. If the flash in her eyes was any indication, she felt it too. But she didn't pull back or acknowledge it beyond that. She let him pull her to her feet before immediately dropping his hand and following him toward the barn.

Cretia blinked hard in a vain attempt to acclimate to the dim light within the barn, assuming Finn was leading her to the sliding door and the house beyond. He was still right in front of her, and she had to fight the urge to reach for his back. He clearly knew his way around, but she'd never even seen the layout. Shuffling her feet to make sure she didn't miss a step, she tried to stay close enough to hear the even fall of his boots against the solid flooring.

When he stopped, she did too. When he stepped to the left, she followed. Rubbing her fingers against her eyes, praying she could make out more than dark shapes, she tiptoed in his direction. And promptly ran right into his shoulder, her nose bouncing off the soft fabric of his Henley.

"Oops." He chuckled, slipping an arm around her back. "You okay there?"

"Yep. Fine. It's just a little bit dark in here."

"Sorry. Some of the animals don't appreciate it if it's too bright."

She tilted her head up and frowned, assuming he could see her. "Joe Jr. and the puppies seemed to have no problem in the sun."

His throaty laugh made her lean in, but she swayed back quickly.

"They don't mind the natural light, but Joe is an animal all his own. And he's spent most of his life in the house. He has no idea what it's like to live in a barn." His voice grew slightly softer as he turned his head. "So I try to make it as comfortable as I can for the rest of them."

"The rest?"

Before Finn could answer her question, something across the open barn bleated. Then again. Then several more times. Or maybe several others. Joined almost immediately by a cow lowing.

Those were definitely not dogs.

She blinked hard and rubbed her fists against her eyes, and when she opened them, a row of stalls along the far wall came almost into focus. The wooden walls between the pens were maybe six feet, but the front gates were more like half that. The enclosures spanned the entire length of the barn, hay and grain spilling over onto the cement floor in front of them.

A bark from the dogs on the other side of the barn made her spin toward the seven happy faces behind chain-link fences. Sunlight glowed through a large opening in the wall beyond them, which seemed to lead to another yard on the outside.

She looked up at Finn and tilted her head toward the stalls. "What's in those other pens?"

He shrugged. "Mostly strays."

Halfway toward the middle pen, she whipped around to him. "But they're not dogs?" The words came out far too much like a question, like she wasn't sure she could trust her ears. Apparently, she didn't.

Another lift of his shoulder. But this one came with a Cheshire cat grin. "Go on. See for yourself."

As she shuffled toward the middle gate, her eyes finally adjusted to the light. She took the last three steps at a jog.

From the other side of the wall, three long, fuzzy faces looked up at her. Their eyes were strange, with horizontal pupils that made her pull back for a second. Then one of the little ones bleated at her, flapping its ears.

She couldn't help but giggle. "Goats. You have goats."

Somehow Finn had made it to her side without her knowing. So when he spoke close enough to stir her hair, she jumped. "And mama goats have babies, which are called . . ."

Heat flushed through her, and she covered her face with both hands, shaking her head. "Kids," she whispered through

83

her fingers. She refused to look up to see the spark of humor in his eyes that she already knew followed that deep chuckle.

"You must think I'm an . . ." She stopped herself and dropped her hands quickly. "Wait. How was I supposed to know you weren't a dad?"

The corner of his mouth ticked up, though it was hard to tell under the volume of his beard. Maybe there was a dimple under there.

Too bad you'll never get to find out.

No. Not too bad. She just wasn't going to know. It was as easy as that. Because she wasn't going to stick around.

She never did.

Not in Barcelona for the waiter. Not in Vienna for the guy who had brought her endless cups of coffee. Not in San Luis for Carlos, her high school boyfriend.

Staying meant having a home. And a home was only good for one thing.

She didn't need that in her life.

Finn cleared his throat, which sounded suspiciously like he was covering another laugh, but it was enough to drag her thoughts back from their wayward track.

"I'm sorry about that," he said. "Everyone around here knows I'll take in just about any animal without a home. But I see how it would be confusing." He sighed. "My mom would much rather I have human kids than the goat variety." His eyes flew open. "I'm sorry again. That was probably way more than you wanted to know." Scrubbing a hand down his face, tugging on his beard at the end of the motion, he quickly moved on. "So this is Jenna and her kids Sonny and Cher."

Cretia raised her eyebrows and shot him a questioning look.

"My mom liked them a lot when she was young. Figured I'd throw her a bone."

She bit her lips together to keep from laughing and gave him a simple nod instead. Sonny and Cher looked up at her through their weird slitted eyes, and she grabbed for the phone in her pocket to capture their sweet faces. It was empty. Which she should have known.

Resigning herself to not recording this moment, she asked, "So are they rescue goats, like the dogs?"

His laugh wrapped around her, full and warm, filling a space in her heart she hadn't realized was empty. "Not so much. Though I don't think anyone has ever tried training them for that job. Maybe we should." Reaching over the gate, he scratched Jenna's head just like he did Joe's. The mama flapped her ears and closed her eyes, and Cretia could swear she smiled. "They're more like rescue goats in that they had nowhere else to go."

"Strays."

"Basically. Jenna belonged to a family near Cavendish, but then they realized their daughter was allergic, and they had to find her a new home. Immediately. Or they were going to have to put her down."

"And Sonny and Cher?"

"Jenna was already pregnant. It was a package deal."

Cretia gasped as a fist around her heart squeezed. "They were going to kill a pregnant goat?" She didn't wait for his response. She didn't need it. "You saved them."

He shrugged. "I had the room."

"That was . . . That was a nice thing to do."

"I guess people around here have me figured out. They know I'm an easy yes when it comes to animals in need." He stabbed his fingers through his hair as he ducked his chin, and if the lighting had been just a little bit better, she had the feeling she'd have seen his cheeks turn pink. "That's how I ended up with Roberta too."

She glanced in the direction he nodded and was greeted by a black face hanging over the door of the last stall. A white patch covered the spot where the cow should have had an eye. Light from the opening behind her gave her a near halo, and she didn't seem concerned with anything but chewing her cud.

"Roberta, huh?"

"She's a good girl." Finn strolled over and scratched the middle of her face. "Her owners let her get sick, and she got an infection and stopped producing milk, so . . ."

"Was she from the dairy farm across the street?"

"Definitely not. Justin Kane takes great care of his herd." With a gentle rub of Roberta's ear, Finn leaned in toward the cow's only eye. "She came from a family that didn't know how to care for animals. And didn't care to learn."

"And you did—I mean, do—know how to care for livestock? It seems different than raising dogs."

He chuckled. "I didn't have a clue what she needed when I got her—Jenna either. But that's the great thing about being friends with a dairy farmer and having a vet on speed dial. I'm willing to learn, and I know who to ask for help."

Cretia wrapped her arms across her middle. Something about the way he spoke and the warmth in his voice felt like a jacket on a cool day—like his dry shirt had around her soaking shoulders the day before.

He spoke simply. Directly. Humbly yet confidently.

He didn't need to brag about his knowledge, yet he undoubtedly knew what he was doing. These animals were safe with him.

And for the immediate future, maybe she was too.

"Come on. You can help me feed the kids." He nodded toward a small room just inside the barn's sliding door. "We just have to heat up their bottles."

"Like baby bottles?" She sounded like an idiot, but he wasn't making sense.

He chuckled again as he strolled toward the room, the sound of his boots dampened by the light coating of hay and dirt across the floor. He pulled a chain hanging from the ceiling, and a single light bulb lit up the square window overlooking the barn.

Cretia took a step after him, and the cow's enormous eye followed her every movement. Roberta's chewing turned more serious, and she stamped a hoof against the ground. Her body swayed into the side of the stall, and the wood groaned.

Throat dry, Cretia shuffled back a step, bumping into a furry body at her hip. "Joe." She forced the word out on a shaky laugh before scratching the dog's back with a few quick strokes. "How long have you been here?"

The dog let out a low bark, which might have been an answer. Or maybe not. Either way, it seemed to make the cow glare at them more intensely, her hooves rustling the hay in the floor of her stall.

Cretia swallowed quickly and pressed a hand over her suddenly speeding heart.

It wasn't like the cow was trying to get out. Or like it could even if it wanted to. And if it could, it probably wasn't going to attack.

Probably.

Not that Cretia had much livestock experience. Or any, really.

She'd visited Pamplona to see the Gothic churches, not the Running of the Bulls. And though she'd received several requests from her followers for videos from a dude ranch in New Mexico, that was a little too close to her childhood and a little far outside her comfort zone.

Dogs were one thing. Dogs were normal animals.

Cows were . . . decidedly not normal.

She gave Roberta a wide berth as she scurried after Finn.

Roberta might not like her, but the cow had every reason to love Finn. There was no way she would attack the guy who had saved her and fed her every day.

Probably.

Seven

inn wasn't exactly sure what was going on between Cretia and Roberta, but he watched their stare down closely for a few minutes after turning on the burner to warm the pot of water. Roberta had ignored his mom and dad, the vet, little Jessie, and pretty much everyone else who had deigned to visit the barn since her arrival the year before.

Not so for Cretia Martin.

Mar-teen. He replayed her introduction a few times in his mind. The gentle roll of the *r*. The subtle Spanish accent that made her name exotic and intriguing. And made him want to ask if she spoke the language. If she'd grown up in a bilingual household. If she still called San Luis home.

Technically, that was none of his business. But it didn't stop the questions from racing through his mind. Roberta wasn't the only one curious about North Rustico's newest—if short-term—resident.

Reaching for one of the big green bottles of milk, he brushed his thumb against the outside of the metal lobster pot sitting on the hot plate. With a hiss, he shoved his thumb into his mouth to ease the immediate sting.

He knew better than to get distracted. He'd nearly dumped the whole pot on himself a week before when he made the mistake of letting Sonny and Cher follow him into the tack room. While a lot less prone to butting against his legs, Cretia was a whole lot more interesting than the kids. And he couldn't seem to look away from her as she shuffled toward Roberta then back, her brown eyes almost as large as the cow's.

Cretia looked up just then, catching his gaze through the window. She nodded toward the cow in question, as though asking if Roberta was safe or if he'd left her with a maniac. Finn dropped his thumb from his mouth and offered a half smile by way of answer.

Cretia didn't seem convinced, keeping one eye on the cow even as she shuffled closer to the tack room.

At the first bubble in the pot, Finn dropped two bottles into the water. He forced his gaze to stay on the task at hand, careful to avoid the splash. He didn't need a serious burn because he couldn't pay attention to his job. Because he couldn't take his eyes off of his visitor.

Setting the little egg timer on the table, he crossed his arms and waited, surveying his workspace. His goat setup wasn't sophisticated—nothing like Justin's dairy across the street. But it got the job done. And considering he'd put most of it together in about twenty-four hours, he was pretty proud of it.

His animals were healthy, cared for, and well fed.

That knowledge didn't stop his gut from twisting when he wondered what his dad would think of it. Or Cretia. Which was absolutely ridiculous. He shouldn't care about her opinion.

He'd made his mom proud, and he hoped he'd earned his dad's respect. He'd saved the animals he could, all while maintaining the business. So what if it wasn't the big, technological production he'd like it to be? No one cared that he was using his mom's hand-me-down kitchen gadgets to make sure the kids got all the nutrients they needed.

Finn was probably the only one who cared that the business wasn't growing. That it functioned much as it had when his grandfather started selling his Princess's puppies to families, farmers, and search and rescue operations across Atlantic Canada.

The dogs were in the same barn, and Finn worked out of the same house—at the same desk—his grandfather had. It all looked pretty much the same except for some new paint, expanded fences, and a few four-legged strays.

But if his setup didn't grow, he'd never be able to put his own stamp on the family legacy. He'd leave exactly the same thing to his own kids. The same moderate success. Just enough to keep going. Just enough to worry about the next month. Not nearly enough to hire help or take a vacation.

Finn scrubbed his hand down his face, combing his fingers through his too shaggy beard.

Something had to change. Even if the banks didn't think he was a worthy investment, he could do something new with this legacy. He just had to figure out what.

Cretia jogged into the tack room, still warily looking over her shoulder. "I don't think your cow likes me."

"On the contrary. Hate isn't the opposite of love."

"Apathy is," she finished for him, a smile tugging at her mouth. "So, you're saying her attentions are an indication of her affection for me."

He grabbed the tongs from the tabletop, poked at the two-liter green bottles that danced in the water, and shrugged. "I mean, she basically ignores everyone else. Clearly, she's fascinated by you."

"By wanting to eat me, you mean."

Finn dropped the bottle he'd pulled halfway up, jumping back to avoid the splash. Laugher rolled out unbidden, and he had to gasp to catch his breath before he could respond. "I don't think she suddenly turned into a carnivore."

"Hmm." Cretia's lips pursed to the side, and she shot another glance at the bovine in question. "Maybe she knows how much I like carne asada and thinks *I* ate one of her cousins."

Where had this woman come from? Equal parts ridiculous and adorable, and he had no idea what to do with her. So he shoved a red oven mitt and a black rubber stopper into her hands.

She raised her eyebrows in an unspoken question.

"For the bottle. Hang on." After sliding on a blue oven mitt—the tip singed black from an incident with a flaming cake when he was nine or ten—he retrieved the bottles and set one in front of her. Then he demonstrated how to put the stopper in.

Cretia mimicked his actions, hesitant at first with the warm bottle, but finally cradled it with the mitt on one hand and shoved the rubber into place.

When the bottles had cooled enough to touch, he said, "Grab your milk." Nodding back toward the pens, he led the way back to the goat enclosure and let himself through the gate. "Wait out here just a second."

Jenna tipped her brown-and-white face up at him before

quickly herding her little ones into the corner. Sonny, mostly white save a tan stripe around his middle, peeked around her. The little guy remained silent but watchful, his eerie amber eyes never blinking.

"Come here, mama," Finn said. Holding out a bit of feed in his hand, he coaxed her toward the gate that led into the eastern pasture. Then, with a practiced movement, he nudged her with his hip until she was outside, only then giving her the treat in his hand. Her tongue was rough and damp, and he wiped his palm down her face and across her long, narrow nose. "Don't worry. We're not going to hurt them."

Jenna bleated her uncertainty, pressing against the gate's metal bars just as Sonny and Cher began their own chorus.

"Is she going to be okay?" Cretia asked.

"She acts like this is the first time, every time. She'll settle down as soon as the kids do." Finn leaned over and scooped up Sonny. The kid kicked for a moment despite the firm grip around his middle. "Come on, big guy. You're just hungry, aren't you?"

Finn doubted the goat had learned the words, but it still responded to his voice, settling into his chest with a sigh even as it reached for the bottle in his other hand. When he swung toward Cretia to let her into the pen, her eyes were wide with something like wonder, but she said nothing as he pointed toward the bright green Adirondack chair in the corner.

"It might be easier to sit down. Cher is pretty gentle, but she gets excited about her milk."

Cretia nodded, perching on the edge of the chair.

She wouldn't stay there long.

Biting back a grin, he tapped the Adirondack's arm,

waving his own bottle. Cher leapt onto the chair, and Cretia pressed a hand to her mouth and muffled a scream as she flew against the back of the seat. The response didn't bother Cher, who hopped onto Cretia's lap, her little mouth already chomping toward the rubber top of the bottle, her little brown rear wiggling with glee.

Cretia's wild eyes darted between him and Cher, uncertainty and a bit of fear evident in the lines of her face. Finn waved his bottle again before holding it in the general vicinity of Sonny's mouth. The kid latched on like the pro he was.

"You don't even have to have good aim. She'll find it."

Face turning serious and eyebrows intent, Cretia tucked one arm around Cher's middle while waving the milk bottle in her other hand. Not to be outdone by her brother, Cher snatched the tip between her lips and immediately began working it.

"If you hold it at an angle—"

As soon as Cretia tilted the bottle, Cher began guzzling, the milk disappearing with each sloppy slurp. Cher swayed a little and then snuggled against Cretia's chest. "Oh."

"All right there?"

The hesitancy in her eyes had been replaced by wonder as she looked up again. "Are they always so . . . ?"

"Yes."

"You didn't even let me ask my question."

He adjusted the little four-legged heater under his arm, scratching the soft fur of Sonny's belly. "However you were going to end that question, the answer is the same. Sweet? Uh-huh. Cuddly? Undoubtedly. Warm? Yes. Adorable? Absolutely."

Cretia's smile morphed into a sardonic grin as Cher sucked down the last drops. "I was going to say *hungry*."

"That too." Finn matched her smile as he bent over to set Sonny down. The kid stumbled like he'd had something stronger than milk to drink, and Finn put a steadying hand on his rear to keep Sonny upright while he gained his footing. "Their mom feeds them throughout the day, but I give them an extra bottle every morning to make sure they're getting enough. And they haven't turned it down once in almost a month."

Cher let go of the bottle with a pop that echoed throughout the barn. The dogs barked in reply, but Cher couldn't be bothered to respond, her eyelids drooping in a milk-induced haze as her body suddenly jerked.

"Is she okay? Did I do—"

"She just has the hiccups."

Cretia smiled at her little lap goat, her hands working their way up and down Cher's back, her fingers slender and clearly calming as the kid folded her legs and settled in more deeply, her body jerking every few seconds.

"I think you've made a friend for life," Finn whispered.

Cretia didn't look up from where she smoothed the kid's back, down the pronounced spine and then back up to the rounded side. "I think I changed my mind. Forget having a puppy. I'd like a pet goat."

Hands on his hips, Finn shook his head. "Until they literally eat everything you own."

"She would never. She's such a good girl."

"Well, tell that to my shoelace she tried to eat last week. And don't let Joe Jr. hear you talking like that. He'll take it as a personal affront."

She giggled, just as he'd hoped she would, the sound flowing out of her like honey.

"If Cher had her way, you'd sit and pet her all day. But I promised you a computer and the internet." Squatting in front of Cretia, Finn carefully extracted the drowsy animal and deposited her on a fluffy mound of hay. When he stood, he held out his hand, but Cretia was already pushing herself up from the chair, dusting off a fresh layer of brown hair.

After opening the gate for Jenna and rinsing the bottles in the tack room, he slid the barn door back and motioned Cretia through. As she stepped into the sunlight, her hair glowed beneath her own personal halo. He had a sudden urge to run his fingers through the long ebony waves that swung from her ponytail down her back. Just to see if they were softer than Sonny's coat. It was science, really.

And potentially ridiculously embarrassing. If she caught him. Which she absolutely would, because he had zero suave.

He'd apparently been absent the day the hockey players learned it at school. Or maybe it was part of their skills training. Coaches taught stick handling, protecting the puck, and how to talk to pretty girls without being a dope.

Too bad he'd never been any good on the ice. He could have used a lesson or two.

A few steps from the door, she began to slow, her feet looking heavy, her steps uncertain.

Figuring she wanted him to take the lead, he scooted around her. "The computer's just inside."

She nodded but didn't move any closer to the house, her arms sliding around her middle and her eyes narrowing on the door. Shifting from foot to foot, she glanced at him, the corner of her lip disappearing beneath her front teeth.

"Cretia?"

She nodded. "Yeah, I'm fine. Yeah. Good." But her gaze

had lost its focus, and she sounded like she was trying to convince herself more than him.

Reaching for the handle of the screen door, he waved her in with his other hand. "Would you rather . . . ?" He wasn't sure what he was asking—or what he was supposed to be asking. He just wanted to find the words to take the wariness from her eyes and ease the lines around her mouth.

She shook her head slowly. "It's fine. Thank you. Thank you for letting me borrow . . ."

"Sure thing. Come on in."

But Cretia didn't step through.

Four years, three months, and—Cretia did a bit of quick math in her mind—fifteen days.

It was a strange statistic to have handy, but the running tally in the back of her mind never stopped. It wasn't like she woke up every morning thinking about the last time she'd been in her mother's house. Anyone's house, actually.

But the number was always accessible, the internal clock forever ticking.

Her streak would end when she stepped into Finn's home. Not a hotel or an inn or a B and B. Just a house. A place filled with a lifetime of memories. A space that would either remind her why she'd chosen her nomadic life or make her second-guess it.

She risked a glance at Finn, who stood at the threshold, his concerned gaze washing over her. But her feet refused to move toward the dim interior beyond the open door.

A wet nose nuzzled into her waist, and she dropped her hand to pet the big furry head. Joe Jr. barked up at her and then nudged her hip, forcing her to take the first step. And then another.

Finn's grin grew until it was evident even behind his shaggy beard.

Then she was inside, the warmth of the sun giving way to the relative darkness. Like in the barn, she paused until she could get her bearings, but Joe had no such hesitancy. He charged around her, bounding and chattering like a child eager to show off a new toy.

"Joe," Finn said. A bite in his tone made the dog still immediately. "Go lie down." He pointed toward a cast-iron stove in the corner of the living room and a large blue pillow on the floor.

Joe looked up at her with sad black eyes, then hung his head and trotted toward his bed. He circled a few times before settling down, his gaze never leaving her.

Cretia swallowed against her dry throat. "It's okay. You didn't need to—"

Finn chuckled. "Trust me. You won't get anything done with Joe by your side. He just wants to play."

The dog's head lifted at the sound of his name.

With a roll of his eyes, Finn walked toward the kitchen. "Don't worry. I'll get him a t-r-e-a-t later."

She checked to see if Joe had learned how to spell while the rest of his litter had been trained for rescue service, but the dog had rested his head back on his paws.

"You're a good boy," she said.

Finn had wandered across the living room, past a brown couch and a single blue recliner, the seat flattened and the fabric worn from years of use. "Trying to make a friend?"

"No, I—"

He held up his hand. "I'm just kidding. Joe already loves you. Clearly." Shooting his dog a faux glare, he said, "I can't get him to look at me like that. I'm just the one who fills his bowl, plays fetch with him, and takes him on a walk every day."

Cretia couldn't hold back a giggle, only then realizing her shoulders had relaxed and her breathing had gone back to normal. After a slow inhale filled with lemon-scented cleaning products, she did a little spin, taking in the room. It wasn't overly large but boasted an open floor plan from long before the DIY television shows had made them popular. The overstuffed couch and recliner faced the fireplace and its round metal pipe, framing the living space. A colorful area rug beneath the coffee table looked like it could have been made from someone's sewing scraps, though Finn didn't seem the type.

A square table made of a dark brown wood and four matching chairs sat between the living room and the kitchen, whose row of hanging cabinets above the peninsular counter were sure to be demolished if any of those reno shows got their hands on this home. Even the appliances were olive green, like something she'd seen on an antiques show.

The house could use an update, for sure.

But it was homey. And clean. No piles of papers or overflowing trash bags or dishes in the sink. Even the hardwood floors beneath her shoes were spotless. Not a sign of Joe's fur or crumbs around the table. Then again, she only used tables at restaurants. Maybe a bachelor living on his own was the same way. Or maybe Joe made sure the crumbs didn't go to waste.

She smiled toward the big guy, who had closed his eyes

and let out heavy breaths that sent his lips and a string of drool flapping.

"The computer is right over here." Finn pointed toward a desk in the corner, tucked beside an unadorned staircase. Ah. This was familiar. This desk was clearly where every wayward scrap of paper went to be lost, stacks upon stacks of envelopes and invoices, bills and Post-its. Whatever sense of organization there might have been had long ago been lost.

The desktop itself wasn't more than four feet wide and mostly dominated by an enormous square monitor like the donated ones in her junior high computer lab. Her class had been the last to use them before the school upgraded.

Leaning over, Finn pressed a button on the black tower sitting on the floor, and the machine whirred to life, chugging and clicking as the screen blinked and shivered.

He clearly hadn't gotten the memo that computers had become portable. And should be.

"It'll just take a minute to wake up."

"To wake up?" She couldn't keep from parroting him. He couldn't be serious. No one worked this way. No one lived this way.

Even her mother had had a laptop the last time Cretia was at her house. Nothing fancy. Nothing overly high-tech. Then again, her mom hadn't had an empty surface large enough to house a computer.

But this was . . .

"This is your computer?"

Finn crossed his arms and nodded.

"Your *only* computer?"

He nodded again. "Why?"

"It's just . . . large."

Giving the setup a quick once-over, Finn shrugged. "It works. Gets me on the internet when I need it. And"—he shot her a glance out of the side of his eye—"at least I don't have to worry about it ending up in the harbor."

"It would probably work just as well after a dip in the water."

Running his fingers over his mouth, he seemed to muffle a snort as he fought to keep a straight face. After a moment, his eyes turned serious, his brows dipping to meet above the bridge of his nose. "Listen, I'd be happy to pay for your new—"

"No." The word came out a bit harsher than she had intended, so she tried to slap a smile into place. "Thank you. But I'm all right. I've got it covered. Insurance and all."

He chewed on his lip for a long moment—clearly trying to decide if it was worth arguing the point—before finally swinging the wheeled office chair out and motioning for her to sit down. "Have at it."

"I don't know." She plopped down in front of him, his breath stirring the hair on top of her head. His body was warm this close, but goose bumps broke out along her arms, and her whole body was racked by a single shiver. Refusing to think about why she insisted on reacting to him so strongly, she forced a teasing smile into place. "I'm not sure I know how to connect with dial-up."

He didn't bother biting back his snort this time. "That was a low blow."

"But honest."

"We're not in the sticks out here. I got a high-speed line a while ago."

"Uh-huh. A while?"

"Two years." He shrugged. "It's high-ish speed."

She chuckled as she moved the mouse to click on the internet icon. It opened—not exactly quickly, but at least it opened. The screen wasn't sharp like her laptop—her ruined laptop—but at least she could make her way to the online Apple store.

Finn gave the back of her chair a couple pats. "I'm going to get Joe some water and his treat." The dog barked on cue, his nails clacking against the hardwood as he raced across the room. "You want anything?"

"I'm good. Thanks."

Finn and Joe disappeared around the end of the stairs and into the kitchen. The faucet had turned on and off before the store page fully loaded. Then, finally, there they were. Sleek silver laptops. The latest tablets. A brand-new phone—the model she hadn't even upgraded to yet—in a gorgeous rose gold.

She hadn't needed upgrades before. But now that she had to start over, she might as well go with the top-of-the-line. Maybe this newer model would even be rated for a dunking in North Rustico Harbour. Though it probably wouldn't survive being smashed against the edge of the dock like her last one.

She picked her pieces and clicked her preferences, topping out on memory and storage space. All of her stuff was automatically backed up to the cloud, but she'd discovered more than a few corners of the world where she couldn't get Wi-Fi or bars on her phone.

She couldn't afford to miss capturing the truly magnificent just because her phone ran out of space. And thanks to 3.2

million followers across all of her platforms, she could afford to get the best equipment.

She quickly filled her cart with not only the electronics but also an extra battery pack. And a waterproof case. Even though she could afford it all, the total that popped up on the screen still packed a punch. But she didn't need a repeat of the day before. Besides, she'd need a new backpack and carry-on too. And the clothes to go in said suitcase.

Looking down at the jeans and fitted blue sweater she wore—the only clothes she owned—she frowned. Her credit cards and cash had been in the bag that ended up in the harbor, had immediately disappeared beneath the surface, and—if Finn was to be believed—were probably washed well into the Atlantic by now. She could shop online in accounts where she'd stored her card numbers or through PayPal. But who knew how long it would take for things to arrive in North Rustico?

Probably not as long as it would take to get her new electronics.

Selecting the express delivery of her items, she held her breath.

Seven to ten days.

She let out a hard sigh between tight lips.

Any way she looked at it, she was stuck on this island. Waiting. Which was not her strong suit. Or even her weak suit. Waiting was not in her skill set. Not anymore anyway.

She'd spent too many years waiting for something better to come along. For something to happen. For her mom to change.

An image of the brown stucco house just north of the Mexican border flashed across her mind's eye. She could order the items to ship there and meet them.

The idea landed on her chest like a brick. Her mother's house was not a possibility. No matter how many times she begged Cretia to come back. Which was pretty much every time she called home—every few months.

Even though Cretia sometimes said she would try to visit, she never had. And she probably never would.

Cretia could be stuck there. Stuck in that little house filled with too many things. Too many memories.

Or she could be stuck here, forced to stay on an island at a cute B and B in the middle of tourist country, down the road from a couple of precious baby goats and squishy puppies. It was a far cry from staying on a dead-end road in a house that barely had room for her. Even for a short time. But the reality didn't stop her insides from wrenching.

Staying in North Rustico wasn't the same as living with her mom all those years ago. It wasn't.

It only felt like that.

Sliding a piece of paper with a bank letterhead out of her way, she rested her elbows on the edge of the desk and pressed her hands to her face. A bead of sweat trickled down the middle of her forehead, and she swiped at it with the back of her hand.

This whole situation wasn't ideal. She could accept that.

But given the choice, she'd pick the Sahara over San Luis. And this tiny village was a far cry from either of those deserts.

She'd wanted to feature the island anyway. With at least a week in the area, she'd have time to find the hidden gems and explore things she would have missed in her planned two-day trip.

Sitting up a little straighter, she clicked on the cart on the screen. This wasn't wasted time. She wouldn't let it be.

"How's it going?" Finn's question came from right behind her, followed almost immediately by Joe's chin plopping on her knee.

She looked up, forcing a smile into place. "Do you know the mailing address of the Red Door Inn?"

Eight

Cretia couldn't remember the last time she hadn't known what to do with her day. Or if she *ever* hadn't. Probably not.

As a kid there had been school and survival. Those were the only things she'd been able to focus on. There had been part-time jobs, a flurry of them, during high school. All overlapping. All to barely keep the swamp cooler running. Then that fateful trip—her first cruise. Nannying for twin seven-year-olds while their parents enjoyed the sun, surf, and casinos.

Those days on the boat had been scheduled down to the minute. But the few seconds she'd found to film the Mexican Riviera had changed her life. Every day since then she'd either been planning a trip or taking it, filming or editing her videos, building her platform or connecting with followers.

Every day had a plan.

Until this one.

Out of habit, she reached for her phone, only to have her fingertips skim the wooden surface of the nightstand.

Right. No phone. The reason for having no plan.

She fell back against the deliciously cozy pillows on the bed in her room at the Red Door and pulled a quilt covered with phrases from L. M. Montgomery's books to her chin. She had to take Marie's word on that since she'd never actually read a book by the island's famed author. A few cloth-bound books on the bookshelf across the room suggested she wouldn't have to go far to brush up on all things Anne.

But not today. Today she needed to figure out what to do with the week that loomed before her.

Okay, so she didn't have a plan, but she had a plan to make a plan. That was a step in the right direction. Rolling out of bed, she stepped into the patch of sunlight coming through the gabled window and stretching across the floorboards. Its warmth seeped through the soles of her feet, up her legs, and stopped somewhere in the region of her heart.

She had a lazy smile plastered on her face when she caught her reflection in the antique mirror over the dresser. It disappeared as soon as she saw the wild tangle that had become her hair.

"Shower first. Then we make a plan."

It didn't take her more than a minute after stepping out from under the steaming spray to know what her first step needed to be. Clothes. Fresh. Clean. Never before worn.

She'd been tempted to order some things on Finn's computer the day before, after placing her Apple order. But she hadn't wanted to pepper his internet history with women's unmentionables, as her grandmother used to call them.

Yesterday she'd been wearing freshly laundered clothes. Today was a different matter.

She'd clear Finn's whole search history for a spare pair of underwear. Scratch that. "I'll buy him a whole new computer," she mumbled as she yanked a borrowed comb through her hair. Dripping wet, it looked blacker than normal, sleek and unhindered by any color. When it dried without the aid of more than a few products, it would probably be almost as wild as her morning hair, but at least it was clean. And she could always pull it back into a ponytail.

Turning her back on the reflection in the foggy bathroom mirror, she sighed. Clothes. Then . . . Her stomach dropped. Her car. She'd been so charmed by Finn's farm that she'd forgotten to call the rental agency the day before. She needed to either return the car today or extend her agreement. If that was even an option.

Maybe the extra expense wasn't worth it, though. Especially not after the zeros she'd paid to the Apple store the day before. If she had a camera of any kind, it would be worth it to explore the island. But she could walk anywhere she wanted in North Rustico.

Or ask Finn for a ride.

Her stomach swooped again. For a totally different reason this time. One she refused to analyze.

Okay, maybe Finn was good-looking.

There's no "maybe" about it, babe.

Fine. He was an objectively attractive man. Who just looked even cuter holding a baby goat or playing with puppies. And, yes, he was kind, helpful. She just did not have time to dwell on his finer qualities. Or how much she had enjoyed spending the day before with him.

As she headed toward the kitchen, young voices singing off-key greeted her. On the last stairstep, she spotted Julia Mae and Jessie sitting at the island, following along to a video on their mom's phone.

Marie looked up from where she was wiping down the counter next to the stainless-steel stove. "Good morning, Cretia. How'd you sleep?"

"Good." Really, surprisingly great. Maybe it was the excitement of the last few days or the walk in the sun or playing with puppies the day before. Whatever the cause, she'd fallen asleep almost as soon as she'd crawled beneath that quilt. For the second night in a row.

"What are you up to today?"

Cretia twisted the hem of her blue sweater. "I was thinking I might walk down to Finn's."

Marie's head whipped around, a knowing glow in her blue eyes. "Oh really."

"To borrow his computer. Maybe do a little more shopping."

Marie offered only a click of her tongue and a saucy smile in response.

"It's not like that. At all."

"Not like what?" Julia Mae chimed in.

"Don't you worry about it," Marie said as she circled the kitchen island and ruffled her daughter's hair. But she didn't look away, and her smile didn't dim.

Cretia scrambled for some way to change the topic. "Do you mind?"

Gently arched eyebrows slowly rose up Marie's forehead, and the sparkle in her eyes turned positively wicked. "Do I mind if you spend time with Finn? Only if you don't tell me about it later."

A chuckle caught her off guard, and Cretia choked it out on a cough. "You're ridiculous. I meant, do you mind if I have a few more things mailed here? I know you said last night that it wasn't a problem for my electronics to come to the inn, but I don't want to add any stress."

Marie's laugh was like sheer curtains blowing in a summer breeze. "You'll be Jessie's favorite person if you give her another chance to see Casper the mailman. He always brings her a treat when he stops by."

Jessie looked up from the screen with round eyes. "'Nack?"

Her mom shook her head. "You just had breakfast."

The little girl's face fell just like Joe's had the day before when Finn sent him to his pillow, and Cretia would have given anything to slip the girl a few crackers. Except she didn't have any snacks on hand. If she had, they would have magically made their way into those chubby little fists.

Not that Jessie was hungry. Cretia had just promised herself that she'd take every chance to say yes to a child, regardless of the actual need. It had been that way with the kids she'd nannied. So much so that their mom had had to tell her to stop giving them gummy bears before dinner. Twice.

It wasn't easy to turn off that switch in her mind, to forget the times she'd been hungry as a child. She'd begged her mom for a blue box of macaroni and cheese and been told to make do with ketchup on crackers. She'd asked for orange soda after tasting it at a birthday party. Her mom had said simply, "No."

For years Cretia had thought that was her mom's favorite word. It was certainly the one she said most often. Until all Cretia wanted to do was say, "Yes."

Stamping down the slew of emotions those memories surfaced, she turned back to Marie. "Thank you. Really. I know you weren't expecting a guest this week. I'll pay you for the room. For your hospitality. For your—"

"Don't even think about it."

Without looking up from her video, Julia Mae chimed in again. "Mama says not to argue with her. And Daddy says 'specially not when she uses that voice."

"Julia Mae Sloan." Marie's barely stifled laughter took the legs out from under her reprimand.

The three-named child in question shrugged. "What? He did." Then she went back to her cartoon as though completely unaware that she'd thrown her dad under the bus.

Rolling her eyes, Marie shook her head. "You know what? I didn't know I needed another adult around here so much until you showed up. Seth is remodeling a house near St. Peter's Bay this month, so you can stay as long as you like. And please make yourself at home. Whatever leftovers are in the fridge are fair game."

Cretia was still smiling over that invitation as she reached Finn's house. She was already staying longer than she would like. But at least she had a comfortable bed and a safe place to sleep. And maybe she didn't mind being teased about going to see Finn.

She'd almost forgotten that feeling of knowing someone well enough to laugh and joke with them. Marie treated her like a lifelong friend. And Cretia didn't have any of those anymore. Not that she'd ever had really close friends, except her high school boyfriend Carlos. It was hard to build friendships when she couldn't invite anyone over, and her friends' houses only served to remind her of what she didn't have.

Like a bedroom that wasn't filled to the ceiling with trash

bags and stuffed animals. A kitchen free of rodent droppings. A parent who cared enough to give their kid a *home*.

After the car accident when Cretia was nine, her mom had lived off disability assistance until Cretia was old enough to work. The government checks had barely been enough to cover the rent.

And the *things*. The figurines and magazines. The Tupperware and unused workout clothes. The baby shoes and cardboard boxes. Cretia still didn't know where it all had come from. Sometimes it seemed to multiply, showing up on their doorstep. Another pile on top of a pile. Always more.

Until there hadn't been room to even breathe. Until she'd had to leave.

She eyed Finn's house with a bit of caution, knowing she'd have to go back inside to use his computer but praying he was out in the barn again. It had been a little easier being inside his home with Joe by her side. And after a bit of goat therapy.

Without a phone, she had no idea what time it was, but maybe she'd made it in time for bottle feeding again.

The sliding barn door was closed, but she bypassed the house and strolled right up to it. A series of barks from the other side greeted her as she pushed it open just far enough to slip in. "Hello?"

She waited for Finn's response, but the barking behind the chain-link fence only grew more frenzied, joined by a few bleats from the goats. Cretia stopped a few feet in as the cow stared her down. Again. She tried to offer a smile, but one big brown eye just looked on unblinking as the cow chewed her cud and stamped her front hoof a few times.

Maybe it was a warning. Maybe it was just an itch. Either

way, Cretia took a circuitous route to the goat pen. The gate inside the barn was locked, but Finn must have opened the back door that morning for Jenna to trot out into the pasture. She didn't even look up as she snacked on lush grass in the bright sunlight.

Sonny and Cher, however, jumped and pranced around their pen, not so eager to go outside. When Cretia leaned over the gate with an outstretched hand, they ran right up to her. Sonny's ears were like silk, and he nuzzled into her hand as she ran her fingers over them. "You're a good boy, aren't you?"

"I like to think I am."

Cretia jumped at the voice behind her, stumbling back a foot and falling right against a familiar form. Strong hands caught her shoulders, and Finn leaned around her to look into her face.

"Morning. I wasn't expecting you to fall for me again today."

Chuckling up at him, she pulled back just a bit, caught in his grip but trying to get a clearer picture of his face. Something had changed. She blinked to focus but couldn't put her finger on it. He still had those bright blue eyes framed by full but not bushy eyebrows. If his nose had been a touch shorter, it would have been too small to balance his wide jaw and blunt chin.

Which she had never noticed before. Because they had been covered.

"You shaved your beard."

The corner of his mouth ticked upward as he let her go and stepped back. "Very observant."

"No, I mean, I like it. It makes your whole face brighter. And you have a little dimple in your chin. It's really very cute. And—" She literally bit her lips together. She had to quit talking so much around him.

But something about Finn invited all of her inside thoughts to pour off her tongue.

"Should have been internal processing?"

She nodded. "Sorry. I didn't mean to make things uncomfortable."

He waved her apology off like a bee on a sunny day. "Seriously? That's the nicest thing anyone's said to me in a while."

"Maybe you need new friends."

Throwing his head back, he let out a laugh that came from deep in his chest, all joy and humor. The sound was like the opposite of the LOLs or silly-face emojis she received in the comments when she posted a blooper video. Those were obligatory, nearly paid for. They were hardly real.

Finn's laughter was filled with life and heart and truth. He didn't hold back, and he didn't seem to want to. It wrapped around her, warm and sustaining. And suddenly she wanted to say something funny again, just to get it to continue.

But her mind was blank, and she could only watch the cords of his throat slowly relax as the sound died down and his Adam's apple stilled.

"Seeing as most of my friends have four legs, I guess I can't blame them."

Flames licked at her cheeks, and she pressed her fingers there to cover them.

Finn reached for a flake of hay and threw it into Roberta's stall. "I doubt you came here to compliment my lack of facial hair, so what can I do for you today?"

"Right, yeah . . . though it is very nice."

LIZ JOHNSON

He gave her a quick wink but didn't comment on her lack of verbal control.

"I was hoping I might be able to use your computer again. I really need some more clothes." With a little flourish of her hand, she showcased the same cropped jeans and blue sweater she'd been wearing for three days.

Finn, on the other hand, was wearing his third outfit in the same amount of time. Another Henley with its super-soft checked texture, sleeves pushed up to his elbows. The one the day before had been stormy gray, but today's shirt was a bright blue that made his eyes nearly glow. And the navy fleece of his vest looked warm enough to cuddle against.

Not that she was considering that.

His wardrobe wasn't exactly going to land him on the cover of GQ, but he sure knew how to pick clothes that showed off his broad shoulders and athletic arms.

Moreover, he had enough clothes. Even if they were mostly Henleys.

Finn glanced over his shoulder toward the house, his eyebrows pinching together. "Yeah, sure. Of course you can . . . but won't that take a few days? You probably want them— need them?—sooner."

Her internal processor finally kicked in, and she bit back the words just before asking him if she smelled funky. Though maybe the smell of the barn and its inhabitants covered whatever was still lingering in her outfit.

"I wish I could, but I don't have any credit cards, or even a phone to do an electronic payment in a store."

Blinking owlish eyes, he chewed on the middle of his lip. "But you have enough money?"

"If you're asking if I'm broke"—she paused to put her

hands on her hips—"the answer is no. If you're asking if I have easy access to the money I do have, the answer is also no."

His mouth twisted into a frown, all trace of his earlier merriment gone. "No, I wasn't— I didn't mean to imply— I just—" He heaved a big sigh. "I could buy you some new clothes. I can take you shopping. Today."

"I don't need you to—"

"Here's the thing. I could use some help putting together a whelping bed, and in exchange—"

"No, that's not the problem. I have the money. It's just stuck in my account until—" She stopped and tilted her head, really looking at him. "But I could transfer it to you."

"What? No. I don't need your money."

That wasn't what she'd glimpsed the day before in the letter from the bank on his desk. She hadn't been trying to read it. But it was hard not to see a big old "We regret to inform you" on the top line. And curiosity had gotten the better of her.

And now she knew he had been denied a loan.

Only, she wasn't supposed to know that. And she had no idea what the loan had been for.

But the man clearly did not have money to buy her new clothes.

Still, he insisted. "I'm offering to help you get some new clothes—in exchange for a little manual labor."

"And I'm telling you I'll transfer the money to you in advance." And maybe throw in a little tip for his troubles.

"And I'm telling *you* that I don't need it." His voice rose.

Hers dropped low. "Quit being so stubborn."

"I'm trying to do something nice."

"You are." She couldn't keep the huff out of her words. "You're going to drive me to somewhere I can buy clothes." "Yes. And I'll buy them for you." His eyes flashed and his tone took on the same note that Marie's had carried earlier that morning. The one that said an argument would not be welcome, at least according to Julia Mae.

But the little girl was nowhere to be seen. And Finn wasn't her boss or giving her a roof over her head. "Then I'll pay you back for them."

He rolled his eyes. "You don't have to."

"I get that. But I am more than capable."

"I'm sure you are." His tone directly contradicted his words.

He clearly didn't understand that she had brought in a healthy six figures the year before and the one before that. In profit. That didn't include her travel, new gear, or other expenses. That was money going into her savings account. Money not going to pay for a house or any of the things to fill it. Money that was invested and growing. Money that meant she didn't have to work for a while if she didn't want to.

Except that she liked what she did. She liked having a plan for her day and her week and her year. She liked seeing the world, finding hidden treasures.

Besides, if she wasn't traveling, she'd be in one spot. Stuck. Collecting only God knew what.

So she was going to keep doing this as long as she could. And she didn't need anyone's help. Least of all Finn's.

The problem was, if they kept arguing, they weren't going to get anywhere near a clothing store today—let alone this week.

"Fine. You win." She held up her hands in surrender.

"Really?"

Pasting on the sweetest smile she could manage, she nodded. "Really."

If she decided to send him an anonymous donation after she left the island, so be it. He wouldn't be able to argue then.

He still looked doubtful but simply said, "Let me feed the dogs. Then we can drive down to Charlottetown."

"Maybe I could return my rental car?"

"Sure. You don't need it as long as you're in North Rustico." With a wink, he added, "I'll take you anywhere you want to go."

Nine

The next day Finn tried to drum up as much excitement about feeding his cow as he'd had arguing with Cretia. The whole drive to the Charlottetown airport, he'd watched her taillights and smiled when he thought of their conversation.

For a moment, he had wondered if she thought he needed her money. He did not. He was probably in a better financial position than she was. Especially since he didn't have to replace his computer, phone, and wardrobe.

He was quite capable of paying for whatever she wanted to purchase at the clothing store his mom had always liked best.

They parted ways at the front door. He found a chair and tried not to stare at her as she wove between racks, pulling out a shirt here and a pair of jeans there. She was efficient and decisive, and then she disappeared into a room in the back and came out with an armful that she thumped down next to the register.

He waited for the clerk to ring up the items, paying close attention to the cars driving in and out of the parking lot until the clothes were all bagged up. He swiped his card and felt a little like a knight slaying the dragon.

Cretia offered a soft "Thank you" as he helped her into his restored army-green Ford pickup. Originally his grandpa's, it was more than sixty years old but drove like a dream after a few thousand dollars and a few months of work. Any sign of rust and wear had been repaired, and the outside shone in the sun. His gut clenched when Cretia's eyes lit with surprise as she settled into the smooth fabric of the seat, taking in the shining chrome and old-school buttons on the dash.

"Nice. Did you do this?" she asked.

He had to bite back a satisfied grin and only nodded in response.

She hadn't argued with him again the whole drive back. They'd chatted about her favorite places to travel and why she loved her unconventional career. "According to you," she'd said.

"She's a better conversationalist than you, Roberta," he said to the cow as he brushed a black spot on her side. The old girl lowed softly. "Prettier too." Roberta stepped away and swung a clearly offended look his way. "Sorry, the truth hurts."

"What truth would that be?"

He whipped around to find the woman he'd been thinking about standing in the doorway, the sun turning her into mostly a silhouette.

"Um, that she's . . . that . . . she's put on a few pounds since she got here."

"Roberta?" Turning toward the cow but keeping plenty of distance, Cretia said, "Don't let him say that about you. You're gorgeous."

Roberta did not appear inclined to buy the compliment from her nemesis. She wandered off through the open gate and disappeared into the pasture beyond the barn.

"To what do I owe this visit?" Finn finally asked, his gaze only then able to focus on Cretia. His jaw dropped. Her new jeans ended several inches above her ankles, but unlike the loose pair she'd been wearing since their first meeting, these hugged her waist and hips and legs in all the right places. Her new shirt—a shade darker than the island's red-dirt roads— made her skin glow and her long hair shine. Even the black slip-on sneakers accentuated her complexion.

"I had to take my new clothes for a test run."

"Mission accomplished," he said. His words were a little too breathy beneath his pounding heart. Quickly clearing his throat, he motioned around the barn. "But if you hang out here, I'm liable to put you to work."

"Good. That's why I'm here. I heard there's a whelping bed you could use a hand with. And I owe you mine."

"Uh-huh."

"Only . . . what's a whelping bed?"

With a snort, his focus returned, and he motioned for her to follow him to the small birthing room opposite the tack room he'd filled with the appliances to prepare the goat bottles. "My dad built these rooms to give our dogs a bit of privacy to labor. And to protect the pups."

Cretia stopped a few steps behind him. "Is giving birth dangerous? For the dogs, I mean?"

"Not usually. But sometimes they give birth to more than ten puppies, and it's easy for a little one to end up between the mom and the side of the box. They can suffocate. We put in a railing to make sure they're protected."

"Okay. Well, then put me to work."

He gave her another once-over. "You sure you want to get your new clothes dirty?"

"I think they're more your clothes than mine at the moment. But since they're probably not going to fit you and I've got to wear something . . ."

Fair point. He grabbed the broom from its spot tucked beside the kennel fence and held it out to her. "Will you sweep out the room? Check for any spiderwebs in the corners and ceilings too."

He half expected her to balk at the mention of clashing with barn pests, but she didn't. She simply took the broom—her fingers brushing his for a split second, like an infusion of caffeine—and set to work gathering up old hay and plenty of dirt. The cap sleeves of her shirt showed off the length of her arms, gentle muscles rolling with each push and pull of the broom.

Suddenly she stopped and looked up at him as though asking if he needed something. He froze for a split second, then whipped around and marched toward where he'd stored the stack of boards after the Fab Four arrived. She didn't say anything, but he thought he heard a low giggle mingling with the scrape of the bristles against the ground.

He carried the walls of the box—almost two meters long and half as wide—two at a time and stacked them just inside the door. Each time he came within a few feet of her, he could smell the soap she'd used. Or maybe the shampoo in all that rich hair. She'd pulled it back into a ponytail, and with each swing of her head, it danced.

He needed to focus on Bella and her pups, not the pretty stranger who had waltzed into his life.

Stopping at Bella's kennel after dropping off the base of the bed, he squatted beside her and ran a hand over her stomach. "Hey, girl. How you doing?"

From her spot lying on fresh hay, she gave a few labored pants and drooled on his boot.

"Pretty exhausted, eh?"

She let him give her another gentle rub, and he could feel the little ones moving around inside. "It won't be long now, girl. We'll get you all set up in a nice spot."

Bella let out a tired woof, and he pushed her water bowl and food dish closer. When he stepped out of the den and locked the door behind him, he caught Cretia staring. Unlike him, she didn't look away. She only leaned on the wooden handle of the broom and cocked her head to the side.

"How soon will it be?"

"Few days. Maybe a week. She won't let me touch her stomach right before they come. But I want to get her bed all set up so she has some time to get settled in."

"You're—" Cretia bit her lip, her eyes narrowing, zeroing in on him until he could feel every bit of her inspection. And he wanted to pass it. "I've never met—" Her eyes flew open, and her tan cheeks took on that rosy tint he'd seen a few times. "I mean, I've never been around dogs like this before. You must love it."

That was not what she'd been about to say. He was one hundred percent sure of that. Maybe she was working on the inside processing. Probably. And maybe he should take a few cues from her in that department.

Biting back all the worries and fears that came with running a family business and carrying on his name's legacy, he merely nodded. "Let me just get my tools, and we can put the bed together."

When he returned from the tack room a moment later, red metal toolbox in hand, she was giving him another intense survey.

"Why do you look like Handy Manny right now?"

"Handy who?"

"Handy Manny. Didn't you watch that cartoon as a kid?"

Setting down his toolbox, he shook his head. "I played outside with the dogs, like little boys should."

"Oh." She blinked a few times, the smile slowly leaking from her eyes. "Right. Of course, that's how kids should grow up."

The sad tug at the corners of her mouth hit him like a bale of hay to the chest. "No, Cretia." He grabbed for her hand but had no idea what to do with it once he had it clasped in his own. "I was kidding. I'm sorry. It was a bad joke. Honestly, my parents were cheap, and we never had cable. And my mom and I were my dad's only help around here. I was outside most of the time, which means I probably missed out on all the good shows."

She fought for a smile. "It was a cartoon about a handy-man with talking tools. It wasn't exactly *Citizen Kane*."

With a shrug, he confessed, "I've never seen that either."

Now she gave him a real smile. Not dazzling, but truthful. "Neither have I."

They stood in silence for a long moment, his hands still cradling hers, suspended between them. She didn't pull away, but neither did she acknowledge it.

All the while, he wanted to know the answer to only one question so he never made the same mistake again.

What did I say to make you so sad?

But he couldn't seem to form that particular question. Instead, he said, "Ready to build a bed?"

Cretia tugged her hand out of his grip with a nod and followed him into the room.

"I'm not so good with building things," she said as he handed her one of the side boards. Finn quickly assured her they'd do it together.

A few minutes in, he knew she had underestimated her own skills. She had a knack for holding the boards just right and seemed to innately know which ends connected and where to hold the metal brackets so he could screw them into place.

Their roles required rather close quarters. Not that he was complaining as her shoulder brushed his again. It was such an innocent touch. So simple. Yet he couldn't help the sudden catch in his breath or the way his stomach pitched. Her presence surrounded him. Filled him. Leveled him.

And he'd only known her for four days.

Granted, they'd started off fairly eventful. More than a little stressful. But the last three days had been almost mundane—just normal life. Running errands and feeding the animals and building a bed for Bella.

Yet they'd been the best three days he could remember.

Which meant either he needed more excitement in his life or Cretia was something special.

His mom would love that. Not that he'd ever tell her. Or that Cretia would ever meet her. Cretia's time on the island had a countdown. As soon as her order from the Apple store arrived, she'd be back in the air, off to parts unknown. Unlikely to return soon.

Or ever.

Finn pressed his shoulder against her arm as he finished attaching the third corner brace. If asked, he would have claimed it was so he could get the right angle for the screw. The silk of her skin against his arm was a happy accident. Mostly. And maybe a tiny reminder that at least for the moment they were in the same room.

Looking up, he caught a genuine smile floating across her face. "You're better at this than you think."

"Or maybe you're just good at telling me what to do."

"Probably that." He added a wink, which drew another grin from her. "You want to hand me that last board?"

Pushing herself off her knees, she stood and strolled over to the last side panel. Though she appeared sturdy and capable, the slat dwarfed her, and she lumbered under its weight.

"Sorry, I should have—" He rose, fully intending to take the wood from her, but walked right into the end of it instead.

Fire seared across his left cheek and up toward his eye as the board clattered to the ground, adding to the sudden pounding at his temple. Blood rushed through his ears, and he clamped a hand over his face, stumbling into the wall.

"Finn. Finn. I'm so sorry. Are you all right?" She was close enough that her breath fanned across the front of his neck where he'd left a few buttons undone. And then her cool hands were on him, firm and urgent, pulling at his wrist and cupping his other cheek. "Talk to me. Can you see? Are you bleeding?"

He couldn't see a thing. But it was because he was pretty sure opening his eyes would be a one-way ticket straight into the arms of an impending headache.

Instead of responding, he sank against the wall, letting his knees bend until he reached the floor. Cretia went with him, her grip unwavering despite her mildly panicked gasps. "Do I need to call someone? What's your emergency number here? I can get an ambulance. Or call Marie. Or—"

Wrapping his free hand around her wrist silenced her for a moment, and he tugged her fingers from his cheek to his chest. Hand splayed against his pounding heart, she scooted closer, her legs tangling with his.

"Finn?" she finally whispered. "Are you . . ."

"Just stunned," he finally managed through gritted teeth, forcing his labored breathing to a more even pace.

"I didn't see you. I'm s-sorry."

It was the little catch in her voice, an almost sob, that made his eyes fly open. Immediately they flooded with tears from the shock and the pain, and he wiped them away just as the headache he'd known was coming pummeled his brain.

Ignoring the pain, he reached for Cretia's face, cupping her cheeks and urging her to look at him. "Hey. Hey." Her long black lashes fluttered, and she finally met his gaze. "It was my own fault. I walked into it. You didn't hit me."

She made no indication that she heard or agreed with him as her expression broke. "Your face!"

"That's what all the girls say."

Clearly, she didn't think him funny. A scowl set into place as she gingerly pressed the pads of her fingers against his cheekbone. They felt more like a sledgehammer, and he jerked back from her touch. Every part of his skull threatened to mutiny. Sighing heavily, he rested his head against the wall behind him, closed his eyes, and held as still as possible.

It might have been two minutes or ten before he realized Cretia hadn't moved. She was still pressed against his side, one hand on his chest and the other smoothing the skin along his jaw with a slow stroke of her thumb.

Cracking one eye open, he watched her watching him, her gaze intent on the left side of his face. He figured he wasn't bleeding or she'd be trying to mop it up. But the skin felt too tight over his cheek, and he'd probably have a black eye in the morning.

Dealing with all of that seemed unimportant compared to sitting in the quiet with Cretia. Her touch was soft, her fingers cool, but they warmed a spot right in the center of his ribs. That heat spread through him, reaching the tips of his fingers and toes. It was all Cretia.

"Finn?"

"Yeah?" He managed to open his other eye far enough to see out of it.

"Are you all right?" Her words were low, hesitant. But she didn't look away from his gaze. Amber flames flickered in her eyes and set off a matching movement low in his belly.

"It's just a bump."

"My abuelita used to kiss my boo-boos." Her voice dropped even more. "Is that what you need?"

He prayed that she couldn't feel his abs clench at the innocent suggestion. She meant nothing by it. Just teasing him.

But his guts didn't get the memo, and his stomach dropped in a not altogether unpleasant way.

She leaned in. His lungs collapsed.

Like the touch of butterfly wings, she pressed her lips to his cheek. She was warm and soft and so gentle that he wanted to curl up in her embrace.

It wasn't possible, but her touch made his face hurt a little less.

"There. Did that help?"

"Never better." Somehow that was the truth.

He dragged his hand from his side to his chest and squeezed her satiny fingers. Her eyes dropped to where their hands met. When she looked up again, her gaze didn't reach his eyes, stopping somewhere in the vicinity of his lips. It was nearly tangible, almost as good as a real kiss.

But not quite.

"Cretia."

"Yeah?"

He didn't have anything else to say. He just liked the way her name tasted on his lips. And he liked the feel of her this close. And he liked the way her hair smelled like flowers. And he liked . . . her. Her humor and her joy and the way she argued with him. And even when she let him win, the look in her eyes that made him think she wasn't finished yet.

And he liked that he knew all of that in four days.

He hated that he might only get another four with her before she left.

This wasn't forever—or even for the long term. But he would hate himself even more if he let her go without knowing more than the taste of just her name.

The pounding across the side of his head seemed to vanish as he slid his thumb around the curve of her ear. As he outlined the smooth line of her jaw with his knuckle, her body trembled against him. Good. He wasn't the only one who felt this thing between them.

In case he hadn't made his intentions clear, he dragged his thumb around the shape of her lips, first the rounded bottom, then the bow of the top. They were impossibly smooth and full, rosy and ripe. Her lashes fluttered closed, resting against the pink of her cheeks. This was his moment.

Leaning forward, he pulled in a quick breath and licked his lips. Only a breath between them. And then less. And somehow even less.

"Finnegan! Guess who came for a visit!"

Ten

Cretia pulled away from Finn so fast that she managed to shove him, and he groaned as the back of his head cracked against the wall. She was barely on her feet when an older couple appeared in the barn. The woman was soft but sturdy—maybe an inch or two over five feet. The man was an exact copy of Finn, plus a few gray hairs and about thirty years' worth of wrinkles.

"Mom?" Finn groaned from his seat on the floor but didn't make a move to get up. "What are you guys doing here?"

"Well, we had an errand over in St. Peter's and thought we'd— What happened to your eye?" His mom looked between Finn's rapidly swelling face and Cretia several times, her eyebrows rising with each glance.

Cretia had never prayed for an earthquake to open the ground until right then. Or maybe for the presence of those European magicians who waved a gold sheet to distract their audience while one of them disappeared. She'd wasted more than a few hours giggling over their videos, and at the moment, she'd happily pay them for a personal demonstration.

To have someone distract Finn and his parents while she bolted out of the barn.

But she had no such luck.

She had to stand there under the weight of Finn's mom's inspection while her whole body probably turned as red as her flaming neck. And all she could think about was how close she'd come to knowing if Finn's kiss was as sweet as the man himself.

And wouldn't that make his mom proud?

"Just a little accident," Finn finally said in answer to his mom's question. He groaned as he pushed himself upright and strolled past Cretia, surreptitiously squeezing her elbow along the way.

Finn's mom was apparently unconvinced by his explanation and grabbed his shoulders, pulling him down to her eye level. "You need to get some ice on that."

"I know. I'll take care of it in a minute. It just happened." He waved his hand toward the partially finished box on the floor. "We were putting together Bella's bed, and I walked into a—"

"*We?*" his dad echoed.

Like a veil had been lifted and Cretia had suddenly appeared, both Mr. and Mrs. Chaffey looked around their son and focused on her.

"This is Cretia. Martin. My . . . um . . . a friend of mine."

His mom's eyes flashed with some understanding. "From the harbor? You're the girl he pushed into the water."

Cretia shook her head quickly. "No. It wasn't like that. It was just an accident. I ran into him, actually, and stumbled. He and Joe saved me."

Mrs. Chaffey grabbed her and pulled her into a tight hug,

arms circling her shoulders like she never intended to let go. "We didn't know you were still here. But we're so—" She glanced back at her husband as though looking for the right way to end that. "Well, it's just lovely to meet you."

Under different circumstances, Cretia would have probably agreed. They were surely a sweet couple, and she couldn't deny a bit of curiosity about Finn's relationship with his parents. But if they'd only arrived five or ten minutes later . . .

Flames licked at her neck while her imagination filled in the gap, the might-have-been. She likely would never know now.

Forcing a smile, she shook Mr. Chaffey's hand. "It's very nice to meet you."

"Call me Thomas. And this is Bea."

"Ma'am," Cretia said with a nod.

"Oh, now, we're not so formal here. Bea is fine. And we're so delighted to get to meet you. Of course, we heard about the accident all the way down in Summerside. But Finnegan seemed to think you weren't going to stick around and we wouldn't get the chance to meet you." Turning to her son, Bea said, "You should have called us sooner. We would have made the trip."

"Well, I . . ." Cretia glanced at Finn, hoping for some rescue. But his face wore the same confusion she felt. "I had to order a new phone and things. And Marie has been very kind to let me stay at the inn while I wait for them to arrive."

"Well, come inside." Bea wrapped an arm around her waist and ushered her toward the house. "Tell us all about yourself. You know, Finn never brought girls home. We didn't get to meet any of his special friends . . ."

As Bea continued prattling on, Cretia saw Finn cringe.

Just for a moment. It was clear he wanted her to stop talking, that she was winding down a road he'd rather not travel. But he never interrupted his mom. He didn't clear his throat or cut in. Or even nudge his dad to end the painful chatter.

Instead, he squeezed his mom's shoulder and kissed the top of her head.

Cretia knew his response wasn't because *she* was a so-called special friend. She wasn't. She wouldn't even begin to assume so.

Finn's actions spoke to his love for his mom. Even when she embarrassed him.

Something pierced straight through her chest that felt a lot like regret. A lot like wishing she had a relationship with her mom that looked even a fraction like Finn and Bea's.

Finn ambled toward the house. With his good eye, he searched for Cretia, who had dislodged herself from his mom's grip and disappeared somewhere out of his range of vision. When he tried to turn to find her, his head spun and he stumbled.

"Finn?" His dad approached from behind him, wrapping an arm around his back. "Steady there."

He was fine. Perfectly fine. Except he couldn't find Cretia or hear her footsteps above the pounding of his heart in his ears. If she'd taken his parents' arrival as an excuse to scoot back to the inn before he could say anything about their almost kiss, he'd kick himself in the seat of the pants.

Because he had wanted to kiss her.

Correction. He still wanted to kiss her.

But obviously not now. Not with his parents hovering around.

Maybe it had just been the moment. The weight of her hand over his heart. The smell of fresh hay. The warmth of her body beside his.

Then he caught sight of her on the far side of his dad, reaching for the screen door to hold it open for them all. The punch to his gut said it hadn't just been the moment. Even as she ducked her chin and tucked an escaped strand of hair behind her ear, she called to him. Whether she meant to or not was still uncertain. But he felt the tug toward her all the same.

As their little parade traipsed inside, he shuffled behind his dad to Cretia's side. Catching her eye, he tried for an apologetic smile, scratching at his missing beard and mouthing a silent *I'm sorry.*

She brushed her fingers along his forearm, light as a feather. He was forgiven. For intruding parents. For interrupted kisses. For a life that must look entirely foreign to her.

"Oh, Finnegan," his mom cried.

He whipped around to look for the disaster that must have provoked his mom's reaction. Maybe Joe had gone after one of the throw pillows or pulled his treats off the counter. That had happened once or twice. But his dog had been in the barn with them, and a quick survey showed his home was just as he'd left it a few hours before.

"Your desk is a mess!" his mom continued, marching in that direction.

Finn almost laughed the comment off until she neared the corner in question. Suddenly his pulse skyrocketed, and a rush of adrenaline raced through him.

He'd dropped the letter from the bank on top of a pile there. He also hadn't bothered to move it since then.

"Mom!" The word came out much sharper than he'd intended. At least it made her stop and turn toward him, so he slapped on the best smile he could manage. "Would you . . . would you . . ." His mind was absolutely blank. He'd like to blame the board he'd taken to the face, but that wasn't at fault. Still, maybe he could use it as an excuse. "Would you get me an ice pack for my eye?"

"Oh, my dear. Yes!" She scurried toward the kitchen, almost immediately rummaging through the freezer. Ice cubes clinked against each other as she poured them into a plastic bag.

He let out a quick sigh of relief, only to see his dad headed in the same direction his mom had been.

"Your father had a pretty good system back in the day," his mom said. "I'm sure he'd help you get it organized."

As if pulled by a rope, his dad strolled toward the desk and the letter he absolutely could not see.

Finn swallowed hard against the sudden pounding of his heart in his throat. "No. No."

His dad turned, halfway across the room, an arched eyebrow asking all the questions he needed to.

"I mean, I know where everything is." Finn offered a lame shrug. "A new system would just make me lose things."

With a laugh, his dad walked back toward him, his motions stiff and slow, and clapped him on the shoulder. "That's my boy." Leaning in, he added in a whisper, "That's what I tell your mom even if I have no idea where things are."

Finn gave the expected chuckle, but a line around his lungs pulled tight, stealing his breath.

"You could hire some help, you know," his mom said as she marched his way, holding out the ice pack wrapped in a dish towel. "I did most of the finances when your dad ran the business."

He accepted the ice and pressed it to his face, the cold making him grimace and reigniting the nerves along his cheek. Keeping his other eye on his dad, Finn watched for any response to the suggestion.

His dad squeezed his shoulder. "That's not a terrible idea."

Finn couldn't tell if that meant his dad thought he could use the help. Or if it meant that he didn't think Finn could do it all on his own.

Probably the latter. Which stung like a wasp. But that hadn't changed in more than ten years. His dad had always questioned his ability to take on the family business. Not so much to his face, but Finn had overheard enough to know the truth.

"I'm doing fine," Finn said. "Things are running as smoothly as ever."

His dad cleared his throat. "I heard from Mike that you're thinking about adding onto the barn."

Finn pressed his ice pack harder against his cheek. It was already numb, but the pressure against his face took his mind off of other stresses. "It's just an idea. I haven't really looked into it." His insides twisted on the lie. But he couldn't handle hearing his dad's thoughts on a possible addition.

The property boundaries hadn't changed since his great-grandfather bought the land. But the once tree-covered fields were now grassy pastures, fenced plots for the dogs—and other animals—to roam. The rolling hills blocked even a hint of a view of the north shore, but on quiet days, Finn imagined he could hear the gentle crash of the bay against the rocky red beaches.

Sometimes, when he let the dogs out to run, he stood in the fields and simply watched the wind ripple through the tall grass, the green flickering and changing with every stroke. Even Roberta enjoyed simply standing in the sunlight that poured over the hills. The animals seemed to know what he had learned long ago. There was something special about this plot of land.

It was made for more.

His dad had seemed content with it as it was. As far as Finn knew, his dad's only hope was that the business would continue, that Finn wouldn't sink what their family had worked so hard to build.

Finn wanted more than survival. He wanted to leave a mark, to raise the trajectory of their family's name.

But until he could prove that he could grow the business into something more than producing a few dozen dogs a year, he wasn't ready to tell his dad about his hopes for expanding the barn.

"Really?" His dad cocked his head to the side. "Mike said you gave him a hand with a repair on his boat and he offered to help you put it up."

Finn responded with a hard shake of his head. "Nah. I'm not there yet. And I'm doing just fine on my own."

"Of course you are." His mom pointed toward the living room. "Come on, let's sit down." She helped her husband into the recliner, and as soon as he sat, the lines around his mouth eased and his shoulders relaxed.

Finn plopped onto the couch, motioning for Cretia to sit

too. Maybe he could get his parents curious about her so they'd forget about his questionable professional skills and quit shooting furtive glances at his desk.

Cretia didn't seem inclined to play along as she shuffled toward the door. "I'm going to just head . . ." She pointed toward the back door.

"Stay," his mom commanded. She was a few inches shorter than Cretia, but she wrapped an arm around her waist and propelled the younger woman toward the couch, nearly depositing her right beside him before perching on the arm of the recliner. "Tell us about yourself."

Thank you, Mom.

Cretia's wide eyes said she wasn't quite so pleased with the situation. Hovering on the edge of the sofa cushion, hands folded between her knees, she gave them a quick smile. "There's not much to say."

"That's not true. Cretia travels around the world for her job."

His mom scooted forward. "Well, that's exciting. What do you do?"

Cretia's glare at him said she did not appreciate having to explain her career to more people who probably wouldn't understand it. But as long as they were focused on her, he didn't have to worry about his parents asking more questions of him.

Eleven

The next few days after Finn's parents' visit ambled by, with Cretia often reaching for her phone, only to be slapped with a fresh reminder that she was still completely disconnected from her work and her life and making plans for both of those things. Her only distractions seemed to be socializing the Fab Four and arriving at the farm just in time to feed Sonny and Cher.

And seeing Finn.

She didn't mind seeing him every day, even though he still sported the black eye that reminded her of her misstep.

The days weren't filled with exciting adventures or major expeditions, but there was a quiet peace to this pace of life. A simple joy to the familiarity of Joe Jr.'s boisterous welcome each time she stopped by, and his warmth by her side when she sat in the grass to play with the puppies.

Her first day in North Rustico, she'd thought that if any place could persuade her to stay, it might be this gentle hamlet on the island's north shore. The longer she stayed, the truer she knew that to be. There was something tempting about the gentle breeze and warm sunshine as she strolled toward

Finn's house this morning. It held a promise she could almost identify, a hope she could almost put into words. Almost.

Yet as soon as she let the idea sneak in, her lungs seized, and she stumbled on the gravel along the side of the road. Shuffling into the grass of the shallow ditch, she pressed her hands to her waist, lifted her face, and took several deep breaths.

"I'm not going to stay here," she whispered to the fluffy cloud swimming across the sky.

But you could.

Finn's face flashed in her mind. His smile. The little dimple in his chin. The crinkles around his eyes when he found something particularly funny. The feeling of her hand encased in his—solid, dependable.

Maybe there could be something real between them. Maybe there were reasons to stick around and explore the could be.

She wouldn't, though. For reasons just as valid. That wasn't her future. She wouldn't settle down somewhere and buy a house and fill it with stuff. She wouldn't pour every last penny into junk she didn't need or things she quickly tired of.

She would not become her mother.

Or any version of her.

Suddenly Cretia couldn't see Finn. Not right then anyway. She needed a minute, just a breath to collect herself. Or she'd be tempted again.

At the moment she wasn't sure she was stronger than his pull. Worse, the silly man probably had no idea what he did to her.

It was probably better that way.

She sucked in a deep breath through her nose, then

released it as she spun a slow circle. Finn's house was only a few dozen yards down the road, his truck parked out front. Between the birds calling to one another, she could almost hear Joe and the puppies playing beyond the barn.

She did not need to fall more in love with those ridiculous dogs either.

Taking a step back toward the inn, she caught sight of the boxy white house across the street. It was simple but clean, its porch nearly an invitation to come over and enjoy the shade, sipping a tall glass of iced tea.

Cretia took several steps in that direction before she even realized it. By then, she could see the small add-on to the end of the barn—the store with the Open sign. Mama Cheese Sandwich's shop.

Picking up her speed, she hurried across the street and down the dirt lane. The wooden door easily swung open and set off a loud moo, which set off her own laughter.

"I'll be right there!" called a voice from the far side of a curtained doorway.

"No rush," Cretia said.

The room was small and simple, white shiplap covering all four walls. The far left corner boasted three round tables, each with two chairs and plenty of scars on their wooden tops. Shelves beside the table held loaves of bread and bags of rolls. Even in their wrappings, they smelled rich and fresh. A large display case and planked countertop dominated the opposite wall. Wheels of cheese in varying shades of yellow and cream sat behind the glass.

She felt like a child pressing her hand to the case, but the memory of this gooey cheese grilled on a lovely sourdough set her tongue to tingling. It hadn't been gourmet or

Michelin-star rated. And maybe it sounded cheesy, but it had been made with love. Or, if not love, at least affection and concern. She had been able to taste those in every meal from Marie's kitchen.

The black curtain in the corner of the room twitched as a woman with gray hair and a quick step walked through. She wore a blue apron and a wide smile. "Welcome to Kane Dairy."

Before Cretia even knew what she was saying, the nickname popped out. "You're Mama Cheese Sandwich."

Somehow the woman's smile grew even brighter, nearly glowing even in the morning sunlight coming through the large windows. "I haven't heard that name in a little while," she said around a chuckle.

"Oh, I'm sorry." Cretia tugged on the hem of her red shirt as she searched for the memory of her name. "Is it Mrs. Kane?"

"Not anymore." There was a note of sadness in her voice, and the light in her pale eyes dimmed. "It's Mrs. Grady now." She waved her left hand, and a modest diamond sparkled on her ring finger. "But the kids around here still call me Mama Kane because the dairy's name hasn't changed. But you . . . you may call me Kathleen. Or Mama Cheese Sandwich if you prefer."

Cretia dipped her chin in understanding. Before she could introduce herself, Kathleen continued on.

"You must be our visitor staying at the inn. Finn's friend."

Heat soared up her neck and settled into her cheeks as she managed another quick nod. She wasn't afraid of being in the spotlight, but she'd already spent years being the person talked about behind her back. The one her classmates suddenly stopped whispering about when she entered a room.

At least she had known what they were saying. Her clothes were always dirty. She lived in a pigsty. Her mother wasn't right.

They hadn't been wrong.

But knowing that her name and something of her story were being whispered among the residents of North Rustico was different. She didn't know what truth or lies they were spreading. Or what people thought of her.

Or what Finn said when he spoke of her.

Or even if *he* was the one talking about her.

Her stomach twisted harshly, and she stumbled a step back, reaching for the door handle behind her. "It was nice to—"

"Please don't go." Kathleen rushed forward and grabbed her free hand. "I have a new cheese that I could use an opinion on. Will you try it with me?"

Cretia fully intended to refuse the offer, but her stomach had other plans, loudly protesting that she'd skipped breakfast.

"I'll take that as a yes." Kathleen beamed, gently tugging her toward the tables. "Please have a seat."

Without much of a choice, Cretia slid into one of the wooden chairs as Kathleen produced the snack of all snacks—a charcuterie board of rich orange cheese slices, various crackers, bunches of red and green grapes, and dried berries.

"I'm sorry, are you expecting someone?" There was no way this woman had prepared this for only herself. And she couldn't have known Cretia would end up here.

Kathleen lifted her round shoulder but shook her head.

"It was a slow morning, and my daughter-in-law has been stopping by lately. I thought I'd be ready just in case—but you'll be a better judge of the cheese. Impartial." The last word came with a decisive nod. "Natalie is married to a dairy farmer, so I can't count on her to be unbiased."

Cretia chuckled as Kathleen pushed the board closer to her. "I might be too hungry to give you an honest opinion too. How do you know you can trust me?"

"Marie has said such wonderful things about you. She loves having you at the inn."

An unexpected warmth filled her chest, and she shoved a buttery cracker into her mouth so she didn't have to respond.

"And Finn too. My son Justin said Finn is glad you've stuck around."

The cracker suddenly turned to sawdust, and a dry cough escaped as Cretia choked on it. Kathleen jumped to her feet, hurried to the display case, and returned in a moment with a cup of lemonade.

"Thanks," Cretia wheezed, sipping the tart drink. It didn't wash away what Kathleen had said, though. Finn was glad she was here. Presumably he'd said as much since she'd given him the black eye. It was possible he still felt that way.

Which made her heart pound a little harder and the rest of her want to scramble off the island.

She still had to go see Finn today, mostly to check on Bella. But also to borrow his computer and check on the arrival of her electronics.

As soon as they arrived, she could leave. Then she wouldn't be tempted with things that weren't for her.

"Tell me about yourself." Kathleen pushed the cheese

closer. "My daughter-in-law says you're internet famous. I don't even know what that means."

———

After spending the whole morning with Kathleen and consuming nearly her body weight in sharp cheddar that melted in her mouth, Cretia eventually visited Finn. She kept her stay short so that she couldn't remember all the lovely things Kathleen told her that Finn had said about her.

They slipped into her mind a few times, though, and Finn caught her smiling. Twice. When he asked what she was thinking about, she mumbled something about the cheese and then begged to borrow his computer again.

The tracking page on her packages said simply "In Transit." No delivery date listed yet. Maybe it just hadn't been updated.

Finn said that wasn't unusual on PEI, especially in the island's small towns. Shipping might be a science, but delivery was an art. One that didn't always go as planned.

As she strolled into the inn that evening, she saw the light on in the kitchen. Marie sat on a wooden stool at the island, hunched over paperwork spread before her.

As she had for several days, Cretia asked without much hope, "Anything arrive for me?"

Marie looked up with the same sad smile. "Not today. But there are leftovers in the fridge if you're hungry."

As though warmed-up lasagna could replace her tardy electronics.

"How long's it been?" Marie asked, her head still bent over her work.

"Seven days." Still within the delivery window. Far outside the realm of her preference. Pretty much an eternity for someone who hadn't stayed in one city for more than six days in over four years.

"Sometimes it takes a while for things to make it up here. I'm sure they'll be here soon."

Cretia punched a button on the microwave, zapping her leftovers back to life. As she watched the plate spin, she tried not to remember the last time she'd had kitchen privileges in an actual home.

Sure, she'd stayed in hotel suites with kitchenettes upon occasion. And she'd warmed mugs of water to make tea or reheated restaurant leftovers. But those kitchens were cold and impersonal, the fridges empty. This room, even with its stainless-steel double ovens and commercial-grade refrigerator, felt like it belonged in a home.

Maybe because it was rarely empty and usually contained the joy of a boisterous family.

"How's Finn doing?"

Cretia glanced over her shoulder, trying to get a read on if Marie was teasing her, but the other woman's face was completely straight. "Fine. Good, I guess."

"And his eye?"

"Healing." She poured herself a glass of water and settled on the opposite side of the island.

Marie raised an eyebrow, and Cretia shoved an entire forkful into her mouth. If she was busy eating, she couldn't answer the questions Marie hadn't gotten around to asking. The ones she almost certainly would.

"What'd you do today?"

She quickly swallowed a bite. "I met Kathleen. Tried some of her cheese."

"She's wonderful, isn't she?"

Cretia nodded as she took another bite. Kathleen had been just as welcoming and kind as every other resident of North Rustico she'd met. But that was starting to feel like a problem.

Because she liked them. Liked all of them.

"It seems like you're enjoying your time here."

"Uh-huh," she managed around a noodle. Marie often lamented her own cooking skills, but this lasagna was tasty. Not like Florence good, but definitely edible. "Did you make this?"

Marie cringed. "No. Seth did."

That figured. With a mock salute of her fork near her temple, she said, "My compliments to the chef."

"I'll be sure to pass that along." Marie's gaze dropped back to her paperwork, then lifted slowly. "So . . . are you thinking about sticking around for a while?"

Her heart slammed against her rib cage, and she pressed a fist to the spot where her last bite had lodged south of her sternum. "Do you need the room back? I can clear out." Out of a weird compulsion, she jerked her plate to her chin and began to shovel the last few bites into her mouth.

Marie's eyes filled with concern. "Not at all."

"Seriously, I can be out of your hair in a minute. You won't even know I've been here."

"Cretia—"

"Let me just clean this plate."

"Cretia!" The single word took on that tone that Julia Mae had said not to argue with, and Cretia froze. Marie crossed her arms on the counter and leaned forward, a smile tugging at her lips. "I'm not asking you to leave. We like having you around."

"You do?" She wanted to swallow those words as soon as they came out—undeniably needy.

"Of course we do." She made it sound like a foregone conclusion, like she didn't even need to consult with the rest of the family. Or maybe she already had. And then, as if she could read her mind, Marie added, "Julia Mae says she likes it when you're here. She says I'm more fun when you're around."

Cretia couldn't form a response, her mouth opening and closing, nothing more than a breath coming and going.

Marie laughed brightly. "There's no pressure or anything on you. It's just that usually when we have guests, I'm so busy taking care of the inn that I don't have much time to play with the kids. But having you here is more like having a friend over for a visit."

"Friend?" She croaked out the word.

"Oh dear! I'm sorry. I've scared you away now, haven't I?" But Marie's grin didn't look sorry. It looked inviting and kind and all the things Cretia hadn't realized she'd missed in friendships.

She'd carved out a good life on the road, but always moving on meant never putting down roots—in a house or with people. She was fine with the former, but just now she realized she might have missed out on the latter.

The friends she'd made online with other travel influencers weren't the same. She'd met a few of them in person when their travel itineraries overlapped. They'd collaborated on posts and promoted each other's events.

But the strange thing about those types of friendships was that they always carried an undercurrent of competition, a worry about if the other's platforms were growing faster or their sponsorship agreements were better.

She had none of that with Marie.

"Not at all. I've enjoyed our— I like coming back to the inn in the evenings and chatting with you." Cretia swallowed her fear. "But you don't want me to leave? I've been here so much longer than I think either of us thought I would be. You won't hurt my feelings if you say you want your house back." Though as she said it, she knew it might not be true. Because it had taken exactly seven seconds for her to latch on to the word *friend* and realize she didn't want to lose that.

Finn's face flashed through her mind. He was her friend too.

A friend she'd nearly kissed. A friend she wouldn't mind kissing. Preferably without interruption.

Her stomach swooped in a repeat of the motion it had made when he'd leaned so close. He'd smelled of wood and grass, and he'd been warmer than the island sun. She'd wanted to curl up into him and hide from the rest of the world for a while.

But still. He was a friend. There was no denying it.

It was possible to have kissing feelings for a friend. She was pretty sure. Even if she hadn't been in that particular situation before.

But she wasn't going to stick around for much longer. She couldn't. This was all a by-product of a broken phone. And slow delivery. The longer she stayed, the more she wanted friendship.

And kissing.

She had no business thinking about that. Friendship was one thing. It could be sustained across unwieldy travel schedules.

Kissing required being face-to-face.

Cretia scrubbed a hand down her cheek. She had no idea why her mind had zipped from friendship to kissing Finn in two seconds, and she tried to shake off the uninvited thoughts.

Marie seemed completely oblivious. "I understand that you can't stay forever, but as long as you're here, you have a home at the Red Door. I won't let you stay anywhere else. For purely selfish reasons." With a wink, she gathered her papers and pushed her stool back. "And I know I'm not the only one who wants you to stick around."

Fingers twisting into the hem of her shirt, Cretia watched her friend stroll toward the office off the back of the kitchen.

Of course Marie had meant Finn. Just as Kathleen had suggested earlier.

Which was lovely and confusing at the same time. On the one hand, she and Marie had an unspoken understanding. Cretia couldn't remember the last time she'd been so sure of what hadn't been said. It was sweet to think that Finn would miss her too.

But she couldn't let herself want those things. She couldn't let herself think of this place as more than another temporary stop. Another place to explore. Another place to leave.

She could enjoy the cool breeze and the smell of the ocean. The warmth of the sunshine and the feeling of grass between her toes. But she would not let herself succumb to that feeling of home. North Rustico, with its friendly people, funny dogs, and one-eyed cow, was an anomaly. Other places had those things. They just didn't tempt her to stay.

It had been more than a week since she'd checked in with her online community. Though she had videos scheduled to post, she hadn't responded to more than a few comments or checked to see what their responses had been. Finn's internet didn't invite lengthy interactions.

It was time to get back online. To find her phone and her laptop and request a new suitcase. A great wide world awaited. And she'd never discover it if she settled.

Her phone, her videos, her online connections. This was the life—with its priorities—that she had chosen. And no fluffy dogs or chin dimples or kitchen gab sessions were going to coax her to start down a path she didn't want.

A roof over her head was all well and nice. But homes were only good for one thing. Accumulating stuff.

And that was a life she refused to accept.

Twelve

very time Finn walked by his desk, he wanted to snatch the taunting page from the top of the stack, crumple it up, and feed it to Jenna. But he wasn't sure a diet high in printer paper would be good for the goat, so he settled for scowling at it. Sometimes he put his hands on his hips and gave it a good glare. On rarer occasions, he turned his back to his desk and tossed Joe Jr. his ball. He should probably at least file the paper so he didn't risk his parents seeing it again.

This morning, though, he barely gave his desk a glance as he scooped up Joe's slimy green tennis ball near the back door. "Come on, boy," he called as he pushed the screen open and trotted into the early morning sunshine. Joe jogged beyond, his breaths loud and damp.

"Go get it," Finn called as he chucked the ball across the lawn. With a happy bark, Joe leapt after it, stumbling over his paws and tumbling in the grass a few times. Finally, his head popped up, the ball lodged between his teeth, tongue hanging out behind it. But instead of coming back to have it thrown again, he curled up in a patch of sun and looked up with big, pleading eyes.

"You gotta bring it back to me if you want to play, dude." Joe barked. But he didn't move from his spot, only rolling over and wiggling on his back.

"I didn't want to play anyway." Finn laughed, and Joe turned his head, apparently confused by the tone of the words. It didn't matter. Besides, he didn't have time to shoot the breeze with his dog. He'd overslept—because he hadn't been able to close his eyes the night before without seeing Cretia's smile. Which had led to daydreams about finishing that kiss that had almost started days before.

He'd missed his alarm, and the sun was already well over the horizon when he kicked off his covers and shoved his feet into his work boots. He'd been pretty sure—even half asleep—that Cretia would be by. She hadn't missed a day since she'd arrived. And he wasn't too proud to admit that he looked forward to her visits—to every curious question about his work and the hints into her life on the road.

The Fab Four could use some leash practice and an introduction to the water, but he really needed a second set of hands for that.

Not true.

He *wanted* a second set of hands. A very specific set of hands.

But he couldn't enjoy the rest of his day until the stalls had been mucked, fresh hay spread out, and food distributed. He might even have time to take Bella on a short walk if she was up for it.

He marched to the barn and snagged the rake stashed just inside the sliding door as he stepped into the coolness. A string of barks welcomed him, followed by some high-pitched bleats.

"I'd like to think you missed me, but I have a feeling you're just hungry."

George and Ringo jumped against their fence, drool dripping from their jowls.

"I guess stalls will wait. Breakfast won't." He grabbed a giant scoop of food and filled the metal bowls in each kennel, the dogs immediately ignoring him for the organic, high-end kibble his dad thought was overpriced. Maybe it was, but Finn was willing to invest in keeping the dogs as healthy as he could.

He'd moved Bella into her finished whelping box, complete with padded flooring and plenty of cozy blankets, two days before. But still there were no puppies. She looked up at him as he stepped into the private room but almost immediately dropped her head back to the padded floor.

"Hey, sweetie." He crouched beside her, running his hand along her side. "You hungry?"

Even as he poured her food into her dish, she didn't move.

"Soon, eh?" He hoped so. For her sake.

Joe barked from outside. Through the window, Finn saw him standing every bit like a guard dog, but intruders were much more likely to end up being slobbered on than attacked.

A second later, the crunch of gravel in the driveway sent Finn walking in that direction. "Who is it, boy?" he asked Joe as he walked by.

Together they jogged around the side of the house, Joe leading then circling back and hiding behind Finn. With another burst of bravery, the dog sprinted ahead toward a sleek silver truck. But when the door swung open, Joe dashed back to safety, nudging Finn forward with his nose.

Finn rubbed the dog's head. "Way to protect the property." Joe's bark said he was just as proud as could be. He clearly didn't understand sarcasm and probably thought he'd really been a good boy all these years.

He didn't have time to analyze his dog's shortcomings as the truck's driver jumped out, shutting the door behind him. Justin Kane waved, shoving the fingers of his other hand through his shaggy black hair before it quickly fell back across his forehead.

"Justin, didn't expect you today. Certainly didn't think you'd make the drive." It probably had taken him longer to get into and out of the truck than it would have to walk across the road from the dairy. "Everything okay? Natalie okay? You all need a hand?"

Justin chuckled as he reached out for a shake. "Everything's fine at home. Natalie's about a month from her due date but refuses to put her feet up."

That sounded about right. Natalie was as stubborn as they came, and she had refused to slow down right up until she delivered their last three kids too.

"My boys have been asking to come over to see your latest litter."

Finn checked the cab of the truck, but Justin's mini-mes weren't in there. "Of course. You can bring 'em by anytime."

"Thanks." Justin dipped his chin. "And thanks for helping out with the new shed at our place."

Finn had spent all of five or six hours over the course of two days, helping Justin frame the thing a few weeks before. "That was no problem. Always happy to pitch in."

"You know, the dairy runs pretty smoothly these days. And we've got plenty of guys on staff. If you ever need a hand over here . . ."

He tried to prop his smile back into place. "I appreciate the offer." And he did. He just couldn't accept it. Not until he'd proven himself. Until he'd made this business into something more.

Justin nodded and pointed toward his truck. "I had some leftover lumber. Thought you might be able to use it on the extension you told me about."

Finn opened his mouth but snapped it closed as the image of that paper on his desk flashed through his mind. Ignoring it didn't make it go away or make the truth any less true. It hit like a two-by-four to the temple.

Somewhere, someone knew the right words to say in this situation, but this was not the place, and he was not that person.

Thanks, but no.

Thank you, but I'm not a good investment. At least that's what the bank said.

Thanks, but I don't need it anymore.

That's really nice of you, but this place isn't expanding anytime soon.

He managed to force what he hoped was a smile—or at least something that looked less like indigestion than it felt—and settled for the simple. "Thank you."

"You want me to drop it off by the barn?" Justin hitched a thumb toward the bed of the truck.

No. Because then he'd have to look at it. And remember the rejection. And remember that under his leadership, this business was going to stay exactly as it had been for the last fifty years. Yeah, that was a great reminder.

Instead, he shoved his hands into his pockets and shrugged. "Sure. Thanks."

As they walked toward the bed of the truck, Joe barked again, the sound pure joy. Three silhouettes appeared against the morning sun, Cretia in the middle and a smaller one on either side.

He knew it was Cretia without even seeing her face. The soft lines of her form and her gait were more than enough to identify her.

And the way his heart slammed into his ribs. Just because.

A genuine smile tugged at his face just before Jack launched himself at Joe. The dog slobbered all over the kid, and there could have been no more excited recipient. "Joe Jr." The two fell to the grass, wrestling and playing, and Jack nearly disappeared under the coat of black fur. But his giggles continued.

"One of these days, that kid is going to get bigger than the dog." Justin laughed. "What's Joe going to do when he's outmatched?"

"Same thing as always." Finn crossed his arms. "Play dumb. Though I don't know how much of it is playing."

As Cretia and Julia Mae strolled up the drive, the little girl clung to Cretia's arm, hiding behind her leg and warily eyeing the dog.

Justin shot him a questioning look out of the side of his eye. "Is this the girl who gave you a black eye for throwing her in the harbor? She's tougher than she looks."

One of the facts of living in a town the size of a postage stamp. Everyone knew everyone and heard everything. Even if the truth morphed the more the story was told.

"You have no idea," Cretia said by way of introduction, stretching out her free hand. "Cretia Martin."

Justin's eyes grew wide—probably surprised by her directness. Then laughter broke across his features. "Justin Kane."

"Of Kane's Dairy?"

He nodded.

"I met your mom yesterday. She treated me to the best cheddar and pepper jack from your dairy. It was even better than the cheese I tasted in Italy."

"I'm glad to hear it." Justin rocked back on his heels, a satisfied smile in place. "Mom said she had a visitor, but she didn't tell me it was someone so famous. You're the most exciting addition to our town in years."

Justin kept going, but Finn noticed the tight lines forming around Cretia's mouth and the way she hugged herself a little bit harder. He opened his mouth to step in when Justin added one more thought.

"My little sister Brooke is a big fan of yours. She said she watches all of your videos and is even trying to get her husband Chuck to take her on your recommended tour of Greece."

"Oh, they should. It's a lovely country!"

Justin motioned down the road toward the shoreline. "You should do some videos of town before you leave."

Cretia beamed. Finn felt seasick.

Something green and nasty boiled inside him, and no number of deep breaths made it simmer down. Maybe it was the way Justin made Cretia smile—which was ridiculous since Justin had been happily married for almost a decade and Natalie was expecting their fourth child.

So what if Finn wanted to be the source of those perfect smiles.

Perhaps it was the simple reminder that Cretia would be leaving.

Soon.

He rubbed a hand to his belly as his gut twisted. It didn't help, and he couldn't fight off the scowl he knew was falling into place. Before he could turn away, Cretia caught his eye. Her mouth opened, and for a second he thought she was going to ask him what was wrong. Then she shook her head and closed her mouth, and he let out a silent sigh.

This was neither the time nor the place to unpack whatever was going on in the depths of his brain—or his stomach.

"Can we pet your goats, Mr. Finn?"

Julia Mae's voice broke through his mental fog, and he squatted down in front of her, scrunching up his eyebrows and putting on a very serious voice. "*You* want to pet Sonny and Cher?"

The little girl giggled and nodded. "And hold your bunnies."

"*And* the bunnies? My, that's asking a lot." Tapping his chin with one finger, he stared up at Cretia, whose smile seemed to have grown. He'd done that. "I tell you what. The bunnies haven't been fed yet. So if you'll help me feed them, you can hold the little ones."

Julia Mae nodded and tugged Cretia toward the barn.

He waved them on. "I'll be there as soon as we unload this."

———

Cretia looked over her shoulder one more time before following Julia Mae into the barn. Something was different about Finn this morning. His smile was staged, forced. And his step had lost its usual bounce.

He'd said the right things. Done the usual things. And he'd

stolen her breath when he crouched to Julia Mae's height and agreed to let her hold the bunnies.

Until that exact moment, she hadn't known that a man getting down to a little girl's level to talk about baby rabbits was so attractive. It wasn't fair that that was all he had to do to make her insides go mad.

But she couldn't shake the feeling that something was off with him. She'd just have to wait until they were alone to ask him what. And she should wait until she accomplished what she'd come down for.

True to his word, he arrived a few minutes later, followed closely by Jack and Joe Jr. Finn pushed the slider closed with a creak before showing Julia Mae how to measure the rabbit food and check their water. When the rabbits were settled, he scooped up a brown ball of fluff and set it in the little girl's embrace. Cretia was pretty sure there had never been a happier five-year-old.

Jack, however, had befriended Roberta, petting the white patch next to her brown eye.

Cretia frowned and shot Roberta a glare. Sure, the old girl liked kids but apparently not digital content creators. For that, she might as well make the cow internet famous.

Reaching for her pocket, she couldn't hold back a smile as her fingers wrapped around the slim rectangle here. She didn't have a case for it yet, and it wasn't connecting to the internet for some reason. But she had a new phone. Delivered an hour ago.

When she'd heard the truck rumbling down the street, she had run for the door and met the driver on the porch—his eyes probably nearly as wild as her morning hair. Oh well. She wasn't going to see him again.

That had pretty much become her motto over the years. Made a fool of herself in front of a group of tourists? Oh well. She wasn't going to see them again.

Spilled spaghetti all over her shirt in front of a cute waiter? Oh well. She wouldn't see him again.

Too busy recording a video to notice the enormous Grecian column before walking right into it? Oh well. She wasn't going to see anyone who had witnessed that mishap again.

It was an all-too-familiar sentiment. Except right now, she wanted to capture the moment. Because she did want to see these dear faces again.

Roberta looked up and mooed just as Cretia snapped a picture of the two friends. The image caught Roberta with her tongue out and Jack throwing his head back in laughter, and Cretia nearly hugged it to her chest. She'd send it to Marie later that night.

"You have a phone?"

She turned to Finn to show off the new arrival, but again, something was off. He looked like he'd bitten into a raw onion, and she couldn't quite place the reason.

"Yep," Julia Mae supplied for her. "It came this morning. Mr. Casper dropped it off and everything."

"Good." Finn's face didn't get the message, though he nodded emphatically. "That's really good."

He was either trying to convince her or himself. And neither seemed to be working.

"Finn? Are you—"

"And your computer? Did it arrive too?"

"Not yet. We came down here so Miss Cretia can use your computer to look for it."

Cretia smiled at the little girl, whose gaze never wavered

from the bunny in her arms. With Julia Mae around, Cretia didn't have to do much talking. Except when Finn looked up with a raised eyebrow.

"My phone isn't connecting to the internet yet. I called tech support, and it's supposed to be fixed today. But I was hoping I could borrow your computer to track down my missing laptop."

"Sure." Finn tromped across the barn floor. "You kids don't let the dogs out until I get back. Then we'll play with the puppies."

Cretia followed a few steps behind, her legs unable to eat up the distance like Finn's did. Within steps she was huffing and puffing. "Finn?"

He didn't slow down. "Yeah?"

"Wait up." She tried to reach for his arm but managed only to brush the edge of his fleece sleeve. Even that sent shock waves through her. "What's the rush?"

"Nothing." His word came out curt and seemed to be the trick to applying the brakes.

She slammed into his back, her cheek hitting his shoulder blade. Bouncing off, she rubbed the side of her face and peered up at him through one open eye. "What's going on? You seem a little . . ." Ornery. Irritable. Cranky. She could have filled in a hundred words but settled for one. "Off."

Finn jabbed a hand through his hair and squinted toward the horizon. "Just got off to a late start this morning. Kind of threw my whole day off."

He didn't know her half as well as she knew him if he thought she was going to buy that.

"You can be honest with me." Laying her hand on his arm, she tried for a gentle smile. "What's going on?"

His gaze narrowed on the spot where her fingers curled into his jacket. "Nothing. *Really.*" He shook his head and slammed his fists into his pockets. "I'm fine."

"I've only known you for about a week, but seriously, you can't expect me to believe that." Sliding a hand from his elbow to his bicep, she squeezed gently. "You can tell me, you know. I won't be here long enough to spill the tea."

For a moment, he looked like he'd swallowed a golf ball. Finally, he cleared his throat. "I'm just worried about Bella. She's three days past her due date, but she's not progressing."

Cretia had to bite back a sigh of relief. For the tiniest moment, she'd thought his mood had something to do with her.

Which was ridiculous.

She had no power to influence Finn Chaffey. How could she?

Forcing a smile, she nodded. "I'm sure she'll be fine. If you need any help when the time comes . . ."

He raised an eyebrow as he took a step toward the house. "You have a lot of experience with that sort of thing?"

"Nope."

Something made him snort. Whether it was her brutal honesty or the exaggerated pop of the *p*, she didn't care. She'd made him grin—even if for just a second.

He opened the back door and strolled inside behind her, his footfalls audibly lighter than they'd been in the barn.

Okay, maybe she had a touch of influence on him.

He turned on the computer, and they waited as it whirred and hummed to life. After the screen turned on and blinked, he nodded toward the chair and backed away. "I'll be in the barn if you need anything."

"Thank you, Finn." It came out all thick and throaty, as though she'd been thinking about things. Like kissing him. Which she had not been thinking about. Until right that minute.

Her cheeks flamed, and she ducked her head.

Mercifully, Finn took that as his cue to exit and disappeared through the back door.

Cretia set to work, entering the tracking number on the delivery service's site. A spinning red circle showed the page was thinking. And thinking. And thinking.

It was either a sign of Finn's ridiculously slow internet or that her laptop had found its way to the other side of the world. Almost certainly the former.

Trying to keep her eyes off the bank letter, she tapped her fingers against the desktop. The circle kept spinning.

"Come on." She sighed, praying for more than the blank page the site had given her the day before.

Her phone had found its destination despite less-than-thorough tracking information. Maybe her laptop was just a day or so behind.

The page refreshed, the circle disappeared, and her stomach shot through the floor.

Estimated Delivery Date: Delayed

She clicked on a button that showed each step and scan of her package's journey. It had started in California. Then moved to Ohio. Then New York.

Then Paris. France.

Then Rustico.

Italy.

Her stomach took a full bounce. Up from the floor to her throat and straight back down.

Italy. Her laptop had somehow been sent to Rustico, Italy, instead of North Rustico, Prince Edward Island, Canada.

Her throat went dry.

There had to be a mistake. Maybe their tracking system was off. It had to be. Yesterday it had been blank. Today it was broken.

After punching the customer service number into her new phone, she waited to be connected to someone who would certainly explain that a glitch in their system had misread the tracking information, and her laptop was just delayed crossing the border from Maine.

That made sense.

Italy did not.

"Thank you for calling International Express Delivery. My name is Neema. How can I assist you today?"

Cretia took a steadying breath before pouring out her ordeal from the harbor all the way through that moment. "I'm stuck in North Rustico, Prince Edward Island, and your tracking says that my computer is in Rustico, Italy."

"Oh my. That is an ordeal." Neema sounded as if she were reading the dictionary. "Can I get your tracking number?"

Cretia read it off to her, Neema's keyboard clacking in the background.

"I am very sorry for the delay, but your package is at our warehouse in Rustico, Italy."

Letting her head fall into her hand, Cretia sighed. "I'm aware."

"Would you like to pick it up at the distribution center?"

"No, I don't want to—" She snapped her mouth closed. "I'm not going all the way to another continent to pick up my package."

Except she could. With a phone and a slightly wrinkled passport, she could get there. Probably a lot faster than the laptop could make it back across the Atlantic.

And then she'd be back up and running. She could get back on schedule to use the visas she'd applied for. Back to her normal life instead of the one she'd slipped so effortlessly into. The life that felt like a dream.

This was a life she'd never even known existed.

It also wasn't real. It couldn't last.

Enjoyable? Yes. Refreshing? Absolutely. Temporary? Without a doubt.

The problem was that the longer she stayed, the more she was tempted to settle. But what happened when a month turned into two or three and the magic began to disappear? Her home base would begin to look cluttered with *stuff*. Her life consumed by things. Surrounded. Imprisoned. Buried.

And the people would be forgotten. Her reason for staying ignored.

The trouble was that she didn't want to leave Finn. Or Marie and the kids. Or the sweet people—like Mama Cheese Sandwich—who peppered the town. But if she was truly honest with herself, her reason for wanting to be in North Rustico would always be Finn.

A stone settled in her stomach, pressing her farther into his office chair.

The sound of children's laughter drifted through the screen door, and she glanced out the window. The Fab Four were chasing Finn around the side pasture, Julia Mae and Jack giggling as they tagged along. Joe Jr. was there too, clearly confused. He darted between the puppies and Finn and then to Jack, his head twitching and jerking and searching for direction, not sure who most needed his attention. Finn scooped Julia Mae over his shoulder, and she squealed with delight as she bounced along, making faces at her brother.

Cretia took a deep breath as her insides twisted hard.

She couldn't stay forever. She wouldn't.

But every minute on Finn's farm made her want to.

Maybe it was better to break ties now. Leave before it got too hard.

But go before Bella had her puppies? Before Cretia found out what had really put Finn in a grumpy mood that morning? Before she got to really and truly kiss him?

She frowned as he led the parade along the fence line.

Neema cleared her throat. "Miss Martin? Are you still there? Would you like us to hold your package in Italy?"

Thirteen

Finn did his best to put on a happy face for the kids and focus on how the puppies were adjusting to new— more—people. But as he scratched Ringo's furry belly, his gaze and mind still darted toward the house.

And Cretia. And the laptop she was tracking down.

He didn't need to know a lick about technology to understand the situation. As soon as Cretia got her laptop, she'd go back to work. On the road.

She probably didn't even need her computer. Her phone would almost certainly suffice. It fit in the palm of her hand but had the ability to run her whole world.

And ruin his.

He scowled at himself and stopped scratching. Ringo barked, demanding more attention, and Finn tried hard to focus. But clearly he was feeling a little bit overdramatic.

He'd only known Cretia for a little over a week. When she left, it would not ruin his life.

His foul mood had much more to do with Justin's delivery. It had been a nice, neighborly gesture. And Justin hadn't known that his loan applications had been turned down and he'd run out of banks to ask.

The arrival of Cretia's phone was just another piece of straw on the proverbial camel's back.

"Mr. Finn!"

He looked over just as Paul jumped against Jack, pushing him to the ground. The boy already had a few grass stains on his jeans and giggled as the puppies all bounded to him, nipping at his sleeves and tugging at his pants. In a few years, this kid could be a help around the business.

All of a sudden, Joe Jr. looked up and loped toward the barn, stopping just as Cretia stepped into the sunlight.

"That cow still hates me," she said as she scratched Joe's ears. "But you don't, do you, boy?"

Finn couldn't stop his smile now as his funk melted away.

"Did you find your com-pupter?" Julia Mae called.

"I did." Cretia's gaze wasn't on the little girl. Instead, she met his, a bit of hesitancy there. It wasn't much, but it was enough to make his stomach drop to the sweet-smelling grass and roll over a few times.

"When's it going to be here?" Jack's words were muffled by the thick black coat practically covering his face.

"It's actually in Italy. Rustico, Italy."

"Italy? Where's that?" Julia Mae asked.

Jack, the older and wiser brother, set about informing his sister of the boot-shaped country across the ocean. But Finn could only hear the word *Italy* ringing over and over in his mind. In a flash, he saw Cretia floating down a canal in a gondola. Saw her strolling over bridges and twirling spaghetti onto a fork.

Without him.

Which was ridiculous. Because he'd never been to Italy, and he had absolutely zero intention to ever visit. It looked nice in pictures and movies, but he was bound to Prince Edward Island and this farm for life. He couldn't imagine living anywhere else—didn't even want to. These pastures, this barn, even the old house was home. They represented roots and family and the things closest to his heart.

He loved this land. He loved when it rained and when the sun shone. He loved it in the summer and when the snow piled clear to the barn's roof. He loved the hard work and the early mornings. He loved the sweet smell of mown grass and the warm welcome of unconditional love from the animals.

He loved the land not just because his dad had but because his dad had taught him to love it too.

And just because he liked Cretia—and liked being near her—didn't mean that she felt the same or was interested in inviting him to tag along on her adventures.

Finn stabbed his fingers through his hair and took a shallow breath, then forced himself to let it out on a silent sigh. "Are you going to pick it up?"

"Across the ocean?" Julia Mae asked. "But that's too far. How will we see you if you're so far away?"

Cretia opened her arm to welcome the little girl's hug about her waist. "Actually, I asked the delivery company to send it to the inn."

Someone yanked a boulder off his chest, and Finn could breathe deeply again.

She looked right into his eyes. "I thought I'd stick around for another week or so."

His smile refused to be subdued, and hers matched.

Spending another week with her was a terrible idea. Saying goodbye in a week would be even harder than it would be now. But for however long she stayed, he was going to enjoy every minute of it.

Cretia finally looked down at the girl hanging on her waist. "Would you mind if I stayed with you a little longer?"

———

Cretia couldn't sleep that night. She paced the confines of her room, pausing every now and then to inspect the sweet antique trinkets that lined the bookshelves or press a key on the ancient typewriter that sat on the desk. But the more she walked, the smaller the room felt.

She had to turn to the side to navigate between the foot of the bed and the desk chair. The bookcase, laden with clothbound tomes, looked like it might tumble over to box her in. Even her brand-new suitcase—identical to the one that had fallen into the harbor—blocked her path.

All the elements that had made the room so homey before now made it feel too small, too cluttered, too *much*.

Her skin itched, tighter than it should be. Her heart thudded so loudly that she feared it would keep Marie and her family awake.

Wringing her hands in the hem of her pajama shirt, she tried not to let her mind wander to the what-ifs. But there were so many of them. Chief among them, what if she'd made the wrong decision?

Maybe she should have gone to Italy.

And never see Finn again?

Her lungs seized at the very thought, and she coughed to force air in.

She barely knew the guy. He was not why she had decided to stay.

He was . . . a perk.

Yeah, keep telling yourself that.

Shaking her head, she slammed her hands on her hips and stared at the ceiling. Even with the light from the bedside lamp, the corners were shrouded in shadows, and she wanted to fall into them. Just to disappear for a little while.

It wasn't too late for Italy.

Snatching her phone from its spot on the nightstand, she thanked God that the customer support had gotten her online. She opened her favorite travel app and started a search for flights to Europe, leaving from Charlottetown in the morning.

Before she could see her options, a bar across the top of her phone popped up. A call. From Finn. The phone vibrated in her hand, on silent mode since earlier that evening.

She froze. It was nearly midnight. He couldn't know she was still awake. Unless he was standing outside her window and saw her light was on.

But that only happened in rom-coms.

Her stomach swooped. Maybe something was wrong. But he wouldn't call *her*. He had an island full of trusted friends and family.

The phone shook again.

With a deep breath, she hit the green button. "Hello?"

"Hey, did I wake you?"

"No. Is something wrong?"

His chuckle was low, quieter than usual. "Not at all. I just thought you might want to know that Bella's making good use of your whelping box."

"She's having her puppies?" Cretia started on a shriek and then quickly dropped her volume to a whisper. "Are you sure?"

"It's going to be tonight. Would you like to come over and see?"

"Yes!"

"See you soon," he said, a smile in his voice. He hung up before she could think better of her decision.

She should be booking a flight. But Bella's puppies were part of the reason she'd decided to stay in the first place. There would be another flight in a day or two. She'd call the shipping service tomorrow to ask them to hold her box in Italy. She'd catch up with it soon enough.

After scrambling out of her pajamas, she threw on a pair of jeans and a hoodie, hopping toward the door. Her shoes were on by the time she made it down the back stairs into the kitchen, and she'd even successfully avoided the squeaky step. She tiptoed around the island and let herself out through the back door, patting the pocket of her jeans to make sure her phone was with her.

As she stepped onto the road, she paused to look up into the inky sky. The half-moon was bright and clear, the stars twinkling with joy. Somehow the night surrounded her, wrapping around her like a blanket, rolling her into its silent peace.

Cretia had a firm rule on her travels. For her own safety she didn't walk alone at night. Anywhere. Often she'd meet up with other travelers and join them on outings. Sometimes other influencers were in the area, and they'd film together for a few days. Most of the time, she stayed in places with an active nightlife. There were always people about, so she had no problem taking a walk to the local gelato place or a famed pub after dark.

North Rustico wasn't one of those places. It was quiet. Only the gentle splash of the water in the harbor broke the silence, the occasional creak of one of the lobster boats tugging on its moorings. Houses were dark, leaving just the sparse streetlights and the old-time iron lamps along the boardwalk to show the way.

Every safety measure she'd forced into habit warned that she should go back inside. She waited for the pounding of her heart or the clipped breathing that always accompanied a healthy dose of fear.

They didn't come. This place wasn't like those others— not just in its stillness but also in its people.

She set off at a quick clip, arms wrapped around her stomach to ward off the damp chill. But with each step she slowed down, savoring the salty smell that hung in the air and the gentle breeze that tugged on her ponytail. Closing her eyes, she lifted her face to the moonlight and breathed deeply.

There was something different about this place.

When she arrived at Finn's property, light shone through a crack in the barn door. She shimmied it open far enough to slip inside, where Roberta immediately gave her a disapproving glare.

"Hello to you too," Cretia mumbled. "Aren't you supposed to be asleep or something?"

Roberta responded with a pathetic low as though she was the one about to give birth, and Cretia turned her back, sneaking toward the birthing room.

She found Finn sitting on the floor, his back against the wall and one arm resting on a bent knee. His gaze didn't waver from the whelping box where Bella lay on the padded flooring, snuggled against a brown felt blanket.

Cretia cleared her throat, and Finn's head snapped in her direction. "Hey," he whispered. "You made it. Come on in." He patted the pillow on the floor beside him and nodded for her to sit too. "Stole these from Mom's old outdoor wicker set. It's long gone, but a stack of these make the floor a little more bearable for long nights."

"Ah, now I see. You invited me over just so you wouldn't have to be miserable by yourself all night." She grinned as she sank to the indicated seat, her shoulder barely brushing his. "You're probably going to put me to work too, aren't you?"

"Well, I mean, now that you're here, it only makes sense. I'd hate to waste your skills."

"And you're sure I have the requisite experience as a midwife?"

"Naw. But you'll never know if you have natural talent unless you try."

He'd said all that in a hushed tone, and she tried to keep her snort low too, clapping a hand over her nose and mouth to muffle it even more. With a playful nudge of her elbow against his, she smiled. "Are you sure it'll happen tonight?"

"Mostly."

"And you're going to stay out here just in case?"

Finn turned toward Bella, whose heavy breathing echoed in the little room. She was restless but exhausted already, and she hadn't even started pushing. "I don't know about you, but I wouldn't want to be alone in a time like this."

"Good point."

They settled into the silence, listening to Bella shift and snort as she tried to find a comfortable position. Finn got up to check on her every now and then, rubbing her head and ears and speaking softly to her. "You're a good girl. You're doing great." She looked up and licked his hand, and he pushed her water bowl closer to her.

When he settled back down beside Cretia, he said, "We probably have about an hour if you want to get some rest."

"No. I'm fine." But her head lolled against the fleece of his jacket. "How do you know how long it will be?"

He lifted the shoulder under her ear. "Bella and I have done this a couple times. And Maisey and Serena and Sunshine and Sadie too."

"How old were you the first time you helped?"

He paused, narrowing his gaze as he pictured a long-ago scene in this very room. "I'm not sure I was much help that first time. Or the second or third. My mom said I needed to stay in bed, but everything in the barn was way too exciting for a six-year-old. So I pulled on my coat and hat and boots and raced out here. I think I had to go back inside half a dozen times just to use the bathroom." He chuckled at the memory. "And I eventually fell asleep before Delilah had her pups."

"Delilah? As in Samson's downfall?"

"Yeah, my mom was on a kick to use names from the Bible, and that litter was mostly girls. It was either going to be Delilah or Sapphira, who I think was struck dead in the book of Acts."

"Sure, well, when that's your other option . . ." Cretia chuckled. "So you missed the big event?"

"But I kept coming back. When I was in high school, I skipped out after lunch one day to be here for Sadie."

"And your mom . . . ?"

"Threatened to make me sleep in the barn if I ever did that again. Didn't matter that I was a foot taller than her by then. Or that it was clear the business would be mine one day."

"Sleeping in the barn doesn't sound so bad." She snuggled against his arm and pulled her jacket a little tighter, her eyes drifting shut.

"Sure. In May. With a blanket." He tossed a soft throw across their laps and tucked it around them both, fighting off the night chill even at this time of year. "It was February. There was a foot of snow on the ground, and the barn wasn't nearly as cozy as it is now."

"You did that, didn't you? Made it cozy?" She looked up in his direction, and he gave her only a grin in response. "Were you afraid your mom was really going to make you sleep out here?"

"Let's just say that wasn't the last time I skipped school to watch after the dogs."

"I'm not surprised, but . . . why?"

Her question wasn't accusatory or belittling, just genuinely curious. It deserved a real answer. One he wasn't quite sure he had handy.

"I mean, it's clear that you love these animals, that you're proud of them and raise them with care. I hardly see you out here cleaning stalls and pens, but they always look nearly spotless. Which means you're probably out here before the sun comes up. And clearly, you're willing to spend your nights out here too." She motioned to their current predicament.

After a long pause, she angled her head to meet his gaze. "I guess it's the same question. Why?"

"I don't suppose I could get away with saying it's because it's what my father did and my grandfather before him. And his father before him. It's in my blood and my bones."

"You could say that. And I would know it's part of the truth."

Leaning his head against the wall at his back, he stared into the wooden rafters for a long second. Cretia's body shivered, and he looked down at her. "Are you cold?"

"Uh-uh."

He stretched his arm around her shoulders anyway, hugging her close, savoring the warmth she provided, the ability to just sit with her. She didn't push or cajole, and she seemed to understand that he needed some time to collect his thoughts, to admit them to himself.

"I've always loved animals. Of all kinds. Not that I don't like people, but animals are easier. They don't ask for or expect anything. Just food and water and the occasional scratch on the head. You can train them—well, most of them—and teach them, and they're all motivated by the same thing."

"Treats."

He chuckled. "Yes. It's easy to know how to make them happy. It's harder to know how to please people."

"Like who? It seems like everyone around here loves you. I'm pretty sure Marie thinks of you as her little brother, and everyone leans on you. Is it hard to be the reliable one?"

"No. Not really. I like that they can count on me, that they call me when there's an animal in need of a home or someone needs help moving a piano or something." He sighed, trying to internally process what he wanted to say. But the words just slid out. "There's an expectation that comes with that. When you're the dependable one, people expect you to be *dependable*. To always show up. To make the situation better than it was."

"Funny how that works."

He squeezed her shoulders, and she snuggled in deeper against him.

"I guess no one has ever expected that of me," she whispered. He wanted to know why that was, but before he could ask, she said, "What's it like?"

"It's good. Mostly. I'm happy to help. I like knowing that I've made someone else's life easier."

"But the rest of the time?"

He sat with that for a long time, rolling over the truth in his mind, trying to shape it into something that would make sense. To her and to himself. It was easy to feel things but a lot harder to give them a name.

"I like helping out my friends and neighbors. But sometimes I feel like I can't ask for help."

"I'm sure they'd be happy to give you a hand."

He nodded. "Probably. But I also feel like I have to prove that I'm capable of running this business on my own."

She shot him a question with her eyes.

"I took over this business a lot younger than my dad did. Everyone loved him. And . . ." He shoved his fingers through his hair. "I guess people didn't expect me to succeed. They thought I'd fail." His dad thought so anyway, and had told at least one of his friends as much. The memory still twisted his insides, but he tried to shake off the feeling. "I've been trying for a long time to never let anyone down. To do enough that I'll hear my dad say he's proud of me."

Cretia squirmed, her legs shifting before settling against his side again. Their breathing had synched up at some point, and with each of his exhales, she inhaled—give and take. Give and take.

"If I ever do hear those words, I'm terrified I'll have reached the pinnacle, afraid of falling from the pedestal. I would have taken the business over from my dad no matter what because I love working with the dogs. But when my dad clamped me on the shoulder and told me he needed me to carry on the family legacy . . . suddenly it wasn't enough just to keep it going. Especially when . . ."

"When what?"

He swallowed the memory that nudged against the back of his mind. The words his dad had spoken. The fear that they might be true.

"I have to make him proud. I have to prove that I can do this on my own. I have to do something more than just keep the shingle out for my son. And what if I can't do that?"

The rhythm of Cretia's breathing changed, and the warm air from her nose against his neck stopped.

"I've made it awkward, haven't I? That should have been inside processing."

She reached for his hand that was draped over her shoulder and gave it a gentle squeeze. "Of course not. I'm glad you told me." With her other hand splayed across his stomach, she tapped a quick pulse. "Is that why you applied for a loan from the bank?"

Every muscle in his torso pulled taut. "You saw the letter on my desk?"

"I didn't mean to read it. I just glanced at it. I know it was private. I didn't mean to pry. I'm sorry."

A slow breath escaped through his teeth on a hiss. "It's okay. Have you told anyone else?"

"Of course not."

He closed his eyes as the muscles in his neck began to relax, blood pumping normally again. "If we could keep that between us, I'd appreciate it."

"Yes. I won't say anything—but why?"

He looked down to meet her gaze, the sincere question in the depths of her brown eyes. "You saw the letter. You know they turned me down."

She nodded slowly. "What were you going to do with the money?"

"Expand. Hire some help. Add onto the barn."

"That's why you were so upset when Justin dropped off the wood. It was to help you expand, wasn't it?"

He chuckled against the top of her hair, smoothing the silky strands across her crown and down her neck. "You read me too well, Cretia. I'm not sure how I feel about that."

"It's not like you try to hide what you're feeling. Or if you do, you do a terrible job of it."

He snorted, probably like she'd wanted him to. He was her puppet, and she knew exactly what to say to pull his strings.

Not that he was complaining.

They sat in silence for a few minutes, and he tried to remember if he'd ever known anyone else who asked such direct questions and spoke such frank truth. She pulled no punches but did so with genuine care and concern.

And she did care. Otherwise she wouldn't ask or listen without interrupting. She wouldn't be out in a barn on a chilly night when she could be cozy in her bed at the inn.

Finally, she took a shallow breath. "I was thinking about how your dad was with you the other day, how hard he hugged you before they left. I'm not an expert or anything"—she swallowed thickly—"seeing as I never met my dad. But it's clear to anyone who takes a glance that your dad loves you. He's not disappointed with you at all. I didn't even have to look hard to see the pride in his eyes. I don't think you have to do anything or be anyone else to earn his respect. He sees you for who you are. And that's a pretty great guy."

He wanted to argue with her. Or maybe make her explain why she was so certain. But mostly, he wanted to know where *her* father was. If he was alive, how he could have missed out on being part of her life?

What an idiot.

Before he could ask, Bella let out a soft whimper, and Finn jumped to his knees beside the box, Cretia scrambling to his side.

Fourteen

Cretia had never witnessed a miracle before. But there was no other word to describe the wonder of Bella delivering ten healthy puppies. The way she cleaned and nuzzled them, snuggling them close, warming them with her body.

She'd settled into the corner opposite the heating lamp that Finn had set up. After all, no woman wanted to give birth under a spotlight.

The puppies wiggled and squeaked, their eyes still tightly pinched shut. All thriving.

Until the last one.

Finn's neck went stiff when the final pup was born, his face drawn tight as he watched Bella. She licked and prodded the puppy, but it didn't respond. It didn't move.

Cretia grabbed Finn's arm. "What's wrong with it?"

"I don't know yet, but will you grab me one of those towels and get the aspirator?"

"The what?" She launched herself at the pile of clean towels, searching for anything that looked remotely like the word sounded.

"The blue thing with the bulb on the end."

She couldn't understand how his voice remained so calm. Her heart thundered against her ribs, and she wanted to scream or cry or do something. Because the puppy still wasn't moving.

As far as she could tell, it wasn't breathing.

She snatched the blue bulb, nearly flinging it and the towel at him as she fell to his side.

Finn's movements were much more measured, his shoulders rising and falling in even breaths. Scooping the little black bundle up in the towel, he rubbed his hands along its sides. But the puppy didn't respond to the stimulation.

Bella lifted her head to see what he was doing, and Cretia smoothed her brow. "It's okay, girl. He's going to take good care of your little one. He's gonna be just fine."

Lord, let that be true.

Cretia couldn't remember the last time she'd consciously prayed. It had probably been about her mom. A cry for God to heal her, to take away the illness that had stolen so much from them.

He hadn't answered then, and Cretia didn't have any indication that he would do so now. Still, she begged him. *Save this little puppy. Please.*

Maybe it was habit, but something made her reach for her phone. She pulled it out and began recording the scene. She'd probably never use this footage. It wasn't about likes or comments or brand deals. This was for Finn. And for herself.

Years down the road, when she thought of him, she'd remember this moment. The gentle way he cradled a helpless puppy, the soft words he spoke over a frightened mom. The confidence of his actions and the steadiness of his hands.

Hers were shaking—the video absolutely unusable even if she had wanted to.

Chewing on her lip, she watched Finn lay the towel over his lap. He stretched the puppy out so its little head hung lower and gravity could help. Squeezing the blue bulb, he pressed the tip into its mouth, released the bulb, and then emptied the contents on the towel. He did it seven or eight times until the tool came back empty.

But the puppy still didn't move.

"Come on, little guy." Finn waited a beat and then lifted the puppy to his mouth. After breathing into its mouth and nose with three gentle blows, he paused again.

Suddenly the dog twitched then squirmed on its own, and a smile wider than the horizon broke across Finn's face as he stood and put the puppy down beside its brothers and sisters.

Bella gave him what could only be a bark of gratitude, and he rubbed her ears. "You did so good, girl."

Cretia wrapped her arms around his waist, resting her forehead against his shoulder and snuggling into the warmth of his fleece sweater—or maybe it was just *his* warmth. "That was incredible. How did you know how . . . ?"

"It wasn't the first time. The vet taught me how to do it—I think so he wouldn't keep getting calls in the middle of the night."

"Will the vet come check on him at least?"

"Yeah. I'll call him in the morning to take a look at all of them. For now, they just need some milk and rest. But it looks like they're all eating." And Bella was asleep with a smile on her face.

Cretia pulled back far enough to look into his face. "Do you wonder whose life you just saved?"

Crevices rolled across his forehead. "What do you mean?"

"I mean, what if that little guy grows up to rescue someone? Maybe someone who fell into a harbor. And he jumps in and rescues them. He wouldn't have been around to do that if you hadn't saved him."

A tired smile crinkled the corners of his eyes as he pulled her in tighter for a hug. "I see your point, but just so you know—if Joe Jr. hadn't been there that day, I would have jumped in to save you myself."

She should leave. The farm. The town. The island.

This was getting dangerous for her heart. It wasn't Bella or the puppies. It wasn't Marie or Little Jack. It wasn't even Joe Jr.'s snuggles.

Finn was the one who would leave her heartbroken.

Actually, she'd be the one to leave. And he'd likely have no idea.

Forcing herself to take a step away from his warmth and the security of his arms, she shoved her hands into the front pocket of her hoodie. "So, what are you going to name them?"

His lips pursed to the side, his eyebrows meeting over the bridge of his nose. "When I was a kid, my dad let me name a litter after Transformers."

"Transformers? Like Megatron?"

Finn snorted. "No. He's a Decepticon. They were Optimus Prime and Bumblebee and Cliffjumper and such."

"And I'm weird because I watched *Handy Manny*?" She gave his elbow a playful push but jerked back almost as soon as she touched him. She couldn't seem to keep her hands to herself when he was around.

Or from fixating on how much she liked it.

Maybe she was simply starved for touch. She'd read once that the average adult needed four hugs a day just to survive. And until she'd wound up in Finn's arms after her dunking in the harbor, she hadn't been hugged in months. Maybe years. That day, he'd proven himself strong, stable, and kind.

That had to explain his magnetic pull.

But it didn't mean she wasn't going to fight it.

She took another step away.

"Is this litter going to get named after toys or cartoons? Strawberry Shortcake or something?"

He squinted at the squeaking puppies. "I was thinking potatoes."

"I'm sorry, what?"

"You know, like Spud, Tater, Chip . . . The island is famous for its potatoes, and the puppies kind of resemble them in shape if not color."

"You couldn't even get halfway through naming all of them."

He waved off her argument. "We'll get creative. We have time."

He had time. She had just long enough for a box to fly over the Atlantic and find its way to the inn with the red door—and that was only if she didn't call the delivery company back and ask them to hold it for her in Italy.

Who was she kidding? She wasn't going to go to Italy. She was going to stay right where she was until her computer arrived.

But until then, she was definitely going to keep as much space as possible between them.

The squirming black spuds caught her eye.

Well, maybe she could come down to the farm for a visit

or two before she left. Julia Mae was sure to want to see the new arrivals.

"Tomorrow will be a busy day for me, what with the vet visit." Finn pushed his hands into his pockets, shrugging. "But I got a call earlier from someone up near the North Point."

She raised her eyebrows in question.

"There's a cow that needs a new home, and I thought maybe you'd like to go pick it up with me in a day or two."

"A cow? Like Roberta? You know how much she hates me."

Finn chuckled. "Roberta doesn't hate you. She just isn't sure what you're doing here."

That made two of them.

"But this one is a miniature Highland cow."

"The little ones with long hair and adorable noses? The ones that have taken social media by storm?"

"I don't know. Maybe."

Right. Because the man basically had a dial-up system on a computer from 1981.

"The owners thought it would make a cute pet."

That sounded right.

"But it's pretty much destroyed their living room. It needs an outside home, some grass, and some room to roam."

"And you want me to go with you?"

Her mother's reminder about drugs popped into her head. *Just say no.*

She did not need to go with him. It wasn't smart. She couldn't really be helpful. And she had just decided to limit her time with him.

This was not limiting her time.

"I'm sure you're—"

He cut her off before she could finish. "I thought I could show you a few of my favorite spots on the island on the way. Maybe they'd make good videos for your work."

Shoot.

⸺

"So, how did you get into . . . what did you call it? Creating stuff?" Finn glanced across the cab of his truck at Cretia, who had been silent for the last ten minutes. It wasn't a strained silence, just quiet. Only the rattle of the stick shift to fill the space. He'd turn on the radio, but he didn't want to risk missing her words when she chose to speak.

Cretia didn't seem to mind the stillness, her head turned toward the window as she watched the bay amble by, its tides coming and going in a gentle rhythm against the big red rocks of the national park shore. Tall pine trees—sentinels of the Gulf of St. Lawrence—sometimes blocked the view, but they didn't dissuade her. She seemed content to just stare at creation. His view of the gray road wasn't quite as engrossing.

Besides, he didn't often have a chance to talk with her without being interrupted by needy puppies or hungry goats. This was his chance to get to know her. After all, he'd sure spilled more than he'd meant to two nights before when they'd stayed up with Bella.

"The content stuff you do?" he tried again.

"I'm a content creator," she said without facing him.

"Right. And what is that again?"

With a reluctant sigh, she turned away from the window. "You know what I do."

He shook his head, treading lightly. He did not need a repeat of his first inquisition about her work. "Honestly, I don't have a clue. I know you travel a lot. I know you need some electronics—phones and computers. But I'm still a little confused about . . . well"—he held his breath—"what you do."

He hoped for a smile but waited for a scowl. Instead, she let out a sweet and full laugh.

"Only you, Finn Chaffey, would have no idea what a content creator does. You and your phone circa 1999."

"You say that like it's a bad thing. It gets the job done. And at least I'm not like those people who go out to a restaurant and never talk to anyone else because their face is in their phone the whole time."

"Those are my people."

"No, they're not."

Her shoulders jerked, and she sat up straighter, turning on the fabric seat to face him. "How do you know?"

"Because those people can't go for a thirty-minute meal without staring at whatever is on their screens." He took his eyes off the road to watch her reaction. "And you went more than a week without a phone and didn't even get twitchy."

"How do you know? Maybe I just hid my twitch well."

He gave her another once-over as she tucked a lock of her jet-black hair behind her ear. The sun through the window made it shimmer and set her whole face aglow. The dark pools of her eyes held a challenge that matched the smirk of her lips.

"You can't hide that kind of thing from Joe. He may be too spastic to be a working therapy dog, and sometimes he stresses out under high-pressure situations, but he knows you. And he likes you. And he isn't agitated by you. Even I can get him worked up when I'm upset."

"That's why he likes Jack so much, isn't it?"

He drummed his fingers against the steering wheel as he thought about her comment. "What do you mean?"

"No stress. No agitation. No fear. Just play. Joe senses that in him."

Well, sweet cinnamon rolls. He'd never put that into words before. But it made perfect sense. Joe loved the boy and never missed a chance to play with him.

Finn was still rolling the thought over in his mind when Cretia whispered, "Maybe I'm not like them, but they are my people."

Yanking his thoughts back to the present and his question for her, he waited.

"I don't get to do what I do without them."

"Which is . . ."

"I create videos about traveling. The beauty. The excitement. The best-kept secrets of popular destinations. Money-saving tips and ways to create the perfect itinerary." There was a smile in her soft sigh. "I try to find the things that would make someone want to visit. The best food. The funnest adventures."

"Adventures?"

"Zip-lining in Costa Rica. Cliff diving in Portugal."

"Running with the bulls in Pamplona?"

She slapped a hand to his arm. "No. Never. Not once. I don't care what Roberta says, that's just stupid." She laughed. "And hard to record yourself without losing life or limb."

His chuckle echoed hers.

"The people who watch my videos, the ones who follow me—they make it possible."

"How does that work? Who pays you?"

She pursed her lips to the side and stared out the window for a long second. "It's a little here and a little bit there. It's kind of confusing."

"I'm a pretty smart guy."

"With absolutely zero interest in the workings of social media."

He shrugged. "All right. That's a fair point. I've never had an interest before. But I'm interested in you."

Her gaze darted back to him, a questioning eyebrow arching high on her forehead as a smug smile fell across her lips.

Flames licked at his throat, and he tugged at the collar of his Henley, wishing he could undo a button without her noticing. "I mean, I'm interested in learning how you do what you do."

"Ri-ight," she singsonged. "Okay. Fine." She seemed to inspect the ceiling of the truck, her eyes darting back and forth. With a deep breath, she waved one finger. "Almost no one makes a living online with one revenue stream. So, while my one job is making videos, where and how I post them can bring in various opportunities for income."

He must have looked confused, because she sighed. "The videos I post on YouTube are monetized through ads. You-Tube pays me to be able to run ads on my content. And the more my videos are watched, the more I make."

"How much are your videos watched?"

"On YouTube? My best video has been watched 4.7 million times."

"Four million people watched you?" He couldn't hide the disbelief hitching a ride in his tone.

"Not necessarily. It's not how many people. It's how many times they watched."

"All right." That made sense. Advertising he understood. He'd sponsored an island youth baseball team to get an ad in their program a couple years before. Basically the same thing, with a little smaller audience. "What are the other streams?"

She ticked off a second finger. "Subscribers. Several thousand people pay five dollars a month to get exclusive content from me."

"Exclusive, like . . ."

"Like pro packing tips to fit everything you need for a weeklong trip in a carry-on. Like suggested itineraries in various cities—for families, romantic vacations, bachelorette parties, and guys' getaways."

"I never thought about that before, but I guess a family trip would look different than a honeymoon trip."

"For sure. Like, so many people think that Nashville is only for bachelorette parties and honky-tonks. And, yes, there are a lot of those. But there's also a ton of history in the area to explore and museums and, of course, live music. There are romantic nooks on rooftop bars and speakeasies that take you back a century. Once a month I do an 'Ask Me Anything' video where I answer my subscribers' specific travel-related questions."

"But not personal questions about you?"

She giggled with a shake of her head. "There's not much to tell about my personal life. I post most of my life on-screen, and I don't have time for much behind-the-scenes stuff."

"Like a romantic situation?" He hadn't meant to say that out loud. More inside processing that had no business being released.

Still, he held his breath. In the almost two weeks he'd known her, she hadn't said anything about having a significant other. But that didn't mean she was single. No matter how much he wanted that to be true.

Pursing her lips to the side, she rolled her eyes at him as though debating if he deserved an answer to his question. Finally, she shook her head. "The only *romantic situation* in my life is helping to plan romantic vacations."

Her words were a bit of a kick to the gut. Only he couldn't tell if it was because she'd confirmed she was single or because she didn't consider their *situation* a romantic one. Not that she should. Nothing had happened. Yet.

"Last year a couple asked me to help them plan an anniversary trip to Middle Tennessee on a budget. So I created a custom itinerary just for them. Cozy hideaways and candlelit restaurants. They sent me a picture of them holding hands on the pedestrian bridge over the Cumberland River, and it was the absolute sweetest."

As she spoke, her eyes lit up and her voice danced, and Finn had the worst urge to take her on one of those custom romantic trips. To make very good use of every dark corner and moonlit stroll so there was no doubt that there was more than friendship between them.

Gripping the steering wheel a little harder, he cleared his throat. "So, advertising and subscribers and what else?"

Cretia blinked, probably at his sudden change of topic, but continued on. "Sponsorships. Companies pay me to spread the word about their products on my platforms."

"Okay, so like infomercials?"

"Oh my gosh. How old are you?" She rolled her eyes again and shoved his shoulder as they turned out of the national park onto a two-lane road and toward the center of the island. "Is that what you were watching instead of *Handy Manny?*"

"Maybe. My gran liked them."

"Okay, well, trust me—sponsorships are not your grandmother's infomercial. If a company wants to sponsor me, I legitimately use their product on a trip. I don't ham it up on-screen or go crazy. I just use it—maybe a bit more obviously than I normally would—and mention how it made my trip easier or better."

"What sorts of products?"

"Anything travel related. I've done hotel chains and neck pillows and even a village in Spain. Most often I'm asked to do luggage—in fact, the suitcase that I lost was from a sponsor."

He cringed, but she smiled.

"It was a good suitcase, and I emailed the company last week to see if they'd replace it. It's already at the inn."

"Wow. You have a magic wand too?"

"It's good for them to have their brand rolling through airports and along cobblestone roads in my videos. Even if I don't mention it by name in every post."

"Have you ever turned down a sponsor?"

She snorted. "What kind of person do you think I am? Of course!"

"Sorry, I didn't—"

"The internet is a wild place, and people come up with really weird things." Her cheeks turned pink, and he was a little bit afraid to ask her to unpack that. In the end, she said just enough. "I've been asked to promote some things that I don't feel comfortable with. Things that might alter someone's state of consciousness or that I'm not sure are safe."

Chewing on her thumbnail for a long second, she sighed. "I know it seems like what I do is frivolous. It's not like I'm training dogs for rescue or therapy, but I do take it seriously."

"It seems like a lot of people trust you."

"Something like three million of them."

He whistled low. That was somehow incredible and also completely understandable. If he was on any of those apps that Justin said his sister was on, he would certainly follow her. And not just because of her gorgeous smile or infectious laugh, but because he already knew the answer to his next question. "And you don't take that lightly, do you?"

"How could I?" Her words took on an earnestness she didn't often use. "They saved me."

Fifteen

Cretia clapped a hand over her mouth, and she couldn't even blink under Finn's intense glance.

"Saved you? From what?"

She shook her head hard, wishing the words back where they'd come from. Wishing she could follow right behind them. Back to nothingness. Certainly back to before she'd admitted the truth, spilled it out so casually.

"Cretia? You can tell me. You don't have to— I won't—"

Judge her?

He couldn't promise that until he knew the whole truth. And then it would be more than a little bit hard not to. Everyone did.

If it wasn't judgment, it was pity. Every time. The school counselors. The man from Child Protective Services. Her teachers. Always with the same look in their eyes. Confusion. Horror. *Pity.*

God knew she didn't need it. She'd spent too many years feeling sorry for herself. And she wasn't going back to that.

She chose every day not to live that life—the one where she was the victim. *And* the one where she turned into her mother. She supposed her mom was a victim in her own right, a victim of her own making and her own mental illness. Cretia refused to be either, let alone both.

And she wasn't going to let Finn feel sorry for her. Not when she had a good life. A full life. Even if she didn't have a full house.

"I don't really want to talk about it."

Pursing his lips to the side, he nodded slowly. "All right. How about we stop at Kildare Capes and walk a little bit?"

"Sure. Yeah."

She didn't know what she was agreeing to, but she wouldn't pass up a moment to catch her breath, to set down the memories that clouded her mind.

Within minutes, he'd parked his old pickup—the army-green one that looked like it belonged in one of those World War II movies—in a little pull-off big enough for just one vehicle. She hopped out as soon as he stopped, closing the door behind her. The sound immediately disappeared, replaced by the clapping waves nearby and the call of the birds. Taking a deep breath through her nose, she inhaled the smell of lush grass and open water, sunshine and serenity.

"Come on." Finn had rounded the hood of the truck and reached out for her hand. She paused for a split second before sliding her palm against his and letting him lead her across the pale sand toward the shore. The call of the wind and the waves revealed exactly where they were headed, and yet when they arrived on the beach, she realized she hadn't had any idea.

It was a small beach, just a little scrap of rich sand tucked between towering walls of red earth. Uneven and messy, they curved and jutted into the water. The beach disappeared and there were only red-rock walls meeting the blue waves, natural sculptures that no artist could compete with. Only the sounds of peace and the smell of earth and sky and a tiny bit of heaven between them.

"What is this place?" she whispered.

He squeezed her hand, his fingers strong but gentle. "This is my home."

He had the same strength as these walls that withstood the endless waves, the same refusal to back down or back away. The same beauty too.

Which was absolutely ridiculous because Finn was not beautiful. He was . . . Finn. He was handsome and rugged and kind and loyal and protective. He was not beautiful. But he and the island were the same. The iron that made the shores red ran through his veins too. And the gentle heart of the land was the same one that beat inside him.

Cretia stopped walking, tugging on his hand so he stayed by her side. "Finn?"

"Yeah?"

"Why did you bring me here?"

"I thought you might like to get some *content*. And . . ." He paused, stepping to face her. She had to look up to meet his eyes, and his gaze searched hers like he was reading a map for the first time. Shivers raced down her bare arms, nearly breaking their hands apart. But he held fast.

"This is one of the most beautiful places on the island— one of my favorites anyway. And I wanted you to see it."

"Because . . ."

"Because even if you're only here for a little while, I don't want to hold anything back. I don't want to miss a chance to share something great with you. To show you how great it could be."

Her heart slammed against her ribs, painful and ecstatic at the same time. He wasn't talking about a slice of coastline on the north shore or a beautiful spring morning. He was talking about sharing something real. Something powerful. Between them.

He dragged his fingers from her shoulder to her elbow, a whisper of a touch that left fire in its path. She gasped and closed her eyes, wanting only to know the feel of him against her skin. Everything else disappeared. The beauty of creation vanished until there was only her and Finn. And maybe God had created them to be in this very moment.

His hand traveled back up her arm, but he didn't stop at her shoulder, his fingers walking over to her neck and dancing up to her jaw. Her stomach swooped like the birds on the ocean wind, and she leaned toward him, grabbing on to the front of his shirt. She had to or she would fall over completely.

Finn's muscles tightened just beyond her knuckles, his breathing above her head soft and erratic.

She was playing with fire. And well aware of it.

He was never going to leave the island, and she wasn't going to stay. But she would always wonder if she walked away in this moment.

Regret was a vicious master. And she refused to let it taunt her. She'd rather know than be left to imagine. Memories were better than remorse.

Licking her lips with the tip of her tongue, she leaned into his warmth, into his strength. His arms wrapped around her waist, tucking her against him. She pressed an ear to his chest and listened to his pounding heart.

"I don't know why I'm nervous," he whispered, though he didn't make a move to let her go. He quickly followed that with a self-deprecating chuckle. "That probably should have been inside processing."

"I am too." She couldn't explain why she also admitted it. But it had been nearly ten years since she'd been kissed. And she'd been held this close by a man exactly never before.

Risking a glance up into his face, she met his gaze. His eyes were intense, but his face held the same kindness she'd known since he'd swooped in to rescue her. He captured a few strands of her hair that had been blown free by the wind and tucked them into place, his fingers brushing against her ear and melting something deep inside her chest.

"Is it okay if I kiss you now?"

"Whenever you're ready."

"Ha. I'm not sure if I am. I just know that I can't not."

Nibbling on the corner of her lip, she said, "I know exactly what you mean."

Apparently that was all the invitation he needed to close the distance between them, pressing his mouth to hers. His lips were tentative at first, as though those nerves he'd mentioned were taking the lead.

But after a moment, he sighed into her, all hesitancy abandoned.

She sank against him, every inch, from her toes to the top of her head, tingling like she'd been dunked in a seltzer bath. Only sweeter and stronger.

Letting go of his shirt, she grabbed his shoulders, then the back of his neck and his chin, running her fingers across the stubble on his face. She couldn't get enough of the stiff texture against her hands, fascinated by the way it changed as she shifted directions. A muscle in his jaw jumped, but he didn't stop. He didn't smile. He only groaned. Kind of the way Joe Jr. did when she scratched him behind the ears.

Which made her wonder if Finn liked to have his head scratched too.

Releasing his chin, she sank her fingers into his butter-soft hair and ran her nails along his scalp. Finn nearly melted into her as he released a low sigh. It was a sound of pleasure, of stress leaving the body. So she did it again.

This time, his muscles went taut, his arms cinching around her and picking her up off her feet. He shifted his head for a better angle and kissed her harder, hungrier. Like a man who had been starving. Like he had no intention of ever being hungry again.

And in the moment, she refused to think about what that meant.

She could only give what he was taking and take what he offered. Which was all of himself. He poured out his whole heart and held nothing back.

When he finally set her down into the shifting sand and pulled away, he let out a stuttering breath. She was somehow both empty and utterly full.

Finn bent his finger, running a knuckle across her highly sensitive cheek. "Cretia." He whispered her name, almost like a prayer. Like he was praying *for* her.

No one had ever prayed for her. At least not to her knowledge. Her mom had watched her prayers as she knelt by her bed in those early years. Before. Before the illness had taken over. Before her mom's mind had become as cluttered as their home. Before the piles had threatened more than their sanity. "I've wanted to do that since the day at the harbor. Since the moment I picked you up and carried you to the inn."

She didn't know how she could be full and somehow accept more, but she did. Her cup overflowing. Too many emotions to name, and all of them centered on the man before her. The one she should never have met. The one who was rapidly becoming far too important.

Then he uttered three little words that flushed out everything he had poured into her. "You could stay."

She shook her head, unable to meet his gaze, unable to stop the trembling in her hands. "I can't. I won't be like her."

"Like who?" He reached for her arm but she stumbled back, her eyes locked on a blue shell poking out of the sand.

Lips twitching and chin jerking, she let out a soft sigh. "I can't be her."

Matching her retreating steps, he tangled their fingers together and pulled her back into his embrace. "You don't have to be anyone but you."

Her eyes drifted shut. She was warm. She was protected. She was safe.

And suddenly there was nothing to hold back the truth.

"I had to leave my home."

"What?"

"That's how I became a content creator. I had to leave. I didn't know we were different when I was a little kid. I didn't realize that other people lived differently."

He nodded slowly into the crown of her head, his arms squeezing slightly.

"I guess I remember there being a time when things were

normal. My abuelita lived with us when I was young, and as long as she was there, she kept after my mom, kept up with her. But she died when I was seven, and after that, my mom gave up. I think she'd lost too many things. Her dad was killed in a car accident when she was young. My dad was her high school boyfriend, and he took off when he found out she was pregnant. And then after her mom . . ."

Cretia tried not to picture the first stacks of magazines she remembered or the trash bags that began to pile up.

Finn smoothed down her hair, cradling her head against him. "Did she hurt you?"

"No. Not like that. Not like you mean." Her stuttered breath released slowly. "She loved me. She just couldn't let go of anything else after that. So she didn't. She kept everything. Every piece of junk mail. Every store receipt. Every piece of clothing that I outgrew. She kept it all. Piles and piles of stuff. Everywhere. I tried to throw things away. I filled up the garbage bin and wheeled it to the curb before I got on the school bus. It was bigger than I was, but I had to do something. When I got home, she screamed at me. How could I have done something so cruel to her? How could I have thrown away the only things she loved?"

Finn took a deep breath above her ear. "What did you throw away?"

"Some catalogs and a few pairs of my abuelita's shoes. They were so worn, and they had holes in them, and no one was ever going to be able to use them. They had been in the back of the closet. But . . . the truth is, I don't even think she knew what I had thrown out. Only that the trash bin had been at the curb when she got up. After that, I couldn't risk it. Mom was the only person I had. And one day, it just took over the house. I don't remember when exactly. Maybe it came on slowly. I just remember waking up on the couch one morning during my senior year of high school—my room was filled from floor to ceiling with stuff—and I couldn't find a path to the kitchen. I could feel the bugs crawling on me, but I couldn't smell the stench of trash anymore. I'd become immune to it." She wrapped her arms around her middle, a feeble attempt to ward off the memories that came flooding back in full Technicolor along with every sound and smell.

"And no one ever noticed?"

"Oh, they noticed. A few teachers took note in junior high when I didn't have basic personal hygiene. They called Child Protective Services. Those who visited the house were horrified. But my mom swore she'd get the house cleaned up. They'd just stopped by on an off day. We were organizing."

Cretia wasn't sure she could handle a look of pity from Finn, but she risked a glance at his face anyway. She didn't find condescension there. Instead, his eyes were filled with genuine sorrow.

"The truth is, I didn't know if I could leave my mom. I just knew I couldn't live like that anymore." Even in his embrace, she managed to shrug. "I had been babysitting for a couple of kids off and on, and I asked their mom if I could stay with them. Just until I finished school."

"So how did you end up with no permanent home?"

"After high school I started nannying for a rich family. They were both doctors and needed live-in help with their two kids. A few years later, they asked me to go on a cruise with them. That's when I shot my first travel videos. Those early ones were tips for making the most of a cruise. I called them 'Cruising with Cretia.' Within a year, I'd earned enough to fund more trips. And more videos. My reach kept growing, and the rest is history."

"And that's how they saved you."

She nodded.

"Where's your mom now?"

"Still in the same house as far as I know. I call to check on her every now and then."

"But you haven't seen her since you moved out?"

She would do anything to block out that memory, but the painful twist in her gut wouldn't let her. Instead of going down that trail, she reached into her back pocket and pulled out her phone. "I guess I should get some video before we have to leave to pick up your cow."

Sixteen

re you trying to make my cow a star?" Finn strolled up behind Cretia, looking over her shoulder at the screen in her hands.

"I'm afraid we're past the trying stage." A note of laughter filled her voice, and relief flooded him.

He'd wanted to know more about her—to understand where she'd come from and how she'd ended up a nomad. But hearing her story, feeling her tremble as the words spilled out on the beach three days before, had nearly torn him in two.

No one should have to carry the weight of memories like those. And the fact that anyone hefting that could find such joy in life, be so quick to laugh and strong in spirit, astounded him. *She* astounded him.

Slipping his arms around her from behind, he nuzzled her neck even as the dogs barked for their breakfast and Roberta glared in their general direction. The new addition to the barn looked up at them with big brown eyes through shaggy russet hair, his nose blowing hot breath at Cretia's camera.

She leaned her head against Finn's, her arms sagging into his embrace, an invitation to hold her close.

He hadn't exactly waited for one. But now he knew he was welcome.

They hadn't talked about the kiss since. He'd been busy settling the mini cow into his new home. She'd been busy fawning all over it, taking more pictures than a mother of a firstborn child. In the pasture. With the kids. And now in the last available stall in his barn.

The top of the cow's head barely reached his waist—though it came a little higher on Cretia. "Perfect hugging height," she'd declared, kneeling in the hay beside it.

He had to admit that the little one was pretty cute and infinitely patient. He'd suffered through Joe Jr.'s forty-point inspection with barely a moo, and when the dog had decided he was acceptable, the new addition was free to roam the grounds.

No wonder a family had thought he was pet material. The problem was, the cow didn't always do his business outdoors. And he wasn't great about staying off the furniture. At not quite five hundred pounds, he'd demolished a few chairs and more than one lamp. The term *bull in a china shop* fit, even if he wasn't a full-size cow.

The family had been happy to hand over their little furniture demolition unit. And Finn was happy to give him a home where he wouldn't have to watch his step.

The only thing he hadn't been able to give him so far was a name. And the cow hadn't been with the family long enough for them to land on one either.

"Past the trying stage?" he asked when Cretia's response

finally sank in. "You've already posted videos of our new friend?"

"Maybe. And they love him. Adore him! And they've suggested thousands of names."

"Like what?"

Cretia punched some buttons on her screen, opened an app, and a video popped up. First, she was alone in the pasture, a chain of dandelions crowning her glistening hair. Her voice from the phone said, "Decided to wear our hair the same so no one can tell us apart." The video cut to the cow wearing the same crown of yellow flowers.

He pressed his lips to her cheek. "You wore it better."

"Careful there, Finn, or someone will think you've been on social media." She gave him a peck on the lips and a saucy wink before turning back to her phone. "I asked my followers what we should name him." She slowly scrolled through the comments, reading off a name here and there. "George. Samson. Abner. Fun-Size. Maple. Half-Pint. Snicker."

As her finger swiped up the screen, a message sailed by. It was longer than the others, but it snagged his attention. "Wait. What did that one say?"

"Nothing." The pink that dotted her cheeks betrayed her. So did the way she tried to drop her phone into her pocket.

"No, I'm serious. What did it say?"

"It's nothing worth getting worked up about."

He spun her around in his arms, hooking a finger under her chin until she met his gaze. "How do you know?"

"Because I already deleted a few dozen of them."

"Of what?"

She rolled her eyes and let out a hard sigh. "Of people telling me I weigh more than the cow. Of people swearing at me for just existing. Of people saying I don't deserve to be alive on the same planet as such a cutie-pie."

Her words came out disconnected and emotionless, but they stirred in him a monster that wanted to rip those jerks apart.

"How could they?" He snorted a hot breath through his nose, not unlike a bull ready to charge. "That was a great video. And they don't . . . they don't even know you." His voice rose until the dogs joined in, their barking setting off Roberta and the goats. Only the little cow remained silent, though he took several quick steps into the corner of his stall.

"Finn." Cretia ran her hand up and down his forearm, teasing the soft hair there. "They're just trolls. They hate their own lives, and they think that saying mean things about someone else will help them feel better." Holding up her phone, she forced a smile as she touched the profile pic of an offender. "I just block them. It's that easy. And now they have no power."

Sure, she'd replay their comments late at night. With only the dark as her companion, she'd wonder if what they'd written was true. She'd wonder if she had no business being on camera. She'd wonder if she really was the size of a full-grown cow.

Her smile began to flicker, and she fought to keep a brave face.

"Really. I barely think about them. It's all part of what I do." She brushed a hand across her shoulder. "I don't let them in."

Most of the time.

Finn nodded slowly, small lines appearing on either side of his mouth. "But they're liars. You know that, right? You know what they're saying isn't true?"

"Of course I do."

Cupping his palm against her cheek, he sifted his fingers into her hair, pulling her a step closer. "You have to know that if they just met you—even for a moment—they'd see how amazing you are. How you bring a smile with you wherever you go. How big and kind your heart is. They'd love you."

Like he did?

Oh, no. It was way too soon to even think about such things. They'd barely known each other for two weeks. Absolutely ridiculous. Truly.

Which did nothing to explain why she hoped he did.

Finn's eyes narrowed, the weight of his gaze like a warm coat on a cold night. "You know how special you are, don't you?"

"You're sweet." A skeptical giggle insisted on following.

"I'm serious."

She smiled and squeezed his arm. But whatever she wanted to say was stuck behind the lump that settled in her throat. Even a single syllable would likely set loose a river of tears from her burning eyes.

Stupid eyes. Stupid tears.

The onslaught of emotion made zero sense. Finn was saying such nice things. She should just smile and say, "Thank you."

But she couldn't get the words out. And she sure couldn't let his words in.

"Lucretia Martin." He laid heavily on the long *e* in her last name. "I've never met anyone like you. And I . . ." As he stepped closer, his scent swept around her, all fresh grass and sunshine, things she'd only recently realized were among her favorites. "What am I going to do with you?"

Keep me?

Nope. That wasn't an option, so with a bat of her eyelashes, she whispered the next best option. "Kiss me?"

He took her invitation, swooping in and claiming her. Any hint of the nerves he'd owned during their first kiss had vanished, replaced by an undeniable hunger for more. More of her. More of *them.*

Wrapping her arms about his waist, she jerked him closer. He stumbled a half step into her, his surprised chuckle muted but joyful.

What was she going to do with him?

Finn didn't have a clue what he was going to do with her. Something deep in his gut cheered on the idea of more kissing. No problem there. *That* he could do. So long as she was on his island, in his barn.

But the after snuck in too. What would he do after she left? After there was no more of them?

Yeah, he was well aware that he was setting himself up for all sorts of heartache. But he'd rather have the memories than the regrets. And he'd keep telling himself that as long as she was in his arms.

Warm and responsive, her lips were smoother than silk and tasted of maple syrup, almost as sweet as the woman herself. Everything he'd said about her was true. Even if the look in her eyes had hinted that she doubted him.

He knew the truth. She wasn't just beautiful—though

she'd certainly been fearfully and wonderfully made, according to the verse his parents had helped him memorize during his Sunday school years. She was creative and funny and independent and generous and stubborn. Traits he'd newly realized he'd always wanted in a partner.

Combing his fingers through her impossibly silky hair, he sighed into her. When he brushed his thumb across her cheekbone, she trembled, her hands grasping first at his shirt, then at his biceps. His skin felt too hot and too small, like the feeling growing inside him needed more space. It was too big to contain.

Not that he wanted to contain it. There wasn't a box big enough or a dam thick enough to keep it in check.

When she hung on his shoulders, a strange sense of pride raced through him. She trusted him enough to lean on him, and he wouldn't risk letting her down.

Or hurting her.

When he wrapped an arm around her waist, he squeezed just hard enough to elicit a giggle, and she pulled back, a bright smile on her face. Pressing his nose to her temple, he sighed. "I like you, Cretia. More than I've liked anyone I've ever met. But I don't want—"

"I know," she whispered into his shoulder, her breath warm through his T-shirt. "This can't end well."

"It could." He nearly bit his tongue off as her entire body stiffened, though she didn't pull away. He had no business saying such things again, and he waited for a long explanation of why he was a fool for even suggesting she stay.

She said only, "No."

Squeezing his eyes closed, he took one more deep breath, memorizing the floral scent of her shampoo. Then, hands at her waist, he pushed her away and took a step back. "I like you too much to make it harder than it has to be."

Something like pain flashed in her eyes, but she blinked it away before he could put a true name to it. She didn't ask him to explain. Instead, she pressed her lips together—lips he could have kissed again if he wasn't such an idiot—and nodded. "You're probably right."

No. He was absolutely right. He was also an absolute fool. That memories-versus-regrets theory had been downright stupid. Because now he fully knew what he was going to miss. For the rest of his life.

And he knew that would come with more than his share of regret. The memories wouldn't warm him from the inside out on cold winter nights. He couldn't hold the memories in his arms, smell their hair, and care for them for a lifetime.

His heart was thinking about forever with a girl who had been part of his life for exactly fifteen days. And his brain only now had the decency to butt in.

Stupid. Stupid. Stupid.

Finn let out a long breath through tight lips. "I'm sorry."

"For what?" Her narrowed gaze insisted on an answer.

At the moment? For wanting to kiss her again. But he bit his tongue on that and gave her question another thought. "For starting something that I can't finish."

"Really? Seems like I'm the one that asked for a kiss."

"Today, maybe. But it's not exactly like you had to twist my arm."

She shrugged a shoulder and shot him a grin. "True. You were a willing participant."

"Very." That was another thought that should have stayed inside.

Her grin turned into a full-on smirk, her eyes glowing as she nudged him with her elbow. "Same."

One word was all it took for his stomach to clench and his breath to release. He had to physically fight the urge to lean in again. But he cared about her too much to let himself get carried away. She deserved more than that. She deserved someone who would—someone who could—help her pursue her dreams. Not someone rooted to this land.

"So." She smoothed down the front of her shirt with flat hands. "Seems like we both enjoyed that. And we agree that it would be wise not to do it again."

"Right. Wise."

But if she stood there staring at him with her great big eyes, he was liable to fall right into those chocolate pools and make all sorts of stupid decisions. He had to change the subject. Pronto.

"Abner."

Cretia's face wrinkled in confusion. Finn didn't know who he'd surprised more—her or himself. But he repeated the name. A little slower the second time, nodding toward the cow that was still staring at them. "Abner."

"That's what you want to name him?"

He shrugged. "Sure. Why not?" It wasn't exactly a ringing endorsement, but to the best of his knowledge, the farm had never had an Abner, little or otherwise.

Cretia turned toward the cow, bending over until their eyes were almost level. "Abner? What do you think?"

The cow shook his head, tossing his hair out of his face, and lowed.

Cretia shot a smile over her shoulder. "I think he likes it. Abner it is. Thank you, internet." Waving Finn toward his newest addition, she said, "Now let me take some pictures of you together."

"I don't know. I'm not very . . ." He stabbed a hand through his hair, which probably already showcased the wind and his work. His hand came away with a piece of hay in it. "See? I'm not cleaned up for pictures."

"Psh." She waved off his comment with as much consideration as a gnat. "You look perfect. Just like a farmer should. The internet is going to eat you up."

"Don't you mean the cow? Um, Abner?"

"I do not." She pursed her lips as she looked at the screen in her hands. "I mean, they'll love Abner. Don't get me wrong—ladies of a certain age will be lining up to adopt one just like him." She frowned for a second. "Come to think of it, videos of cows like Abner looking all cute and cuddly are probably how the poor guy ended up as a pet."

"Seriously?" he grumbled. "What's wrong with people?" He knew firsthand that some people took in animals they couldn't care for. That was how he'd gotten Jenna and the kids. And the rabbits. And several cats as a child.

"They think something this cute must be a house pet." Holding her phone at arm's length, she swooped it around them. "Can you blame them?"

"Yeah, well." He ran his fingers through Abner's mane, scratching behind his horns for good measure. Abner swung his head, and Finn jerked away just in time to keep from being smacked in the arm by one of those horns. "You'd think that whoever sold him would have warned them against it."

"You'd think. But for now, just try to look like a good farmer."

Ten-year-old Finn would have stuck his tongue out at her.

"I'm not a farmer. I don't own a tractor, and I've never sowed a seed outside of my mom's garden. I own about four acres of land. That's not enough to be called a farm by any stretch of the imagination."

Her face twisted into a silly grin. "Very well, then. What should I call you when I post this video?"

"You're not really going to—"

"What should I call you?" Her tone sounded an awful lot like a teacher's. Like Marie's when she'd had to correct Julia Mae one too many times.

"Your followers don't care about me. They want to see you and Abner."

"All right, Farmer Finn it is."

"I'm a business owner. A dog breeder. An adopter of strays." He spat the words out as fast as he could. Anything but Farmer Finn.

"I'll see what I can do, but you may have missed your window of opportunity." Her eyes twinkled and her cheeks twitched as she bit her lips until they nearly disappeared. "We'll see what the council says."

"The council?"

She shrugged, putting on a facade of boredom.

"And who exactly is on this council that decides my online persona?"

"Me and Roberta."

There wasn't a dam in the world that could have held back his snorted laugh, and he grabbed her sides, tickling mercilessly as he pulled her to his chest. She screamed and squirmed and fought him with laughter-limp arms.

"Take it back. Roberta would never betray me!"

"I will not. I thi-think she's warm-warming up to me." As

her giggles cut off her words, he spun her in his arms. She ended up pressed against his chest, breathing heavily, and smiling into his face. Just where he wanted her. Just how he wanted her.

Longing slammed through him, an unwelcome visitor. Holding her hands at his chest, he sucked in a deep breath. Every one of his noble intentions lined up to march right out the door.

One more kiss couldn't hurt. It wouldn't really change anything. They both knew that a *they* could never last. They also knew how sweet it could be between them. Another kiss would just . . .

It's not an option.

He'd chant those words over and over again until he believed them. For her sake. For her heart.

He would regret kissing her again. And he would regret not kissing her.

He'd be miserable no matter what. But maybe he'd be a little less so if he knew that he'd done his best to show her just how much he cared.

Strange that not kissing her was the way to do that.

With a half smile, he let go of her hands and stepped back.

"Giving up, I see," she goaded him. "I'll confer with Roberta and let you know our decision later."

Jabbing his fingers through his hair, he said, "You're ridiculous."

"And?"

"And it's no wonder that three million people watch your videos."

"And now three million people are going to watch you."

She was like Joe with a bone. "How many times do I have to tell you that they want to see Abner?"

"*They?*" Her forehead wrinkled at the same time she lifted her phone to block the rest of her face. "They include a bunch of twenty- and thirty-something women, who would be just as happy to adopt Farmer Finn as they would Abner."

"Ridiculous."

"What can I say?" She fanned her face with her phone and raised her eyebrows a few times in an exaggerated motion. When she added in a wolf whistle, he laughed.

Dropping to his knee next to Abner, he hugged the little guy around his neck. "Tell her, boy. You're the one everyone will want to see."

Cretia took a few smooth steps in a half circle around them, her motions slow and controlled as she looked right into her screen. "Care to make a friendly wager on that?"

Finn had never been a gambler. That required time and money he was willing to throw away. Two things usually in short supply around his place. But Cretia didn't look like she was trying to empty his wallet. In fact, her grin suggested much higher stakes.

"What'd you have in mind?"

She clicked her tongue. "I'll post this video tonight. If it has a hundred thousand views within twenty-four hours, you have to let me name Bella's puppies."

Squinting at her, he crossed his arms. "Potato names?"

"Every single one. From Sprout to Tuber."

"Tuber? You're not serious."

"You're one to be talking." She dropped her phone to her side, her other hand planted on the curve of her hip. "You wanted to name one Tater."

"As in Tater Tot. It makes sense."

"Why not just name him Tot, then?"

"Be—" His words disappeared, and he shrugged. "I don't know. I guess either would work."

"Exactly. Clearly you haven't thought this through. So let me name them." "I promise to give the task my full consideration."

He eyed her carefully. "And if the video doesn't get a hundred thousand views?"

"I'll muck out Roberta's stall for a week."

Finn gasped so hard that he nearly swallowed his tongue, barely managing to choke out a gravelly chortle while his brain repeated one word. *Week.* She was planning to stay another week.

His misery had a reprieve. Seven more days. At least.

"I'm determined to make that bovine my friend. Just like Abner is." Scratching the cow's chin, Cretia got a sloppy kiss on her wrist, which made her nose wrinkle and her smile grow. "But I'm not going to have to clean up her stall. Because you're going to get more views than you can imagine."

"And you'll mention the business name?"

"Chaffey's Newfoundlands." She held out her hand to shake.

Slipping his palm against hers, he squeezed softly. "And you won't call me Farmer Finn."

"Oh, I can't promise that. Roberta still has to have a say."

Seventeen

told you!" Cretia crowed as she pranced into the barn the next morning, waving her phone over her head.

Bent over a stall door and dumping a bucket of oats in Abner's dish, Finn mumbled something under his breath for the mini cow. For her, he said, "It hasn't even been twenty-four hours."

"I know. But I stayed up half the night thinking of potato names."

He stood, the black bucket hanging by its handle from his fingers as he leaned his hip against the wooden planks of the wall. "Evidence first." A half grin began to tug at his lips, but his nose twitched as he seemed to fight it.

"You don't believe me?" She pressed a hand to her chest in feigned distress.

"It's not you I distrust. It's the very idea that a hundred thousand people would be interested in a miniature cow."

"You forget the small-town farmer from the island."

His smile disappeared into a scowl. "I'm still not a farmer."

"*I* know that," she said, all innocence, forced to bite back the giggle that bubbled in her chest. "But the ladies of the internet would not be denied. They came up with Farmer Finn all on their own."

"Uh-huh." He sucked on a tooth and clicked his tongue. "You're a terrible liar." Holding out his hand, he curled his fingers. "Let's see it."

Instead of passing over her phone, she walked over to him and spun until her back was almost against his chest. A catch in his breath stirred her hair, and she tried not to smile. He was warm and solid and all the things that had attracted her to him since the day they met.

Kissing was off the table. He'd made that abundantly clear. It was probably the right choice.

But if she happened to know that her hair smelled especially good after Marie shared a bottle of coconut shampoo with her, shouldn't Finn get to appreciate it too? And if it made him reconsider his stance on kissing her again . . .

Some things couldn't be helped.

Besides, she'd tracked her laptop shipment that morning. It had arrived in New Jersey, headed for Toronto. Estimated arrival to the Red Door, three days.

Her teasing smile took a hard hit at the reminder, and she ducked her head to keep him from noticing. She had only three days left on this sweet island. Three days left with Finn. She already knew that not kissing him wasn't going to make it any easier to leave. She just didn't have a choice.

Adjusting the brightness of the screen in her hand to accommodate for the relative dimness inside the barn, she held it up before them. First she played the video of Abner munching on hay and then strolling up to her until all the camera could see were his cute nostrils and infinitely boopable nose. Then the shot cut to Finn kneeling next to the cow, his arm around Abner's back and his other hand invisible in his thatch of long hair. The cow swung his head in time to the background music she'd added—a popular song by a folk singer—and Finn scratched under his chin before looking right at the camera and giving her a slow grin.

Honestly, she'd slowed that last bit of the video down because she knew the girls would go wild for it. She had too. But just a little bit.

The difference was that she knew the man behind the smile. She knew he was so much more than broad shoulders and a handsome face—though that dimple in his chin still made her stomach swoop when she caught it at the right angle.

And she wasn't above using his good looks to win her bet.

Finn grunted when the video ended. "Did you write something about it? Something about the business?"

"Of course." She scrolled beneath the video and read it aloud. "'Prince Edward Island is more than stunning landscapes and red-rock beaches. It's home to beautiful farmland and some of the cutest creatures on earth. Meet Abner and Finn—owner of Chaffey's Newfoundlands, a dog-training business and staple in the community of North Rustico.'" She looked up and behind her to meet his gaze. "Zero mention of you being a farmer. Are you happy?"

His gaze narrowed and he shook his head. "Not yet. How many views?"

"One hundred and thirty-three thousand. Oh!" She looked again at the number that had gone up since that morning. "One hundred and forty-six thousand."

"That's ridiculous. It can't be true."

"The Instagram insights don't lie." When she pointed to the number beneath the play button, his jaw dropped.

"So, I'm thinking Spud, Tater, Sprout, Chip, Fry, Scallop, Tuber, Starch, Russet, Red, and Mash."

Finn didn't move, his eyes still focused on her phone.

"Finn?"

Finally, he sighed. "How did you do that?"

"Do what? Make the video? That was easy. There's all sorts of editing software, but my phone has most of it built in."

"No, I mean . . ." He stabbed his fingers through his hair. "How did you make that many people watch me and Abner?"

"I didn't make anyone do anything. I just gave the people what they already wanted."

"How do you know?"

She gave him a wicked laugh. "Oh, you want me to open the floodgates. My pleasure." Clearing her throat and putting on her best suburban accent, she began reading some of the three thousand comments.

"*Girl, please. You need to warn us about cuteness overload.*"

"*Starts looking for real estate on PEI.*"

"*Must get one of those hugs. And cows.*"

"*Can I visit on my next trip to the island?*"

"*I'm packing my bags right now.*"

"*That's the cutest thing I've ever seen. The cow's pretty adorable too.*"

Finn began to cough, and Cretia turned around to find his face was the color of a beet.

"I told you," she singsonged. "Just giving the internet what it wants. They already gobble up accounts about hot guys with dogs and hot guys reading books and . . . well, generally, hot guys. Add in ridiculously adorable animals,

and they don't know what to do with themselves, except . . ."
As she skimmed through a few more comments, her smile
began to dim and her brain churned.

When Finn finally got control of himself, he mumbled,
"Except what?"

"They want to come visit. Not just you but your cow. And
I would bet your goats too. Can you imagine if you let them
bottle-feed the kids?"

"Why would I do that?"

"For the experience. People pay for experiences. They
want to see and hold and touch and feel and experience
life with real animals. You could show them what it takes
to care for animals and how cows—even mini ones—aren't
really inside pets. You could teach them about caring for the
animals and raising them well and let them get in the stalls
and make furry friends."

"Who?" He sounded like he thought she'd gone completely off the rails.

Waving her phone in his face, she said, "Them. These
people. The ones who come here on vacation and want something fun to do with their families. There are millions of kids
just like Jack, who love animals and would love to spend an
afternoon on this property."

Finn began shaking his head before she even finished. "I
can't . . . I didn't take these guys in to show them off. They
just needed a home."

"I know. But that doesn't mean you *couldn't* show them
off."

Scrubbing a hand down his face and scraping across his
whiskers, he shook his head again. "I have to focus on the
dogs. The business is my priority."

"But this could be an extension of your business. You could keep breeding and training the dogs, and you could make that part of teaching visitors about how Newfoundlands are such a special breed. And you could get local kids to help out—it'd be better than camp for them. I bet kids from all over the island would come to help. Or you could hire someone."

"No."

She blinked rapidly at the volume of his voice. She'd never heard him shout before, but the single word silenced even the barn crickets for a moment before the dogs began barking and even Roberta let out a concerned bellow.

"Finn?" She took a hesitant step in his direction and rested her hand on his forearm, the muscles there bunched up and tense.

"I don't need help," he said between clenched teeth. "I can make this business grow on my own."

"I-I know you can. But the point is you don't have to. Justin doesn't run his whole dairy by himself. Even your dad had you to help when he ran this business. A little change, an extra hand, could open a big door for you."

Finn forced his fists to unclench at his sides, flexing his fingers and taking a deep breath through his nose. Still his hands trembled, and his pulse pounded in his ears. A band around his chest had pulled tight, and he didn't know how to release it. Or how to explain it to the woman with eyes full of questions.

"I'm sorry." His voice barely carried the mere distance between them.

"It's okay. But did I say something . . . or . . . ?" Cretia cocked her head to the side as she squeezed his arm. Her careful inspection bored into the secret parts of his heart.

He wanted to step away or hide. But his feet refused to budge. "I need to do this on my own."

"But why? There are so many people here who care about you, who would be happy to help you. And your parents love you. I'm sure they'd be happy to—I don't know—cosign a loan application for you or something."

Begging his parents for help would just prove that what his dad had said to Milo McGinniss was right. It was not going to happen.

Letting out a slow breath through tight lips was all he could manage for a moment as he remembered that day, those words. It had been more than a decade ago, but somehow, they still rang through him.

He tried to shut them up and fill in the space with a joke. "That's rich coming from someone who tried to refuse help when she had a twisted ankle and was dripping from head to toe."

Cretia didn't laugh. She didn't even smile. "But I did accept your help."

"You were forced to let me help you that day because you couldn't manage on your own. I can do this alone."

"No one doubts that. But—"

"Yes, they do."

Cretia's mouth snapped shut, whatever argument she'd been trying to make dying on her pursed lips. Slowly she put her hands on her hips and looked him up and down. "Who?"

"It doesn't matter," he spat out.

"I beg to differ. I've never seen you so upset."

"Yeah, well." He swung his head around and turned his back on her as his heart thundered. "You've known me for all of two weeks and some change. What do you expect?"

She sucked in a small gasp, and he turned around, expecting her to be halfway across the barn and headed back to the Red Door. Instead, she was right in front of him, two fingers pressed to her mouth, failing to cover a ridiculous smile.

"Why are you smiling?"

"Because I like fighting with you."

"You like it when I'm mad?"

She shook her head as she stepped into his arms, which automatically wrapped around her back. "I don't like that you're upset, but I like that I know you're always going to turn back to me. I like that you don't walk away. I like that even when you're mad, you still hold me." She pressed her forehead against his breastbone. "I like that you still let me hold you."

He stared up at the open rafters as the backs of his eyes began to burn. He didn't understand how she could know him so well, but she did. So he held on to her and let her hold on to him. And together, maybe they could make sense of the things that didn't.

Like the feelings that were supposed to be easing with distance but were only growing.

For several long minutes, only the sounds of the barn filled the space—the munching of hay and the bleating of goats and the yips of eleven baby Newfoundland pups.

Just as his heartbeat returned to its normal pace, she whispered against his shirt, "What happened to make you think you have to do this all alone?"

He'd never told a soul. Not his best friend or his cousins.

Especially not his dad. Yet Cretia asked with such sincerity and certainty that she seemed to know there was something to tell. She'd opened up to him about her mom. This was the least he could do.

"Growing up, I always knew that this business had been passed down from father to son. But my dad told me many times that I didn't have to take it if I didn't want it, that I could choose any career. He said he'd be proud to pass it along to me, but he'd never force it on me. When I was seventeen, I told him that when he was ready to retire, I'd be ready to take it on. He told me I didn't have to decide yet. There was still time to change my mind, and he wouldn't blame me if I wanted to pursue something else. But I told him I would do whatever it took to keep our family's legacy going strong. He just smiled at me and said he had no doubt that I would."

Finn swallowed the lump that lodged in his throat at the surprisingly emotional memory. He could still feel the weight of his dad's hand on his shoulder and see the trust in the older man's eyes.

"That's really sweet," Cretia said. "But I don't—"

"A few years later Dad started getting stiff, and he couldn't do some of the physical parts of the job. He was diagnosed with rheumatoid arthritis. It's not terminal. It just makes it harder for him to get around. Harder to get on the ground with the puppies. Harder to be on the move all the time. I think he'd planned on working the business until he was eighty, but his body just gave out. And Mom told him in no uncertain terms that they were going to retire and move to Summerside, where she'd grown up. I think she missed the convenience of living in a city. And more than that, I think she wanted to be near a hospital in case something happened. It was probably best for Dad, and I knew I was going to miss them, but I was sure that I could handle things. I'd watched my grandpa and my dad run this business since I was a kid. I knew what I was doing."

Cretia nuzzled her head against his chest. "What changed? Because as far as I can tell, you do know what you're doing, and the business is doing well."

"One morning I came outside, and I saw a truck in the driveway. It was a friend of my dad's—a guy named Milo McGinniss. He used to live on the farm right next to ours. I didn't see him and my dad around, so I headed toward the barn to do morning chores, and I was in the tack room when they walked in. I know they didn't see me there, and I know I wasn't supposed to hear what they said, but it's seared into my brain now."

She didn't speak, but her back became tense even as she pulled him closer. Almost like she thought she could spare him the pain again.

"Milo told my dad that I wasn't up to running the business. 'You know your son can't handle it. Are you ready to see everything your family has worked for go down the drain because you left it to a kid?'" Finn sucked in a stabilizing breath. "I couldn't see them, so I don't know what my dad did, but I know he said, 'You think you're the first to say that?'"

Finn swallowed hard before forcing out the rest of the memory. "My dad said he didn't expect much out of me. I was barely twenty at the time, but I felt like I'd shown that I was worthy by working hard all through my childhood. In that moment, I knew I hadn't."

"So you're here—working all by yourself, refusing to ask for help—because you're trying to prove your dad wrong?"

"Something like that."

"But . . ." Cretia pulled back only far enough to stare up into his face. "I know I only met your dad once, but that doesn't sound like him. He's so proud of you."

"Maybe. Or maybe he's just surprised that I haven't failed yet."

Eighteen

The next three days flew by, and Cretia stuffed as many memories as she could into every moment. She captured many of them on her phone—Joe Jr. leading a parade of furry black dogs through the tall pasture grass, Abner rolling around in the sunshine, and Sonny and Cher prancing around the barn.

Some she couldn't record—like the smell of the harbor as she and Finn walked Joe and the Fab Four down the boardwalk. The way it was easier to breathe in the island air than any other place she'd visited. The way the faces and greetings of the locals had become familiar and welcome.

Some memories, though, were only for herself—the smell of Finn's aftershave, the strength of his embrace, and the safety she felt at his side. Even if she could have recorded those, she wouldn't have shared them with anyone else.

She'd come to this island to share it with her followers. But some memories were only hers.

And some things would break her heart.

Like her love for Finn.

So when Jack yelled up the stairs that a box had arrived

for her, Cretia could barely pluck up an ounce of excitement at the news. Yanking the quilt over her head, she closed her eyes and prayed for a reprieve. Just another day. Another week. Another year.

It would never be enough. She would always hate leaving. But just because she hated doing it didn't mean it wasn't the right thing. She'd made that decision long ago.

Rolling out of bed, she ran a hand through her hair and then slipped on the same gray hoodie she'd worn the night Bella gave birth. She paused only long enough to duck into the bathroom and brush her teeth before slumping down to the kitchen.

Jack had disappeared, but Marie puttered around the kitchen, wiping down countertops as Jessie sat in a wooden high chair inspecting and then eating individual Cheerios from the tray before her. Her pudgy fingers were damp and probably sticky and ridiculously adorable as she jabbered in her seat.

Marie looked up as Cretia reached the bottom step. "I thought maybe you'd already gone to Finn's this morning."

Cretia shrugged as she reached the island and stared at the mailing label on the brown box before her. Someone had scribbled "CANADA" in black marker above an extra sticker or three. The corners of the box were a little roughed up, but she had no doubt that the white box inside it was still in pristine condition. The tech company always packed her equipment carefully.

"I'm not going to lie. I half expected you to hug that box when it finally arrived." Marie began to chuckle at herself but stopped short.

Three weeks ago, she would have. Without a doubt, she'd have scooped it up, pulled together every meager thing she owned, gotten a ride to Charlottetown, and hopped on the next plane to anywhere else.

"You don't even look pleased that it's here," Marie said.

"I am." The lie slipped out far too easily.

"Are you hungry? I can make you some frozen waffles or something."

Her stomach threatened to mutiny at the very thought of food of any kind. "No thanks. Let me help you." She marched to the dishwasher and began unloading it, never once having to ask where something went. A perk and a responsibility of kitchen privileges.

Marie shot her a smile as she put away a stack of plates. "We're going to miss you around here."

"No, you're not." Though she liked the idea of someone missing her more than she cared to admit. "Your guests will start arriving with the tourist season, and then you'll be way too busy to think about me."

"Oh, that's not true." Marie wet a washcloth under the faucet and wiped up Jessie's mouth and fingers. "I guarantee you that guests don't help clean up the kitchen."

"So you just want me for my manual labor?"

Marie laughed. "Not at all. If I thought it would influence your decision, I'd offer to let you stay here as a real guest— with no manual labor—for as long as you wanted."

The weight of Marie's words settled heavily on her chest, and Cretia rubbed at the spot over her heart. "That's very kind of you," she managed to get out.

"You don't have to go, you know."

"Yes. I do." Cretia pulled out the top rack of the dishwasher and grabbed a towel to dry off the plastic sippy cups and colorful plates. "But if it matters at all, this is the first place I've ever wished that wasn't true. No place has ever felt quite so safe. And you and Finn—I've never had friends like you before."

Marie took a slow breath as she released Jessie from her high chair and set the toddler on the floor. "Forgive me, but I don't understand. I mean, I get that your job requires you to travel. But couldn't you have a home base, a place—people—to come home to?"

Cretia turned away as her eyes began to burn, but staring at the ceiling didn't ease the stinging. It all sounded so lovely.

In theory.

"I tried to."

Marie froze, the teakettle suspended in her hand over the stovetop. She opened her mouth and then quickly closed it again, questions flashing across her face.

Cretia closed the dishwasher, leaned a hip against the counter, and turned to face her hostess. Fighting for at least a hint of a smile, she gulped a little breath. "My mom is . . . difficult. She's the only parent I've ever known, but after my abuelita—my grandma—died when I was seven, my mom changed. She'd lost so much that she refused to get rid of anything else. We never used the term, but she became a hoarder. There's no other way to describe it."

Marie's eyebrows pinched together, and she whispered, "I'm so sorry. That must have been so hard."

"It certainly wasn't a picnic." She snapped her mouth closed and glanced up apologetically. "I'm sorry. I shouldn't have said it like that."

Marie waved off her apology. "Family relationships are hard. Sometimes they bring out the worst in us."

Cretia nodded slowly. Finn hadn't said it in as many words,

but he was trying to make his father proud and prove him wrong at the same time. It wasn't bringing out his best either. Apparently, they had more in common than she'd thought.

"I moved out when I was a senior in high school and worked a live-in nanny job for a few years. The family asked me to go on a cruise with them, and that's where I began taking videos and picking up travel tips. My platforms grew from there, and before I knew it, so did my income."

When the kettle whistled, Marie nodded to it, an unspoken question between them.

"Yes, please."

Marie got out two cups and set them on the counter. "So, you started making money?"

Cretia couldn't hold back a good-natured snort. "That's putting it mildly. I grew up in a border town, living in a two-bedroom stucco house with no air-conditioning and temperamental plumbing. I barely graduated from high school, and I thought making fifteen hundred dollars a month as a nanny in addition to a room was upper-class. But I discovered a whole section of the internet eager for tips and tools to make travel easier, more affordable, more enjoyable. And I could give them that. I did my research. I explored the world. I was real about what I liked and what I didn't. Pretty soon I had a million followers. And that year, I made almost that much money. Of course, most of it goes into traveling and equipment. But my followers kept growing, and with them the opportunities and income."

With a chuckle, Marie said, "Natalie and Brooke said you were famous, but I didn't realize. Here we've been hosting a star, and we didn't even know it."

Cretia responded with a laugh of her own. "Absolutely not.

I'm not a star. I just found my niche, my people. And I thought I could use that money to help my mom. I thought maybe I could have a place to go home to." Her smile melted away, and her lips trembled as the memory surged through her.

Pressing a flat hand to her back, Marie ushered Cretia to a stool at the counter and set a steaming cup of tea before her. "What happened with her?"

She shook her head, not sure if she could speak the truth, or even begin to convey the way her mom's face had twisted with rage or the way her screech had rung through the house. "I-I-I hired a professional organizer. A team, really. I called my mom and told her we were coming. That we were going to help her take her home back. And that I could come visit—stay with her when I wasn't traveling—if she would just clean it up and throw out the trash." Cretia took a sip of her tea, the warmth sliding down her chest to her stomach. "It didn't work."

"What do you mean? She couldn't keep it clean?"

"No. She wouldn't even let us start."

Marie looked stricken, though Cretia didn't know why. It wasn't like Marie's mom was so far gone.

"When the team picked up a trash bag—even before they threw it into the giant dumpster they'd brought with them—my mom lost it. Crying and raging, screaming and throwing things at us." Cretia wrapped her arms around her middle, trying to ward off the memories that, once begun, flowed off her tongue. "I tried to calm her down. I tried to rationalize with her. I even resorted to blackmail. If she didn't get her house in order, I told her I would never set foot on her property again. It didn't matter. She couldn't hear me. She wouldn't. She'd made her choice. She'd rather have her junk than have me in her life. And just before I left that day, she screamed that everyone always said I was just like her. And I was going to end up in a house just like hers."

From the other side of the island, Marie reached out a gentle hand. "Oh, sweetie, I am so sorry."

"This is the part where you tell me that she's the only mother I'm ever going to have and I need to try again."

Marie's forehead wrinkled along her hairline. "Not at all. Why would you think that?"

"Because that's what the organizer said. She said I should wait a few months and call her so we could try again."

"Well, it sounds like that organizer didn't come from a dysfunctional family."

Cretia shrugged. Probably not. But she was also one of the few people who had witnessed her mom's meltdown.

"Can I tell you about my relationship with my dad?" Marie asked.

She nodded silently, hiding her trembling lips behind her teacup.

"My dad is difficult too. He's a wealthy and powerful real-estate developer in Boston, and when I was twenty-eight, he tried to use the worst thing that has ever happened to me to get a land deal."

Cretia nearly spit out her tea. That wasn't difficult. That was despicable. "What happened?"

"I ran away from home and ended up on PEI." Marie smiled, though her eyes still held a dose of sadness. "I met Seth's uncle Big Jack on the ferry here. I wish you could meet him. He took his wife Aretha to the Bahamas for an extended vacation. But he's the type of man who recognized my pain and looked for a way to heal it. He asked me to help him get the Red Door Inn open. Seth was here too—and despite my best efforts, he won my heart. Maybe you know what I mean?"

Finn. Why did her mind always go back to Finn?

"So what happened with your dad?"

"My mom passed away when I was sixteen, and since then, my dad has tried to make my life miserable. It's like he wants company in his own misery. And for years, I thought that's how fathers were. I thought that's what family was—dragging each other down. But Big Jack showed me a different love. He showed me that family isn't always the one you're born into. Sometimes it's the ones you choose to love. The ones who choose to love you back. My dad always chose money over people. And that's not love. That's greed."

"Do you still speak to your dad?"

"No. And my kids won't know him either. But they know the love of their dad Seth and their adopted grandfather Big Jack. And they know that God loves them more than anyone here on earth could."

"You just cut your dad off?"

Marie dunked her tea bag a few times as she chewed on her bottom lip. When she looked up, there was a certainty in her eyes. "No matter what I chose, it was always going to be hard. I could choose to keep him in my life and deal with the way he treated me and my family. Or I could set boundaries so that I wouldn't continue to let him hurt me—and so he wouldn't ever hurt my children. Both would be hard. But I chose the one that was best for my kids. I can't change him. I can pray for him. I can hope the best for him. But I can't deny what he's done and how he's hurt those around him. I can't make him into a different man, but I can choose how

I will respond. I can choose how I will treat those I love."
Marie leaned forward, her gaze heavy and solemn. "And I choose not to carry on any of those hurtful traits."

So can you.

Marie hadn't spoken the words, but they hung between them as loud as if she had.

Cretia cringed. It wasn't that easy. She'd spent eighteen years in a broken house with a broken mom. Eleven years with just the two of them. The fractured parts were ingrained in her. If she never settled down, she couldn't succumb to them. And she couldn't pass them on to anyone else.

"I'm sorry you've had such a hard relationship with your mom," Marie said. "But there are people here who would welcome you into their family. I saw Kathleen again today, and she was still talking about how much she enjoyed your visit. *I* would love it if you stayed. And I have a feeling that there's a certain dog breeder down the road who would be pretty happy if you stuck around too."

Just say yes.

That was all she had to do. Say she would stay. Choose the island. Choose a home. Choose them.

Choose this hard instead of the hard of not having a home.

Her hands began to tremble, and she snatched them into her lap before they could betray the battle within.

"I appreciate you saying that," she whispered.

"Just know that you always have a place here when you come to visit. And I do hope you will."

"Thank you." Cretia grabbed her box and hugged it to her chest with a swift farewell. Then she ran up to her bedroom, closed the door, and did what she should have done more than a week before. She bought a plane ticket off the island.

Nineteen

When Cretia strolled into his barn that afternoon, Finn knew something was wrong. Though she greeted him in her normal way and gave Roberta a wide berth per usual, there was a stiffness in her shoulders that he'd never seen before. Not even on that first day. That day, after the incident in the harbor, she'd been hesitant with him, unsure how to respond.

Today, there was a chasm between them.

He pretended otherwise, busying himself with cleaning the rabbit hutch, and only glanced up to ask, "Later than usual today. Everything all right?"

"Mm-hmm." Her hands fidgeted with the hem of her blue sweater, the one she'd worn that first fateful day. "You?"

"Good." He dragged the word out, not sure if he should nudge her for a bit of the truth. Eventually her inside processing would slip out, so he didn't push.

"Can I help with something?"

"Want to warm up the bottles for Sonny and Cher?"

She nodded and disappeared silently into the tack room.

Joe watched her go, then sent Finn a worried look before trotting after her. The big dog wasn't the only one concerned. The next few hours followed with much of the same. They fed the goats, and Cretia brushed Abner's coat, giving him a gentle kiss on the forehead as she finished. They took the Fab Four out to the pasture and played with them, tossing balls and bones and cheering them on as they brought back the toys. After pulling out her phone, Cretia captured some video of the would-be Muppets, which drew her first real smile of the day. But as Finn opened the door to their pen, her smile disappeared. She hugged and squeezed first Paul, then George, then Ringo, and finally John, giving him a firm scratch on his belly.

She didn't wait for Finn to head into the whelping room, and by the time he reached her side, she'd knelt next to Bella. "You're such a good mom," Cretia whispered, rubbing the big girl's ears. "And these little guys are—" For a moment, it sounded like her voice broke on a sob, and Finn touched her shoulder. Shrugging off his hand, she petted one of the pups. Their eyes had just opened, but they still scooted around the box, mostly blind. "Which one did you save?" she asked.

Finn looked at the eleven pups—eight of them all black, their markings nearly indistinguishable, and two of them brown. Finally, he spotted the gray one and plucked him up. "This is Tater."

Her lips twitched, but her smile didn't reach her eyes. As she took him and held him to her chest, he squirmed and squeaked against her. "Hey there, little guy. You had quite the start, but I know you're going to be a great rescuer. Grow big and strong and do exactly what Finn tells you to. All right?"

That was when the truth landed, nearly buckling his knees

and stealing his breath. She was saying goodbye. First to the animals—and soon to him. The week he'd thought he would have had been cut in half. Their time together had been stolen. And he didn't know who to ask for it back.

"Your laptop came in, didn't it?"

She nodded.

"So you're leaving?"

She didn't look up from the wiggling puppy trying to suck on the collar of her shirt. "That's always been the plan."

"When?" The word sounded like it had been raked over gravel.

"Tomorrow morning. I have a flight out of Charlottetown."

This was supposed to be easier. He'd set up boundaries—albeit a little bit late—to make this manageable. To make the goodbye natural.

The problem was that he didn't *only* like kissing her. Of course he enjoyed it. He wasn't a complete fool.

But kissing wasn't even his favorite thing about her or the thing he would miss most. After she left, who would argue with him and tease him and make him laugh? Who would nudge him and prod him and drive to the other side of the island to pick up a cow with him? Who would fill his days with chatter and nonsense and creativity?

He'd thought he didn't need any help, but those were things he couldn't do for or by himself. Cretia filled a place in his heart that he hadn't even known was empty until she clung to his neck and shivered against him on that first walk to the Red Door.

His dad had always said that God had made his mom just for him. Now Finn understood what that meant. But if God had made Cretia for him, was he just expected to let her go?

His future stretched out before him, dim and bleak. He wanted to pull her into his arms and beg her to stay. He wanted to hold on to her for the rest of forever.

He just didn't know how to do that without asking her to give up who she was or what she wanted.

So he asked the only question he could think of. "Can I drive you to the airport?"

She shook her head. "It'll be really early, and you have puppies and cows and goats relying on you." She tried for a smile that didn't land. "I've already lined up a taxi to pick me up."

The chasm was growing, and he didn't know if he should just let it or if he should fight for their last minutes together. There was no answer, only painful choices. One option hurt now. The other would hurt later.

Maybe it was better to give her space. "I guess you'll need to pack and get a good night's sleep tonight."

"Yep." She leaned over the box's wall and set Tater back into his spot. "I should probably get to it."

He tried to bite his tongue, to swallow the words that insisted on being spoken, but he couldn't. "Can I walk you back to the inn?"

When she finally met his gaze, her eyes were glassy and filled with sadness. She bit her lips together, maybe because her vocal cords felt paralyzed too. Finally, she nodded.

By the time he locked up the barn and called Joe to join them, the sun had reached the horizon, splashing orange and pink stripes across the evening sky. They walked in silence, past the lobster boats in the harbor and the spot where they'd first met. When they reached the beginning of the boardwalk, Finn grabbed her hand, needing something to remind him that she was still there, still a part of his life. Even if only for a few more minutes.

His boots echoed on the wooden planks, and he nodded a greeting to the Huntingtons, who were out walking their dog. Joe barked but didn't leave Cretia's side. He had to sense the change coming too.

When they reached the set of stairs halfway down the boardwalk, he tugged on Cretia's hand, stopping her on the first step. Nearly eye to eye with her, he couldn't deny the misery in her trembling smile.

"You could stay," he whispered. "I *want* you to stay."

With a shake of her head, she said, "You could come with me." But there was no hope in her words.

"I can't leave. I have too many mouths counting on me."

"I know." She blinked, and a tear escaped down the pink of her cheek, leaving a silver track in its wake. "I thought I'd ask, just in case."

Cupping her face in his hands, he leaned his forehead ever so gently against hers and inhaled deeply. "Cretia Martin, you are the most amazing woman. I'm so glad that I got to know you." Pinching his eyes closed, he dropped his hands and pressed his lips against her cheek for a long second before stepping back.

"I'll be forever grateful you were there at the harbor. You and Joe." She squatted down in front of Joe and hugged his neck as he licked her cheek and slobbered on her shoulder. "Thank you, buddy. You're the best boy."

Then she turned, walked up the steps, and disappeared from sight. Leaving him adrift, with no one to pull him out of the water.

Finn woke the next morning with a wild urge to see his parents. Maybe he hoped there would be some magic in his mom's hug or a word of wisdom from his dad. But as always, the chores wouldn't wait. The animals had to eat, and he couldn't leave them alone, even for one night.

As he checked on Bella and her pups, an odd idea popped into his head. It sounded a lot like Cretia's voice. *You don't have to do it alone.*

Maybe that was right, but practically speaking, the work had to be done. And there was no one else to do it.

He rinsed out and replaced Bella's water bowl and made sure she had plenty of kibble before scratching her head. "Doing okay, girl?" She barked, and her pups yipped their agreement. Everyone was good and healthy.

Maybe he could . . . It would just be for a night. He wasn't abandoning them or foisting his responsibilities on anyone else. Everyone needed a day off every now and then. Everyone got sick once in a while.

He hadn't had a day off in more than ten years. Maybe it was time.

After the stalls were mucked and every one of the animals fed and watered, Finn trudged back to the house and collapsed in his desk chair. Maybe it was his imagination, but he could almost smell Cretia's shampoo lingering at this spot where she'd ordered her new electronics, tracked down her laptop, and looked like she fit right into his home.

Scraping his nails across his whiskers, he blew out a giant breath as Joe sauntered up to him and plopped his big head on his leg. "I miss her too, boy."

Sitting around his house wasn't going to fix the ache in his chest, so he flipped open his phone and punched in the number to the landline across the street. His fingers still remembered the pattern his mom had made him memorize.

"Hello?"

"Hey, Natalie, it's Finn. Is Justin around?"

"Yeah, let me get him for you." There was a noisy handoff on the other side, first Natalie calling for her husband and then a few whispered words that sounded an awful lot like, "Cretia left this morning."

Good to know the town grapevine was in perfect working order.

"Finn, what's up?" Justin said.

"Listen, I was thinking about—that is, if you're available—"

He scrubbed a hand through his hair and rolled his eyes at himself. He sounded like an imbecile. Cretia would probably tell him it was because he was out of practice. He just needed to get his inside processing out, so he took a deep breath and released his words with it.

"Would you mind feeding my animals tonight and tomorrow morning?"

Justin laughed. "Man, we've been neighbors our whole lives, and I've been waiting for you to ask. You've helped me out with a dozen projects the last few years, and Natalie said I was taking advantage of you."

Finn cracked a smile. "Thanks. I appreciate it."

"I'll be over in a minute, and you can show me where your feed is and who gets what."

Finn completed the quick tour, thanked Justin for his help, packed a bag, and was on the road within an hour.

Joe Jr. sat shotgun, his fur waving in the wind as he stuck his head out the rolled-down window. Finn savored the midday sun and the fresh air as they tooled along the highway, but he still felt a strange weight on his shoulders. It wasn't precisely tied to Cretia, though her words echoed in his mind. *"I only met your dad once, but that doesn't sound like him."*

For his whole adult life, he'd believed his dad questioned his ability to carry on their legacy. But with one sentence, Cretia had planted a seed of doubt in that certainty.

She was right. It didn't sound like him. There was a lie somewhere, and only one person could tell him the truth.

The ambling two-lane roads of the island carried him south, past rolling hills of alfalfa and potatoes and farmhouses in the blues, reds, and oranges of the island sunrise. The noon rays overhead turned yellow fields of canola more brilliant than the sun itself.

Joe barked and spun around in his seat until Finn buried his hand into his thick coat. "Easy, boy. We're almost there."

As he pulled up to the curb outside his parents' home, he saw his dad standing in the front yard, a hand on his hip and his head cocked at a strange angle.

"I wasn't expecting to see you today, son," he called as soon as Finn hopped out of the truck.

"Thought I'd come for a little visit. That okay?"

"Of course. But if we'd known you were coming, your mom wouldn't have gone to the ladies' tea at the church, and you wouldn't be stuck with just me."

Finn offered a half smile. "I brought some companionship

too." He let Joe out of the truck, and the dog bounded across the yard, spinning circles around his dad.

His dad held up the garden hose he'd been using to water his wife's flowers, and Joe bit at the slow stream like it was lunch. "Good to see some things haven't changed." He chuckled as he held his arms wide for a hug.

Finn stepped into the embrace, the force of his dad's clap against his back setting something loose and shoring up something else.

"Where's that pretty girl we met? She didn't come with you? Your mom liked her, you know."

Finn nodded. "I liked her too. But she left."

"You run her off?" His dad absolutely meant it in jest, but the words still made something inside him ache.

"I hope not." He didn't even try for a smile. "I asked her to stay."

The jovial grin that was so much a part of his dad's face dimmed, and he bent over slowly to turn off the water. "And she left anyway? I thought she really liked you."

He lifted one shoulder. She had liked him. Just not enough.

"Sit with me for a little while." His dad groaned as he lowered himself to the top of the three steps leading to the white front door. They'd chosen a cute bungalow the color of bricks, just one story so he didn't have to navigate the stairs. They'd been in the house more than eight years, and somehow, it still didn't feel like their home to Finn. The green farmhouse beside the red barn was where he always pictured them.

Maybe because sometimes he still felt like he was just watching over things while his parents were on holiday.

"You want to talk about her?"

When his dad was settled, Finn dropped down next to him and watched Joe find a shady spot in the grass to roll around. "Not really." Of course, that didn't stop him from thinking—or dreaming—about her. "I thought maybe I'd spend the night, though."

Finn studied his dad's reaction, looking for any sign of disappointment. Instead, his dad's smile grew. "Well, that's new. You haven't spent a night away from the old house since you took over." Then his eyes narrowed, his bushy gray eyebrows bunching together in the middle of his forehead. "Is everything all right? Is this about your girlfriend leaving?"

"She wasn't my girlfriend."

His dad made a sound deep in his throat that said he begged to differ.

Finn pushed on before his dad could argue the point. "Do you remember Milo McGinniss?"

"'Course I do. We were neighbors most of my life. He sold his property and moved to the mainland years ago. What made you think of him?"

"I know . . . I just . . ." Finn folded his hands before him, resting his forearms on his knees and taking a deep breath. Cretia had gotten him into the habit of voicing his inside processing—or at least thinking about it like that. But considering it and actually doing it required entirely different muscle groups. And the muscles he needed to pluck up the nerve to speak had atrophied somewhere along the line.

"Son?" His dad clapped a hand on the back of his shoulder. "You can tell me anything."

This was the side of his dad that he'd known most of his life. Encouraging. Kind. Caring. It just didn't line up with his memory of that day in the barn—which was somehow so much easier to believe. He'd heard once that character was what you did when no one was watching. And Finn had always figured that true feelings were what you said about someone when they couldn't hear you. Or—in the case of Cretia's trolls—what they wouldn't say to your face.

Cretia could knock them down with a simple block button. Finn couldn't exactly block his dad. But if he knew the truth, then maybe he'd know what he had to do to truly earn his dad's respect.

Closing his eyes, he opened his mouth and prayed the words would make sense. "I was about twenty, I think, and I was doing chores in the barn one morning. I didn't mean to eavesdrop, but you and Milo walked in, and I heard him tell you that I couldn't handle the business. That I was going to run it into the ground and ruin our family's legacy."

With the truth finally out there, Finn held his breath.

His dad nodded slowly. "That sounds about right."

Finn's head spun, and his pulse thundered in his ears.

So his dad *had* agreed with Milo.

"Best as I recall, he wasn't the first one to come to me saying those things either."

His dad had clearly agreed with the others too.

Finn launched from the stoop, wringing his hands in the front of his shirt as he paced the width of the lawn and back. Joe looked up from his back scratch on the grass but didn't bother coming to his side. Joe could probably feel the tension flying off of him in waves and wanted no part of it.

For once, he was a smart dog.

"Finn?" His dad pushed himself up, slower and stiffer. "What's gotten into you?"

Finn flung his hand out in the direction of the past. "You

told him you didn't expect anything from me. It was like you were telling him you were certain I was going to fail."

His dad caught his arm in a firm grip, but Finn couldn't match his gaze, his periphery turning cloudy.

"I did say that. I said that to every single one of the men who came sniffing around after my diagnosis."

Finn blinked hard to clear his eyes. "Sniffing around for what?"

"The business. They wanted to buy it from me. They thought you were too young to take it on, to make it succeed, to carry it into the future."

"And you didn't expect much from me because . . ."

"Because I didn't want them sniffin' around you, waiting for you to fail. I figured if they thought the status quo was all I was hoping for, they'd know I wasn't going to be disappointed if the business didn't take off right away under your leadership. You and I both know that there are good years and not-as-good years. But I knew you'd figure it out. I just didn't want you to have to deal with guys coming after your business—especially right after you took over—saying I thought you should sell."

Planting his hands on his hips and hunching his shoulders, Finn let out a long sigh. "Why didn't you ever tell me?"

"I didn't want you to worry that I'd regret not selling it. Or that you'd think there was something you could do that wouldn't make me proud of you." His dad paused, his head tilting to the side. "Did you think all this time that I thought you couldn't handle the dogs? That you would somehow ruin what my dad built? Psh. Not likely."

Finn clapped a hand to the back of his neck. "I don't get it. What is it that you expect from me?"

His dad licked his lips slowly and scratched his chin. "Well, I suppose I want you to love God and treat others with respect. I expect you to work hard and care for those under your watch. Your mom would sure approve if you fell in love and gave us a few grandbabies."

"Dad."

"I'm serious. She would."

With a shake of his head, Finn met his dad's gaze. "I've been trying for years to expand the business on my own—to build onto the barn and take in more dogs. To somehow prove you wrong *and* make you proud of me."

Something like compassion sparked in his dad's eyes. "You can stop trying. I will always be proud of you. You're my son. And even if you weren't, you're a man of integrity and generosity. You help your neighbors and rescue damsels from the harbor."

His cheeks burned at the memory, and his heart squeezed at the reminder. But he forced himself to stay in the conversation. "So, you don't care that I'm just making ends meet? Or that most of the profit goes to feeding ornery cattle? Or that I just took in a mini Highland cow?"

His dad's eyebrow rose. "Your mom will want to meet him."

Finn stared him down until his dad's smile broke free.

"I couldn't care less. I want you to be all of the things you already are, and I want you to enjoy your life. If that means filling the barn with stray animals, fine. I wanted to pass something of value to you. Whatever you choose to do with it is up to you."

Finn looked down then, a smile tugging at his mouth as freedom settled on his shoulders. "Cretia had this wild idea.

The neighbor kids like to come over to visit the animals, and she said she thought that tourists would pay to visit the property, to bottle-feed baby goats and, you know . . . pet furry cows."

His dad chuckled—not a laugh of disbelief or derision but a laugh of pure joy. "I bet they would. Come on inside and tell me more."

Twenty

As flights went, her trip to London was the worst Cretia had ever experienced. It wasn't that it was so terribly long. The ones to Australia had taken more than twice the time. It wasn't even that she had a bad seatmate. Her frequent flier status had added up to pretty consistent first-class upgrades. On this flight, the window seat beside her had been taken by a petite woman in a button-down blouse and crepe skirt. She'd refused a drink from the flight attendant, pulled a sleeping mask from her carry-on, and promptly fallen asleep.

On any other plane, Cretia would have thanked God for the peace. But this particular plane had absolutely nothing that could hold her attention.

Of course, it had all of the usual gadgets—a screen on the back of the seat in front of her stocked with every B-list movie from the previous five years, endless channels of music, and even old-school magazines in the seat pocket.

When she'd first started traveling, those magazines had been her inspiration. They offered clues and suggestions for countries she'd never even heard of. She'd scribbled down their names and looked them up later. Articles in those magazines made her curious if the street tacos in Madrid could truly rival the best Michelin-star restaurants or if cliff diving was as wonderfully freeing as it looked.

They did and it was.

But there wasn't a single thing on this flight from Toronto to Heathrow that could distract her from the pain in the pit of her stomach. It wasn't hunger—though she hadn't eaten in almost a day. It wasn't physical either—though every joint in her body screamed for relief.

It was all in her head.

Or, more accurately, in her heart.

That left her to shift from side to side, trying to find a comfortable position for sleep. But even with her eyes closed, a pillow under her head, and a blanket tucked beneath her chin, all she could see was the pain in Finn's eyes right before he'd kissed her cheek and she'd walked away.

Worst. Flight. Ever.

The sun was already fighting its way through the London clouds when they landed. Her phone said it was 6:32 on a Saturday morning. Her heart said it might as well be noon on a Thursday.

Somewhere in the critical-thinking part of her brain, she knew she should capture some content of the morning in the historic city. But as she dragged her carry-on off the plane and through customs, only one thing kept her feet moving—the hope of a cozy bed and dreamless sleep.

Outside the terminal, she hailed one of the city's famous black cabs and crawled into the back.

"Where to, miss?"

"Leonardo Royal—" She stumbled on the words, her

tongue as sluggish as the rest of her. "The hotel by St. Paul's?" She'd almost skipped making a reservation during her layover in Toronto, but now she wanted to hug her past self. Present Cretia could barely sit upright, let alone find a room for the night.

"Of course. I know it well." Her driver's accent was thick but friendly, and he smiled at her as he pulled away from the curb and into traffic on the wrong side of the road. "Is this your first time in London?"

"No." Just the first time she desperately wanted to be elsewhere. Her previous three trips had been packed with exploring the history and architecture and culture of vibrant London. This trip was an escape—the first flight she could get. Far enough away that she wouldn't be tempted to go right back to the island. Right back to Finn.

Squeezing her eyes shut only released a few tears, and she knuckled them away, telling herself that she was just tired and that the reflection of the sun off the other cars bothered her eyes. Whatever lie she had to tell herself to get through the day. The next few days.

The bed in her room at the Leonardo Royal was everything she'd hoped it would be. Soft and cozy. Warm and soothing. Except for the location. About three thousand miles west would be better. Under the roof of the Red Door Inn.

Slamming a pillow over her face, she screamed into it. It wasn't fair. She wasn't supposed to meet someone so *right*. Someone so good and kind and perfect for her. Someone who made her wish her life could be different.

She'd been thoroughly satisfied—more than content—right up until Finn Chaffey had scooped her up on that boardwalk and carried her to safety.

The tears came in earnest then. Tears of anger and pain, denial and grief. She didn't bother trying to stem their flow, just letting them come. Great big, silent tears that leaked out of the corners of her eyes and pooled on the white Egyptian cotton pillowcase.

Cretia awoke with a start. The room was pitch-black, but she immediately knew it wasn't *her* room, the one at the Red Door anyway. She blinked against the darkness, her eyelids clearly lined with sandpaper. Pressing her hands to her eyes, she tried to make them tear up, but nothing came. Apparently, the crying jag before she'd fallen asleep had dried up all of her reserves.

Forcing herself to roll out of bed, she stumbled toward the bathroom, nearly losing a toe to the leg of the bed in the process. Pain shot across her foot, and she shoved her fist to her mouth to keep from terrifying the guests in the room next door. Flicking on the light, she shrank from its brilliance, then turned from the hideous reflection in the mirror. Eyes swollen and red, hair a disaster, face puffy, cheeks splotchy. Every bit was the worst version of herself.

At least her outsides matched her insides.

With a sigh, she turned on the exquisitely scrolled silver faucet, filled up the white marble sink, and splashed cold water on her face. When she looked up again, the mirror still showed the very worst version of herself, only wet.

She had two choices. Wallow or do her job.

The first was pointless. Especially since all of this was the result of a choice she'd already made. Leaving had been the right choice. Even if it hurt for a little while. Or a long while.

She had a feeling that she'd think of Finn years from now and remember what might have been. By then the sharp edges would be softer, the pain replaced only by fond memories. For now, she needed a distraction.

After a steaming shower that fogged up the mirror and wrinkled her fingers and toes, Cretia got dressed and applied enough makeup to look human—though nothing was going to make her camera-ready. But that was okay. She didn't need to be in the video when she was mere steps from St. Paul's Cathedral, Christopher Wren's architectural masterpiece. She'd never captured it, though she didn't quite know why. She'd been in this area before, stayed in this same hotel.

She'd rectify that this morning.

Grabbing her backpack with all of her new equipment, she stepped into the hallway, only then realizing the silence. The plush hallway was empty, no other doors opening or closing. She glanced at her phone. Probably because it was 4:35 in the morning. Any normal person was sleeping.

Ignoring her growling stomach, she tiptoed through the corridor toward the elevator, then through the lobby. Outside, the cool morning air greeted her with the scent of the Thames, and her hunger pangs immediately vanished.

She couldn't help but compare London to her precious north shore, to the smell of fresh air and salt water that greeted her, to the sunshine and life of the island. Which wasn't fair. No place was like Prince Edward Island, but London had plenty to its credit, like the massive building that loomed before her. Its enormous dome and outstretched wings shone like a beacon even in the relative darkness.

The street was nearly empty, save a few cars slipping by on their way to somewhere more important. The lights of a coffee shop flickered on as a shadow inside flipped a placard to "Open." Signs of life.

Cretia strolled west along the street and paused when she came to a bench. There she set up her phone on her retractable tripod, changing the settings to capture a time-lapse video. Then she waited.

The sun began its warm morning embrace as it reached between the city's buildings—both ancient and new—turning the sky pink and peach and settling a gentle glow over the day. As it rose, even behind gray clouds, people came. First, a few walking into the cathedral—perhaps the choir or the ushers. Then more. And more. And just before eight, flocks came. Families with children, little girls in hats and dads straightening their sons' ties. Distinguished gentlemen leaning heavily on canes. Young women in floral dresses and high heels.

Cretia looked down at her tan linen pants, blue blouse, and slip-on sneakers. She wasn't dressed for a visit to St. Paul's, but something about it called to her, invited her inside. Church attendance hadn't been a regular part of her life after her abuelita died, and she couldn't remember the last time she'd sat through a whole service. But she believed there was truth in the Scriptures. Perhaps—like Marie had said—there was a God who loved her more than her mother had ever been capable of.

If she walked inside, maybe she'd hear more of that. And she wanted more of it in her life.

She packed up her gear, stuffed it into her backpack, and hurried across the street toward the entrance. A driver laid on his horn as she rushed in front of his car, and she waved her apology, too eager to be inside to stop.

When she reached the black-and-white-checkered marble

floor beyond the enormous wooden door, she froze. Hun-dreds upon hundreds of chairs filled the cathedral floor in neat rows, all facing a wooden platform at the front. And be-yond the podium, the choir stood singing like she'd thought only angels could.

She slipped into a seat in the last row, closed her eyes, and listened. She could have sat there for hours, the choir's sweet hymns of praise wrapping around her, soothing the dark spots of her heart.

She was still lost in their perfect melodies when a young priest with dark hair and olive skin walked up the steps and into an intricately carved box lined with vibrant red fabric. He placed his hands on either side of the pulpit and took a deep breath.

"John 3:16: 'For God so loved the world, that he gave his only begotten Son, that whosoever believeth in him should not perish, but have everlasting life.'" The priest's voice rang out soothing and clear. "One of the most well-known verses in all of the Bible. We quote it, we memorize it, yet we often miss its truth. God loved the world so much that he gave up what he loved most."

Cretia swallowed against a suddenly dry throat, squeezing her folded hands together in her lap. She'd heard that verse a hundred times, memorized it in Sunday school many years before. But she'd never thought about it in that way.

"Later in the Gospel of John, we read, 'Greater love hath no man than this, that a man lay down his life for his friends.' My friends, this much is clear in these two verses. The heart of love is always sacrifice. When was the last time you gave up something precious to you to love someone else well?"

The priest paused, but his words rang in her ears over and over, striking at her heart.

The heart of love is always sacrifice.

Finn had let her go. He'd done everything he could to make it easier on them both. He'd sacrificed his desires for her best chance at happiness. Not because he didn't care but because he cared so much that he was willing to lay down his own wants, the longings of his own heart. So Cretia could pursue her dreams.

And what had she given up?

Not a single thing.

The tear ducts that had been dry earlier that morning flooded again, and her bottom lip trembled as she held her hand over her mouth. If she wanted to be with Finn, she'd have to sacrifice. Her lifestyle. Her job. Her growing community.

All of that she could give up. None of it mattered nearly as much as Finn.

But it wasn't enough.

If she wanted a future with him, she'd have to put down roots on the island. She'd have to have a home and stuff and *junk.*

If she really loved Finn, she'd have to sacrifice the fear of turning into her mom.

But there was no question that she loved Finn. If only she could show him how much.

Twenty-One

When Finn arrived back home Sunday afternoon, he hopped out of the cab of his truck, Joe Jr. close behind him. The barn and the house were still standing. That was a good sign. As he opened the sliding door to the barn, the scent of fresh hay greeted him. The dogs barked in greeting from their kennels, no real urgency or need in their voices.

Squatting down, he checked their water bowls. Fresh and full. Bella and her puppies were good too. Sonny and Cher bleated their greeting, and Abner scraped his horns along the wall of his pen. The rabbits squeaked their greetings too. Even Roberta practically smiled at him as he rubbed her face.

Probably because Cretia wasn't with him.

The thought simultaneously made him laugh and made his heart hurt.

"It's going to be like that for a while," he said out loud as he pressed a fist to the middle of his chest. Joe shot him a concerned look, but he waved it off. Cretia had said she talked to herself sometimes—that was how she had processed much of her life while traveling alone.

Well, he figured he was just as much on his own as she was most of the time. And if a little bit of his inside thoughts made it out into the barn, there was no one else to bother.

"But there could be."

Closing his eyes, he saw Cretia's face right before him and heard the urgency in her voice when he'd told her he needed to prove to his dad that he could make the business into something more. *"You don't have to."*

His dad had said the same thing the night before. His mom too.

He didn't have to do it all by himself.

And he didn't have to do it just like his dad and his grandfather before him. He could do something different. Something special. Something new.

Taking a slow spin around the barn, he looked at all the changes he'd made over the years and the animals he'd rescued. This wasn't the barn his dad had managed. The walls and the roof may have been the same, but there was more to this place.

Just like Cretia had said.

He snapped open his phone and called Justin to thank him for helping out for a second night.

"Anytime," Justin said. "Seriously. I mean it."

Finn smiled. "I'll take you up on that offer sometime." Then he closed his phone and tucked it in his pocket.

Another thought rocked through him—a familiar face around his barn, the spindly arms of a boy hanging around Joe's neck. He'd thought Jack might be helpful in a few years. But maybe . . . with a little bit of training . . .

Patting his leg, Finn called Joe to follow him, and the big dog bounded around the house and down the lane, eager to stretch his legs after the ride in the car. They walked around the dock, past the spot where Cretia had fallen in, and along the boardwalk.

For just a moment Finn let himself remember what it had felt like to carry her in his arms, the weight of her body against his, the warmth of her hands on his shoulders. She'd smelled like seawater and fish, and somehow it was still the sweetest memory.

He let himself remember it—remember her—even as he traipsed up the steps where she had said goodbye. Where he'd kissed her cheek and let her go.

He wanted to call himself every name in the book, but it had been the right decision. Begging her to stay, making her feel guilty that she couldn't—that wouldn't help either of them. Or make the impossible possible.

Her memory wasn't going anywhere anytime soon. But it might help him to have something else to focus on.

That had been his mom's suggestion. And, of course, his dad had agreed with her.

As Finn topped the stairs up the embankment in front of the inn, Joe let out a bark and raced across the street, dashing over the Red Door's lush lawn to bowl over an unsuspecting Jack. The kid cried out in excitement as Joe landed on top of him, the two of them wrestling.

"You okay, Jack?" Finn called.

The only response was a laugh as the dog licked his face.

Yeah, this could work.

"Finn, you're back!" Marie waved from one of the white Adirondack chairs on the inn's porch, Seth by her side. "We missed you at church this morning, but Kathleen said you stayed an extra night with your folks."

Finn smiled and nodded. Maybe he didn't even need to share his plans with them. Once he'd thought them, the whole town probably knew about them.

Bounding up the steps, he reached out to shake the other man's hand. "Good to see you, Seth."

"How are your parents? Everything okay?" Marie's words were laced with fear. Probably because she knew that he'd asked Justin to take care of his animals at the last minute.

Finn quickly waved off her concerns as he leaned against the porch's white railing. "Everyone's fine. I just needed a . . . I needed a little breather."

"Oh, sure." Marie's face fell, and he knew he'd never have to speak Cretia's name if he didn't want to.

Which he didn't.

Except he did.

"Have you heard from her?" He cringed as the question slipped out, like far too much inside processing had lately.

Marie glanced at her husband, who reached over and squeezed her hand. "She wired me some money for her room at the inn. She must have sent it as soon as she landed in Toronto because she'd barely been gone six hours. The message just said 'Thanks.'"

That sounded right. Cretia, who didn't want to rely on anyone else, had called him out on his own unwillingness to ask for assistance. He'd point out her pot calling his kettle black the next time he saw her.

If he ever saw her again.

He needed that distraction. Big-time. "I guess that means I still owe her a favor if she paid for her own room. And you still owe me one."

Marie's smile broke through. "I don't know about that."

"Hear me out? I have an idea."

Seth leaned forward, resting his forearms on his knees, and Finn took that as an open invitation.

"Cretia had this idea that tourists might want to come see my barn. Maybe I could teach them about how to care for the animals and give them a whole experience. Let them hold bunnies and pet cows and bottle-feed kids."

"Oh, Finn." Marie jumped to her feet. "That's a wonderful idea. We can recommend you to all of our guests. When will you open?"

"I'm hoping for next summer."

"Oh." Marie's excitement simmered. "I guess we can wait."

"But I'm going to need some help around my place. There'll be a lot to do to get set up, and I didn't know if"—he shot a look over his shoulder at Jack and Joe—"maybe Jack would like to help me out. It might be a little more work than summer camp, but I could use another set of hands. Especially with eleven puppies to train."

"Really? You want me to help train puppies?" Jack's footsteps pounded up the stairs as he barreled toward his dad, his dark curls blowing in the wind. "Can I? Please!"

Seth looked up at his wife, who didn't even try to hide her smile. "Are you sure, Finn?"

"Jack's as good with the dogs as I was at his age."

Joe joined them on the porch, bumping his nose against Finn for attention. He gave the dog a good scratch behind his ears. "I'm pretty sure Joe agrees."

Marie caught her husband's gaze, unspoken words passing between them.

"I'm thinking three or four hours a day, five days a week.

I can pick him up and drop him off, and I'll pay him a small salary."

That offer made Marie choke out a laugh. "Are you serious? You can't pay him to have more fun than he'd have anyway."

"Besides, if you pay him, how are we doing you a favor?" Seth asked.

"Well . . . um . . ." Finn scratched at the couple days of growth on his chin. "He still needs your permission."

"Fine."

Jack let out a whoop of joy and ran up to hug him about the waist. "Thank you, Mr. Finn. I promise, I'll work hard and listen and take the best care of your dogs."

Putting a hand on top of the kid's mop of hair, Finn smiled. He was sure he would.

Finn woke early the next morning before the sun had even deigned to make an appearance, not exactly eager to get out of bed. But at least he had a goal in mind, something to work toward. And he knew he had his father's respect and his approval to try a new business model.

He attempted to drum up some excitement about the day, but as he pulled on his Henley and his fleece vest, he couldn't find more than his usual obligatory motivation. The animals would be hungry, and they'd need fresh water. They were his responsibility—even if he'd rather stay in bed and pull the covers over his head and pretend that his heart wasn't still trying to find its new rhythm.

He stamped his feet into his boots by the back door and trudged across the yard. Joe followed him, though maybe he could sense his master's lethargy because he kept his distance, more than a few paces back.

Suddenly Joe shot past him, racing for the barn and barking at the closed door. His feet skittered, and his hind parts wiggled a strange dance.

"Joe? What's up?"

But the dog only gave a low, needy woof. And then again, as though to make sure that Finn understood the urgency.

It was probably a skunk or a fox or something. "Calm down. It's fine." But when he reached the barn door, it was unlocked. Only a handful of people knew he even locked his barn—let alone where the key was stashed in a small hidey-hole in the barn wall. And he didn't think his parents or Justin had made the trip to care for his animals.

His heart hammered against his ribs. He had definitely locked the barn the night before.

"Joe," he hissed, wrestling the dog behind his leg. "Get out of the way." Of what, he wasn't exactly sure. But he wouldn't let Joe be in the direct line of whatever fire might come. Or be the first to stumble upon whatever was inside.

Sliding the door open a crack, he poked his head around it. The light inside cast a yellow glow over the kennels and pens. And a big former milk cow wandered around the middle of the floor.

"Roberta?" He spoke her name as though she would explain how she had gotten loose and why she was roaming around the barn, one big brown eye focused on the Fab Four, who all stood on hind legs, faces pressed against the fence.

"I had to let her out so I could muck her stall."

The familiar voice was like a long-forgotten hymn, filling him up and stealing his breath in one note.

"Cretia," he breathed as he raced in the direction of her voice, stopping short of tumbling into the wheelbarrow containing the remnants of Roberta's pen. Inside, the woman who had filled so many of his thoughts the last few days and long before that leaned against the wooden handle of his rake, a smile tugging at the corner of her mouth.

"Cretia?" He said her name again to make sure that it was really her, that she was truly back. "How did you . . . Where did you . . . Why . . . ?" He couldn't complete any of his thoughts when she smiled at him like that, coy and flirty and joyful.

"I flew back last night. Marie had said if I ever needed a place to stay on the island, she'd be offended if I didn't stay with her. Then this morning, I had an epiphany, and I had to come to the barn."

He took a small step toward her, longing to close the distance between them for good. "An epiphany, huh? Sounds important."

"I figured out why Roberta didn't like me."

"What?" Cretia was back. His heart was full again. And she wanted to talk about an ornery cow?

"She couldn't see me. I kept sneaking up on her blind side, and she didn't know I was a friend. The whole time I was away, I kept thinking that something had to be wrong. There was no way that every other animal in this barn liked me except her. So I came over this morning to show her I'm on her side."

"You came back to the island because of my cow?"

"Well . . ." Cretia shrugged, her face fighting a smile that he could have seen coming from across the harbor. "Among other things. But Roberta was a key factor."

As her shoulders shook with silent laughter, he realized what she was wearing—the yellow plaid flannel that he'd wrapped around her once upon a time. She'd rolled up the sleeves to her elbows and tied the hem in a cute bow. But he still knew it as his own.

"What is this?" He tugged at the collar of the shirt.

"I found it in the tack room. And I have a limited wardrobe. Plus, I didn't want to get my clothes dirty. I figured if you'd shared once, maybe you'd be willing to share again. Besides, maybe Roberta would think I was you long enough to let me show her I'm a friend."

So reasonable. So ridiculous. So Cretia.

"Sweet cinnamon rolls, I've missed you." The words came out on a sigh as he charged into the stall, walking her back until she dropped the rake. When she ran into the wooden wall, he captured her face in his hands.

She bit her lower lip as he smoothed down her hair, twisting his fingers into its loose waves. "I missed you too, Finn."

He barely heard her as his own words came out in a deluge. "I should have begged you to stay. I should have told you I'd give up anything to keep you here. Even if it's not forever. Even if it's just a place you come back to between trips. I don't want to clip your wings. I'm not trying to fence you in, but I need you."

Despite a sudden lump in his throat, he pressed on. "I need your laughter. And I need your creativity. And I need your kindness. And your stubbornness too. And I need *you*. All of you. I should have told you that before you left. I'm so sorry. I was just . . . I thought I needed to let you go, but I don't think I can. I was trying so hard to do this whole thing alone. To do life alone. But I can't. And I don't want to."

"Finn."

The single whispered word cut through him, stopping him short. As her fingers walked up the front of his shirt, they pulled something like hope with them.

"I was in St. Paul's Cathedral in London. It was beautiful and historic, and I went to get a shot of the exterior. But then I felt this tug, like I should be inside." Her gaze dropped to his chin, her eyes narrowing. "When I went in, the priest was talking about love. He said the heart of love is always sacrifice. And it made me wonder if . . ." She swallowed thickly. "I wondered if maybe you let me go because you cared more about my happiness than your own. Because maybe you loved me a little bit?"

Heaven help him, he'd never heard anything more true in his life. But he couldn't manage to get a word past his lips, so he settled for a jerky nod.

"Then I thought about what I hadn't been willing to sacrifice for you." A tear slipped down her cheek, and he caught it with his thumb. "I was afraid. I was afraid of turning into my mom. Of being consumed by stuff. Of having a *home*." She let out a stuttered breath. "I think wherever you are is my home. And it turns out that all I have to sacrifice for you is my fear. I have to give it up if I want to be with you." She shrugged one shoulder. "I don't know what this is going to look like, what our lives are going to look like, but I pick you, Finn Chaffey. I pick you over any fear. I pick you and this island and your life here."

Pulse thundering, he pressed his forehead against hers, wiping away even more streaks across her cheeks. "I'm falling in love with you."

"I'm so glad to hear that, or I wasted a lot of frequent flier miles coming back here."

As he was sure she intended, he chuckled low. "I suppose we better make good use of them then," he whispered against her mouth, their lips barely brushing.

It seemed that was all the invitation Cretia needed to throw her arms about his neck. She met his kiss without fear or reservation and held him tight, and he knew they'd figure it out. Whatever his life was going to look like, it would be so much brighter with her by his side.

After several long kisses, and more than a moment of disbelief that this was really happening, Finn pulled back just far enough to say, "I'm so glad you came back."

"Well, I had to. Roberta and I needed to confer about your online name. I'm sorry to report that she's not budging. I'm afraid from here on out, you're going to be Farmer Finn."

Epilogue

Three Years Later

Morning, wife."

Cretia looked up from the phone in her hands as Finn strolled into the living room, his hair standing up on one side and a few extra days on his five o'clock shadow. He still made her heart pound and her stomach take a lazy barrel roll. "Good morning, sleepyhead."

He leaned across the arm of the cozy couch and hovered over her for a moment before pressing his minty lips to hers.

"I thought you were going to sleep the whole day," she teased as Joe Jr. nestled closer to her, his head on her lap.

"I was thinking about it. You know, I need my beauty rest." He ran a hand over his ruffled hair with a grin. "Ruby and Jack only do morning chores one day a week, so I've got to take advantage of it. But the bed got cold without you." His eyes filled with a heat stronger than fire, and she lifted her lips for another kiss. Finn graciously obliged.

Saturdays had become her favorite day of the week, not because it was the weekend—the work on the farm never ended—but because Finn had hired Ruby, a retired schoolteacher, and

Jack to handle the morning chores each week. More often than not, Jack stuck around to play with the dogs, learning everything that Finn could teach him about training the big guys.

But Saturday mornings were for her and Finn. They were for sleeping late and snuggling side by side. They were for long sips of coffee and lazy smiles. They were for enjoying their home, which was full of the most important things—love, hope, and laughter.

And they were for long moments of gratitude for a life so much richer than she'd ever dreamed. No exotic destination or luxury hotel could compare to the joy of building a life with the one she loved.

In the end, she hadn't really sacrificed much of anything. Sure, her day-to-day had shifted some. She spent more time creating videos of animals than she did jetting off to new locations—though Finn had joined her on a travel adventure since they had gotten married two and a half years before. He'd suggested running with the bulls. She'd suggested a relaxing beach. They'd compromised and gone to Fiji.

Now she put her skills to use growing Chaffey's social media channels—one dedicated to the dogs and one for Finn's Farm, which drew hundreds of visitors each summer for the chance to pet the animals, learn about caring for them, and even bottle-feed baby goats.

The internet couldn't get enough of the little cuties.

If she were honest, neither could she. There were six kids this year and bound to be more next year, as she and Finn had driven to a farm near the West Point Lighthouse to pick up a few more goats in need of a home only the week before. It was a good thing their online income had more than covered the cost of the new addition to the barn. At the rate that Finn brought in new strays, they were going to need even more space soon. A lovely problem to have.

At least they'd have some more help this summer. It wasn't officially a camp yet, but four local children were lined up to come every weekday for two weeks beginning on Monday. Jack would teach them how to feed the animals and brush their coats and care for their needs. They'd play with the dogs and socialize Bella's latest litter—all girls, all named after PEI wildflowers.

This year was an experiment. But several moms at church had already asked her if their kids could participate next summer.

"What are you working on?" Finn asked as he settled onto the arm of the couch and looked over her shoulder.

"The St. John's Rescue team sent over a video of Tater at work this week. I was editing it for our channel." She held up her screen, and Finn smiled as the big gray dog jumped into the water off the Newfoundland coast and swam straight for a child struggling to keep his head above the water. Tater reached him within seconds, and the kid hung on to a special vest as he was towed back to shore and safety.

"Good boy," Finn muttered. He probably didn't even know he said it, the encouragement was so ingrained in him. One of the things she liked best about him.

Running her hand across his knee, she smiled. "Remind you of another harbor and another rescue?"

"Best day of my life."

"I'm sure." She giggled. "I was sopping wet and covered you in harbor water."

"If I hadn't bumped you into the harbor, I never would

have met you. And you never would have stayed. And I never would have known how great my life could be." He leaned in and pressed his lips gently to her forehead. His voice dropped low as he whispered, "Like I said, best day of my life."

"And you really would have jumped in after me if Joe hadn't been there?"

"One hundred percent." Finn ruffled the big dog's ears, which garnered a deep woof of appreciation. "But I'm glad he was."

"Me too, boy. You were a pretty good matchmaker."

Joe looked up at her with enormous eyes, his tongue lolling out the front of his mouth, then rested his head back on her lap, his ear pressed to her stomach. Smoothing her hand over his head and down his back, she let out a soft sigh. He'd been extra clingy the last few weeks—and now she knew why—but she didn't mind his warmth on a cool spring morning.

"Have you already fed him?"

She nodded. "But he hasn't had a treat."

Joe's whole body jerked up, and he jumped to the floor, his head swinging between them as though asking who would be providing the promised snack.

Finn pushed himself off the couch and nodded toward the kitchen, which still smelled of the pine-scented cleaner he'd used to mop the floor the day before. "Come on, Joe. I guess you've earned it." As he trotted toward the kitchen, he looked over his shoulder. "Can I make you a cup of coffee?"

Cretia paused, pressing a hand to her stomach. "I'm not sure."

"Are you feeling okay?" Worry laced his voice. "You said

Julia Mae was sick when you went over to the Red Door a couple days ago. You think you picked something up?"

She couldn't fight a smile. "No. I don't think it's contagious. I'm just not sure if I'm supposed to."

A cupboard door banged closed. "Supposed to what?"

"Drink coffee."

"Why wouldn't you . . . ?"

Her insides did a little jig—not like they had as she'd leaned over the toilet that morning and the one before. This was a happy dance as Finn marched back into the living room and stood before her, eyes wide and unblinking, Joe at his side and clearly confused as to why he hadn't yet gotten his treat.

"You said you weren't sure if you were ready to try."

With a giggle, she shook her head. "I don't think it matters."

"So, you're . . . ?"

She nodded, and he fell to his knees in front of her, resting his forehead on her legs, eyes pinched closed.

"Finn? Are you all right?" Combing her fingers through his hair, she tried to soothe the lines at the corners of his eyes. "I thought you'd be happy."

"I'm so far beyond happy. I can't even— There are no— I don't know how to—" He sighed heavily before taking a deep breath and opening his glassy eyes.

"Finn." She cupped his cheek, her voice trembling with unexpected nerves. "Talk to me."

He lifted his head, biting his lips for a moment until a smile finally broke free, full and bright and as wide as the island. "Happy? That's not half of it." He grabbed her hands and pressed them to his trembling lips. "I love you so much, and I can't wait to share our life with our kids."

"Well, just one kid for now. I'm not pulling a Bella or anything."

"Fine. Our *kid*. *Our* kid. I've dreamed of building something worth passing along to him. And he's going to love this land and these animals and our life." He swallowed thickly.

"It could be a girl, you know."

He chuckled, then sobered slightly. "Are you happy?"

"Me?" She chewed on her lip for a moment. "Well, the morning sickness isn't great so far. But the idea of starting a family with you? That's pretty amazing."

"Are you glad you gave it up? The travel and the nomadic life? Living out of a suitcase and always on the move? Do you feel like you settled for this life?"

She scooted to the edge of the couch cushion and cupped her hands around his face, staring right into his eyes. "Finn Chaffey, when I met you, I thought home was a place to store junk, just a roof over *stuff*. But a home isn't a building or a location. It's the people you love. And the only thing I had to give up to find my home was my fear. I would choose that over and over again." Pressing her lips against his, she whispered, "I love you. And I want this life with you. Forever. For always."

He wrapped her up in his strong embrace and whispered the same to her.

Forever. For always.

Acknowledgments

My many thanks to Farmer Flory and the amazing team at Island Hill Farm in Hampshire, Prince Edward Island. I scheduled a visit there to bottle-feed baby goats for my animal-loving niece on a trip to the island two years ago. But the truth is, I was more excited than she was. We loved our goat experience. And holding baby bunnies and petting wild-haired mini horses and avoiding spitting alpacas and even hugging full-size cows. Don't worry—none were as ornery as Roberta.

My whole family was so impressed with the care and creativity that have gone into this working goat farm. They make goat-milk soap there too, and the gift shop smells like heaven.

Island Hill Farm inspired me to give Finn a bigger dream and to expand his horizons beyond the family business he'd inherited. While you can't visit Finn's Farm on a trip to the island, I hope you'll consider a visit to Island Hill Farm. I think you'll have a wonderful time!

So much gratitude to the readers who have trekked back to the island with me. Your prayers and words of encouragement have buoyed me through dark seasons. Thank you!

A special thank-you goes to the readers who joined me on a tour of Prince Edward Island last summer. I was planning our trip while writing this book. It was a dream to get to share the island with you in person. And to my mom, who is always game for another trip and another adventure. Thanks for always having your passport ready.

Rachel Kent and Books & Such Literary Management, thank you for believing in my stories. Thank you for the way you invest in your authors and have built such an amazing community. I'm forever proud to be a Bookie!

The amazing team at Revell, you are incredible. Thank you for making this book better than I could have made it on my own. Kelsey, Jessica, Joyce, Karen, Hannah, and the rest of the team, my endless appreciation. Thank you for suggesting a return to the Red Door Inn.

The Panera ladies, my fellow writers, confidantes, and friends. You are one of the truest blessings of this writing life. I couldn't do it without you! Thank you for showing up faithfully in my life, Lindsay Harrel, Sara Carrington, Jennifer Deibel, Sarah Popovich, Erin McFarland, Ruth Douthitt, Tari Faris, Kim Wilkes, and Breana Johnson. Thank you for helping me dream big dreams and encouraging me to go after them.

My family, who still tolerates my writing schedule and gladly travels abroad when I say it's time we go back to the island. I missed more than one birthday party and plenty of Friday night dinners while writing this book. Yet you still welcome me home with open arms when the writing wraps up and the story comes to a close. I'm forever grateful to be part of the Johnson/Whitson clan. You're still my favorite.

This book is in your hands only because of God's goodness. As with nearly every book I've written, I got to the halfway point and wondered how it could possibly come together. How could these disparate storylines weave together into something bigger than what I had imagined on my own? Only through him.

One

I t was the best of times, it was the worst of times.

And she was definitely in the wrong Dickens story. Because this was really, very much the worst of times. At least the worst possible time for her house to fall apart. Not even the shimmering snow swirling outside the window and the scent of the real pine tree in the living room could transport her into old Bob Cratchit's kitchen.

With a grunt, Whitney Garrett kicked her oven door closed and threw herself against the stovetop. The downright chilly stovetop. The one that should have been toasty warm by now since she'd turned the oven on to preheat twenty minutes before.

Resting her head on her crossed arms, she groaned in the direction of the nearest burner.

It probably didn't work either.

The stupid oven had been on the fritz for months. But she'd thought it would hang on at least a little while longer. Just through the Christmas season. That was all she needed. Five weeks. That was not too much to ask.

Except, apparently it was.

She kicked the white metal frame and promptly screamed as her big toe throbbed. Stumbling toward the adjacent counter, she hopped on one foot until the pain subsided.

Letting out a soft sigh, she stared at the three pies—uncooked as they were—sitting on her counter. All apple cherry with precise lattice tops and rippled rims. But they were missing the golden color and rich scent that made everyone's mouths water.

She shot one more scowl at her broken appliance for good measure.

Whitney had called her landlord, Craig, about getting the oven looked at a week ago. He'd stopped by and fiddled with something near the pilot light. And it had worked for exactly five days.

He'd done the same thing with her washing machine the summer before. It had lasted for three weeks. Craig was one of those guys who insisted on being the first line of defense. He wouldn't pay for a repairman until he'd tried to fix it himself.

Picking up her phone, she punched in Craig's office number. It rang and rang, and no amount of tapping her toe made him answer. She was just about to hang up when his voicemail kicked in.

"Hey, this is Craig. The missus and me are in the Maldives for our fortieth anniversary. Leave me a message, and I'll get back to you when we get home the middle of December."

Whitney put her phone on the counter and glared at it. "Seriously?"

Craig was literally halfway around the world and clearly not checking voicemails. For three weeks. Those were weeks she couldn't spare. Not when she could bake only a couple pies at a time. And when she'd already paid for her stall at the Summerside farmers' market in two weeks.

Staring at her phone for a long moment, she debated her

next move. She snatched it up and put it back down just as quickly.

Just call them.

No.

Maybe they'll change their minds.

Her fingers brushed her phone before she yanked them back. Her dad had been more than clear.

But these are extenuating circumstances.

Every other absolute failure had had extenuating circumstances too.

Her parents weren't going to bail her out of another harebrained scheme—and she'd had many of them. Even though she'd fully thought through her plan to attend the culinary institute in the spring, if things fell apart, she'd already used up every single favor a daughter could ask for.

With a huff, she pushed her phone across the rust-colored counter and turned to the pies, already picturing the way the cherries would bubble and turn the apples bright red. She just needed a place to cook them.

An image flashed across her mind. Double ovens built into the wall. Stainless steel. Meticulously maintained. Enough room for even the biggest Christmas feast.

The very best place to cook in North Rustico was Rose's Red Door Inn. Everyone knew Caden Holt Jacobs's kitchen was charmed. Maybe it was Caden who brought the magic.

Whitney had certainly thought so as a high school student learning to cook from the inn's chef herself. Maybe Caden had left some fairy dust behind. And the inn was closed this time of year—really any time of year that threatened frost.

Which meant . . .

Whitney barely dared to hope. But it was her only chance

to save her stall at the farmers' market. To save her business this season.

After carefully tucking the pies into her fridge, she pulled on her thick jacket and tied her scarf around her neck. Wind whipped inside when she opened the kitchen door, but she stepped into the ankle-deep snow and hurried along the path toward the big blue house with the bright red door.

<hr />

Whitney let the warmth of the inn's mudroom fully embrace her before loosening her homemade blue scarf. Thumping her boots on the floor, she knocked off as much snow as she could, but not enough to risk tracking it beyond the tiled floor. So she toed off each fur-lined boot and crept into the kitchen.

The inn was oddly silent. At least upstairs. The echo of children's play seeped through the floorboards, shrieks of laughter and delight. But Marie and Seth Sloan, proprietors of Rose's Red Door Inn for nearly ten seasons now, didn't seem to be around.

Whitney tiptoed through the immaculate kitchen, giving the stainless-steel double oven an envious glance before making her way down the short hall to the office. The big wooden door stood wide open, revealing a desk piled with papers in nearly every color of the rainbow. The sleek computer monitor was on, but the little room was empty.

She turned back to the kitchen and stopped mid-stride.

Chubby cheeks and a near-toothless grin greeted her from the hardwood floor. Squishy hands grabbed at the air as the baby reached up. "Nee-nee. Nee-nee."

Whitney scooped up the little doll, pulled her into a tight

hug, and pressed a kiss to her silky brown hair. "Well, hello there, Miss Jessie. Where's your mama?"

The little girl blew a series of bubbles in response and giggled with glee, her rosy cheeks positively pinchable.

"Should we go find her?"

Jessie blew some more bubbles, which Whitney took as agreement, and they trotted around the rest of the main floor. Decorating had already begun in the parlor, which featured an evergreen in the corner, adorned with ribbons and bows and strings of popcorn. A warm fire crackled in the hearth, a cozy blanket laid across the oversized chair. It looked ready to welcome any and all guests.

Except the inn was officially closed. It wouldn't open up again until tourists returned in May.

Suddenly a cry split the air. "Jessie. Je-essie!" Footsteps pounded down the back stairs, and Whitney raced to meet them in the kitchen.

"She's here. She's fine."

Marie landed on the bottom step with a sigh of relief, swinging her mass of brown waves out of her face as she put her hands on her hips and frowned at her youngest. "Her brother thinks it's funny to take her downstairs and then promptly forgets about her."

Whitney chuckled. That sounded about right.

Only then did Marie seem to realize she hadn't even greeted her visitor. "I wasn't expecting company today," she said, giving Whitney a quick side hug. "How are you?" She offered a smile that hadn't changed much since they'd met so many years ago. Perhaps there were a few new wrinkles around her eyes, but if she had any gray hairs, she hid them well. "Would you like a cup of tea?"

Whitney flashed hot beneath her puffy coat, but she nodded anyway. "Please."

Marie set about putting the copper kettle on the gas stove before wiping her forehead with the back of her hand. "You can pick your flavor." She nodded toward the cupboard. Whitney knew it well.

But when she pulled the metal tea box down, it was suspiciously light. She flipped open the lid to discover exactly one package—a sleepytime tea.

Marie's entire face went red. "Oh no. I'm so sorry. I thought I had . . . I guess I need to add that to my list. I'm just . . ." She rolled her eyes at herself. "I can't seem to keep up with anything right now. The kids. The house. The guests."

Jessie began to squirm at the stress in her mom's voice, and Whitney bounced her until she calmed down. "Guests?"

Marie opened another white cupboard and produced two white packets. "Will instant hot cocoa do?"

Whitney nodded, her eyebrows still pinched together. "What guests? Aren't you closed?"

"We should be. But Aretha needs a favor, and you know I can't say no to her." Marie swiped at a frizzy curl, suddenly looking more unraveled than she had just a moment before. "So now I have two guests checking in in a week, a Christmas pageant to direct, and I promised Little Jack that we'd make gingerbread houses and go see the lights. Plus, I'm supposed to host the cookie exchange this year, and I need to buy presents for the kids. Seth too, I suppose."

The way she tacked her husband's name on as an afterthought made Whitney chuckle, but the deep lines of stress around Marie's mouth quickly sobered her.

This was the worst time to beg for a favor—yet Marie

was the only person she could think to ask. If her parents hadn't just moved into the condo in Charlottetown, she'd have asked to borrow their oven. Borrowing an appliance wasn't quite like being bailed out. It was just a little bit of assistance.

But her mom and dad were tucked into their cozy two-bedroom along the harbor, where they insisted they would revel in their pension years.

And if all went as planned, she'd be moving to Charlottetown shortly after the first of the year too. That just didn't solve her immediate dilemma.

Whitney pressed the tip of her thumb to the corner of her mouth and chewed gently on her nail, which tasted suspiciously like cinnamon. She frowned at her finger, and Jessie seemed to giggle at her problem.

Fine. That earned the little cherub a one-way trip to the floor. Which was apparently not punishment. Jessie scooted across the floorboards, opened the first cupboard she encountered, and immediately pulled plastic containers and their mismatched lids to the floor.

"I'm sorry." Whitney rushed to retrieve Jessie, but Marie stopped her with a hand to the arm.

"Don't worry about it. Jessie has long since decimated whatever organizational system Caden had in place in those bottom shelves. Better she's making a mess in here than exploring the Christmas tree again." Marie released a long-suffering sigh, pairing it with a smile that looked a lot like love for her youngest.

As she stirred the cocoa mix into two steaming mugs, spoon clanking, Marie looked over her shoulder. "So, what brings you by?"

"Oh, um . . ." Whitney was unable to form even the most basic words, her tongue having lost its way.

Marie held out one of the green mugs. The ring around the base was clearly the island's famous red clay. It was probably from Mama Potts's Red Clay Shoppe. Marie sold their plates and platters, bowls, and other dishes to guests all summer long.

Whitney wrapped her fingers around the warmth of the mug and inhaled the sugary steam. The sides of the cup were just a little bit uneven, a testament to the way each piece was crafted by hand.

From her place tucked into the corner of the counter, Marie raised her eyebrows as she sipped her own drink. "Are you all right since your folks moved? Are they doing okay?"

"Oh. Yes. They're great. They're . . . I guess they really like living in the city."

Marie's dark eyebrows dipped together over her perfect nose. "I haven't seen you at church the last couple weeks. Is everything . . ."

"I've been selling my pies at farmers' markets around the island."

Marie's face relaxed, and she blew into her mug, sending steam spiraling.

"But that's . . . kind of why I'm here." Whitney released the last words in a quick stream, still afraid to ask, yet terrified not to. She couldn't back out now. "My oven broke. Again. And I can't make more pies if I don't have an oven. And I need . . ."

Her mom had always said that it was uncouth to talk about money. But she needed it.

The Culinary Institute of Canada in Charlottetown had

no problem talking about money. And asking for it. And reminding her that if she wanted her spot to remain reserved, she needed to make a payment. That just wasn't going to happen without an oven—a fully functioning one at that.

"Oh, Whitney. I'm sorry about your oven. How can we help?"

Great. Marie was going to make her say the words. It would only take five of them. But really, couldn't she just offer?

Whitney took an unsteady sip of her cocoa. It was watery and fairly flavorless, but at least it gave her something to do while she stared at the floor and plucked up all her courage. "Maybe . . . if it wouldn't be too much trouble . . . would it be okay if . . ."

Marie's eyebrows pinched all the way together, confusion clearly written across her face.

Taking a deep breath, Whitney closed her eyes and opened her mouth and prayed that the words that came out would make sense. "Would it be okay for me to maybe use the inn's oven to bake my pies?"

"Oh." Marie's mouth hung open, her eyebrows raising nearly to her hairline.

The silence between them fell heavier than a blanket of wet snow, and Whitney rushed to fill it, but Marie beat her.

"I mean, I'd love to help you out. It's just . . ." Her arm waved toward Jessie happily clapping pan lids together like cymbals. "It's such a . . ."

Busy time.

Marie didn't need to fill in the words. The whole island was nearly buzzing in anticipation of Christmas and all the activities the season held. And Marie's season was going to be extra full.

After struggling so much to find the words only minutes before, Whitney had no trouble spitting out a wholly unexpected trade. "I could watch your kids while you have guests."

She was certain she looked as shocked as Marie in that moment. She liked Marie and Seth's little ones more than any others in their little hamlet, but she didn't know much about caring for kids. Her own sister was only eighteen months younger, and there were no nieces or nephews in the family yet.

The offer hung there like week-old laundry on the line, nearly forgotten but refusing to be ignored.

A slow smile stretched across Marie's face, her eyes lit by a flame within. "Really? That would be amazing. Even a few hours a day—like when I'm at the church for rehearsals or going shopping. Seth has been focused on a remodeling job in Cavendish, and he's trying to wrap it up before Christmas. He's been leaving early in the mornings. And we agreed to the job before Aretha told us about her guests." Marie sighed as though she'd set down a heavy weight. "Do you truly have time?"

A glimmer of hope flickered inside. Whitney didn't have time not to, so she nodded quickly. "Sure thing. I'd be happy to."

"And you would just need to borrow the oven?"

Hesitating to stretch the request, Whitney swallowed softly. "And maybe the kitchen to do some prep." Caden had top-notch tools that could make her even more productive.

Marie took a step forward, resting her mug on the island. "And maybe cook some breakfasts?"

Her mouth went dry, and no amount of sipping rapidly cooling cocoa could change that.

"The Lord knows Caden is a wonderful teacher, but she hasn't taught me squat." Marie chuckled. "Nearly ten years of friendship and I can barely cook scrambled eggs. I'd like to be able to offer our guests a little something more."

"You want me to fill in for Caden?" Whitney began shaking her head to answer the question before she had even finished asking it. "I don't think I'd be . . ."

Marie slipped around the edge of the island and leaned in close. "But you're a natural. And you were part of Caden's first class of summer school students. I'm not asking for much. There are only two guests. It doesn't have to be elaborate. Simple. Edible."

"So, if I watch the kids and make breakfast, I can use the whole kitchen?"

Blue eyes flashing bright, Marie nodded. "Please."

This wasn't exactly how she'd planned to spend the Christmas season. Then again, she hadn't really made *any* plans. She had booked farmers' markets and festivals all the way up until December 22. Then, if the roads were clear, she'd venture down to the city to see her parents.

Suddenly the next five weeks stretched before her, all bags of flour and cups of sugar, fresh fruit and warm pies.

Just her. And some pastries.

Jessie pulled a pot from the cupboard, and it crashed to the floor, making both women jump. Setting down her mug, Whitney scooped up the little girl and looked at her mom. This didn't have to be a lonely holiday season. And if spending the upcoming weeks helping at the Red Door meant access to Caden's kitchen, she couldn't possibly refuse.

"All right. I'll do it."

Liz Johnson is the *New York Times* bestselling author of more than twenty novels, including *The Red Door Inn*, other Prince Edward Island–based books, and the Georgia Coast Romance series. She works in marketing, makes her home in Phoenix, Arizona, and daydreams of summer days on PEI's shores. Learn more at LizJohnsonBooks.com.

Meet
LIZ JOHNSON

LizJohnsonBooks.com

Be the first to hear about new books from Revell!

Stay up to date with our authors and books by signing up for our newsletters at

RevellBooks.com/SignUp

FOLLOW US ON SOCIAL MEDIA

   @RevellFiction